Praise fo. .ιc *Body Next Door*

"A heartfelt, funny novel of suspense and romance, with a dead body thrown in. My favorite kind! Kudos to Ms. Yellen." —Pamela Fagan Hutchins, author of the bestselling series *What Doesn't Kill You*.

"Treat yourself to this romantic, vivid and skillfully-crafted mystery!" —Patricia Flaherty Pagan, author of *Trailways Pilgrims: Stories*.

"This is a true page-turner. I highly recommend The Body Next Door!" —Rebecca Nolen, best-selling author of *Deadly Thyme*.

Praise for *The Body Business*

"Sure to keep you on your toes. All the loose ends come to a close in a thrilling climax." —*Insite Magazine*

"There were heart-pounding, oh my gosh moments, some intense sabotage, and the writing was good, too!" —*Otakutwins Reviews*

"The Cruella DeVille of the year: that's who author Gay Yellen has expertly re-created as antagonist in The Body Business . . . one of those characters you just love to hate. And sticks with you long after the story ends." —*InD'Tale*

THE BODY NEXT DOOR

A SAMANTHA NEWMAN NOVEL

Gay Yellen

GYDR PRESS
www.GYDR.com

This book is a work of fiction. Any references to historical or
current events, real people, or real places are used fictitiously.
Other names, characters, places, and events are products of
the author's imagination, and any resemblance to actual
events, persons or places are entirely coincidental.

Cover design: Heidi Dorey

The Body Next Door/ Gay Yellen. -- 1st ed.
ISBN 978-0-9978915-0-8

To my parents, with love and gratitude.

Chapters

CHAPTER ONE

Twenty-Fifth Hour

On the moonless highway, a thundering convoy of eighteen-wheelers barreled up out of nowhere and surrounded my compact rental, threatening to crush it between their hurtling wheels. My teeth vibrated to the roar of diesel engines. Trapped at eighty miles an hour, I gripped the steering wheel and held on tight.

It was probably crazy to try to make it all the way from Nebraska in one go, but after two days of rehashing the second-worst chapter in my life, I had to get home—or what passed for home these days: Carter Chapman's condominium apartment in Houston, on loan until I got back on my feet.

In a colossal moment of bad timing, my phone lit. Risking death by trailer-truck, I slid my focus to the caller ID.

Condo.

Only two people could possibly be calling from there: a) Carter, my mystery-man of a boyfriend, or b) Gertrude Gold, my former secretary. She'd been staying with me while they tented her house for termites.

The semis heaved around me like freight trains. I held my breath and squeezed the little car—a Ford Frito, or Ferret, or something like that—through a narrow gap and into the right-hand lane. A rolling stockyard rocketed past my headlights. As it sped by, its cargo of hapless cattle raked their startled eyes through slits in the trailer's corrugated wall.

The dashboard clock read 4:59 a.m., a weird hour for

Gertie to be calling. Most likely it was Carter, returned from wherever he'd disappeared to and on his way back to the city, or at least, to his ranch outside of town. Even so, five a.m. . . . .

The convoy moved on. Safe on the shoulder, I pressed the connect button. "Hello?"

"Hold on, Samantha, I—"

Not Carter, though I could barely hear Gertie's voice above a piercing yowl that cut through the earpiece. "Gertie? What's happening?"

"Sorry for the hour, dear, but I'm at my wit's end. There's a situation here with your neighbor and, well, I don't want to have to call 9-1-1."

"My neighbor? Which one?"

Another wail drowned Gertie's answer. I took a guess. "Is she thirty-something, brunette and big-bosomed?"

"Yes."

"Brandy."

"Last thing she needs is another drink."

"It's her name. Brandy."

"Oh. Well, she's a mess. I let her come in for a minute, and now she won't go home."

I should have warned Gertie about potential trouble down the hall. Brandy Bayne and her husband Irwin had marital issues, or alcohol issues, or both, as far as I could tell from their middle-of-the-night yelling. Sometimes she ended up on the wrong side of their front door, pounding and begging Irwin to let her in.

Whatever the problem was, quiet soon prevailed, so I'd always stayed out of it. But tenderhearted Gertie had likely opened our door to see if she could help, only to be sucked into the drama.

"Make her drink lots of water."

"I did. But I think—" The roar and hiss from another hauler blocked the rest.

"Say again?"

Her words came in a whisper. "I think she has a bigger a problem. There's blood."

Blood? "Are you sure you shouldn't call 9-1-1?"

"She begged me not to, and she doesn't seem to be bleeding now. Besides, Mr. Chapman wouldn't like the intrusion. You know how private he is."

He was private all right, enough to run off without saying why, or where to, or when he'd return. Still, Gertie was his assistant now. Surely she could get a message through. "Call him and explain. He'll understand."

"He's not to be disturbed, unfortunately."

I shut my eyes and shifted to Plan B for handling a drunken fool. I'd acquired an unfortunate wealth of experience from managing my friend Lista's binges, back when we were college roommates and up to the last day I saw her alive. My mind rewound to the sight of her grieving parents, huddled over her grave only a dozen hours ago.

I shook the memory. "Can you get Brandy's clothes off and put her in the shower?"

"She was naked when I found her."

"Naked?"

"It was a shock, believe me. I cleaned her up the best I could. I know you can't do much from Nebraska, but if you have any other ideas . . ."

"Actually, I'm on the road, about an hour away. Call 9-1-1. They'll get there quickly. Carter will understand. Just keep her off the furniture, okay?"

I disconnected and banged my head on the steering wheel. I'd pushed myself to get home, and for what? Practically everyone important in my life was gone. The career I'd worked so hard to build, ruined. And the person I thought could be the man of my dreams, vanished. Yet here I was, bee-lining it back to the city where it all went down.

The highway stretched ahead, dark and deserted. I drained the last of my Super-Sized Java from the All-Nite in Denton, switched the radio to hard rock, and turned the volume up to ear-bleed. Singing my head off to *Mercy*, I pulled the Ferret onto the road again.

The Wellbourne condominium rose along a broad, leafy boulevard in the Houston Museum District, a premiere high-rise in the center of the sprawling city. In the early morning hour, its silhouette cut sharply into the steely sky. I could see the familiar elliptical roof lights from blocks away, blinking red against a smear of oyster clouds.

At the last stoplight, I scanned the grid of cantilevered balconies and darkened glass on the building's stone-skinned façade, trying to pinpoint Carter's condo. At that hour, only a handful of windows were lit from inside. Looking up at it made me dizzy.

Either I was losing my bearings after the long drive, or my kryptonite fear of heights had taken hold. Acrophobia, it's called, and it can strike me just thinking about high places. Living thirteen floors up at the condo had taken some serious self-talk.

I forced my eyes back to the street. Eleven hours glued to the road had them feeling like red-hot samosas. Only a block to go.

I pulled under The Wellbourne's circular porte-cochere behind the only other vehicle, an ambulance. The EMTs were packing to leave.

There was no time to search for the hair tie I'd torn

off miles back and tossed who knows where inside the car. I hooked a thick stray behind my ear, unfolded my stiff legs onto the pavement and sprinted to catch the crew before they pulled away.

I banged on the driver's window and yelled. "Were you here for someone in 13G?"

The window rolled down. He leaned out and gave me the same once over I'd endured from the truckers at the All-Nite. What was it with these guys? My rumpled, coffee-stained tee and general road-trip funk hardly resembled an invitation to tango.

I tried again. "13G. That's where I live. What's happening?"

He raised his eyes to my face. "Well ma'am, the lady seems okay. No apparent wounds, just minor bruises. We've got another call, so we're leaving it for the cops to sort out." He shut the door and peeled away.

The cops. As if I hadn't had enough of law enforcement types to last the rest of my life.

Not that I'm anti-police. I'm just sick of being mired in one sad situation after another, each one beyond my control. The last one had triggered one of the biggest corporate takedowns in history, and it almost got me killed in the process. Yet all I'd wanted to do was find a missing friend.

The night concierge wasn't at the front desk, and there was no valet in sight. I hauled my luggage out of the hatchback and tugged it through the grand foyer toward the elevators.

Mirrored walls tracked my awkward progress over the buffed terrazzo floor. My scruffy reflection was an eyesore among the high-fashion, tight leather benches, chrome tables and modern art in cool shades of gray that ruled the expanse. It always surprised me to be living there, even if it was temporary.

on as the elevator doors opened, I barged forward smacked flat into the hard body of a valet who was trying to exit. A big *oof!* escaped my lungs.

He backed away.

He'd been playing a game on his phone, by the look of it. "S'cuse me. Didn't expect anyone down here so early."

He stuck his heavily muscled brown arm between the closing doors and forced them open again.

I hurried in.

"Have a good day," he said.

As the elevator carried me upward, I shut my eyes and took a deep breath. Would there be any good in a day that was ticking into its twenty-fifth hour?

I was turning the key to enter the apartment when I heard another door shut down the hall. A newspaper delivery boy ambled around the corner with his stack. When he saw me, he hesitated.

"I'll take it." I grabbed a paper just as Gertie opened the door.

The three of us stood blinking at one another until the distressed look on Gertie's face broke the spell. Her normally neat halo of tight gray curls corkscrewed away from her head willy-nilly. She looked a little pale.

I stepped into the apartment, but as soon as the door was shut, there was a knock on it.

"Um, sorry," the paperboy mumbled. "You don't get that paper. It's for next door."

"Oh." I handed it back to him and shut the door again. The apartment was quiet. "I don't hear any crying. Is Brandy gone?"

Gertie re-tied the sash on the pink gingham robe around her grandmotherly frame and took a deep breath. "She refused to go home. The paramedics cleaned her up and calmed her down, at least. She's in the second guest room. Asleep, I hope."

"I need to pee. And then I need caffeine."

"But there's something else you should know—"

"Sorry, I gotta go." I headed down the hall toward the nearest bathroom.

On the way back, I paused at the door to the guest room where Gertie had put Brandy. All was quiet. No sense trying to wake a sleeping drunk. I tiptoed the rest of the way.

Gertie was in the kitchen making coffee. "I'm sorry I made you rush back. I just didn't know what else to do."

I squelched the urge to say that maybe she shouldn't have opened the door in the first place. She'd stood by me when De Theret International, the company I had positioned as a paragon of corporate virtue, crumbled in infamy. She and hundreds of others—including me, the former V.P. of Media Relations—had lost our jobs and life savings. No way I'd make Gertie feel any worse than she already did.

I lowered my achy backside onto a stool at the breakfast island. "Brandy and her husband drink and yell at each other some nights. Next day in the elevator, they're all lovey-dove. That's how they roll, apparently, so I've steered clear of getting involved. Until now."

Gertie looked at me, sad-eyed. "I probably shouldn't have tried to help. Now I've dragged you—us—into heaven knows what."

"My fault. I forgot to warn you. Nothing to do now but get through this. It'll probably blow over, as usual."

She pulled mugs from the cabinet, filled them with coffee and handed one to me. Her hands were trembling. "I'm afraid there's more to it, Samantha."

"Like what?"

"I tried to tell you when you arrived. Before the paramedics left, they said they were alerting the police."

I set my mug down. "I know. I ran into them downstairs. It doesn't make sense, though. If Brandy wasn't really hurt, why would they call the police?"

"Because when they checked her over, they discovered that she's not bleeding anywhere." Her eyes grew wide. "They said the blood isn't hers."

CHAPTER TWO

The Neighbors

The kitchen phone jangled. Gertie jumped, sending a tidal wave of coffee over the counter and onto the floor. I sprang to answer.

"Ms. Newman?" It was the night security manager. "Apologies for the early call, but . . . did you notice anything odd in the hallway?"

"No."

"Is Mrs. Bayne still at your place? There may be an issue with her apartment, and no one is answering their phone."

"What kind of issue?" I leaned my head against the cupboard and prepared to hear the words that would likely stretch yesterday and today into infinity.

"Well, the police are here, and—"

I lowered the receiver to my chest. Compared to this, spending another night at that depressing motel in Hebron would have been heaven.

A thought wormed its way through. If I could persuade our unwanted guest to return to her own apartment, she and Irwin could meet the police there, and Gertie and I wouldn't have to be involved. I raised the phone again. "Hold on a minute."

I handed the phone to Gertie and headed for the guest room.

Brandy sat up in the bed, whimpering. A purplish bruise underscored her left eye. She made no attempt to cover her naked breasts.

Hers was a body men looked twice at, all curves, like the Hollywood bombshells of the nineteen-fifties. Dark bangs, crystal blue irises and non-stop dimples gave her a china doll quality. I've had my share of head swivels from men, but she was a full-on eye magnet.

"Hello Brandy." I tried to ignore the wet fluttery eyelashes she offered and picked up the bedside phone. "There's a call for you from downstairs. The police want to enter your apartment." I held the receiver out to her.

She recoiled from the phone like it was a cobra and shook her head. "I can't."

"Just talk to them. Tell them everything's fine."

She started to cry. "But it's not! It's not fine . . ." The rest was gibberish.

I began to understand what Gertie had been dealing with. In a voice so calm it surprised me, I spoke into the phone. "Mrs. Bayne isn't feeling well. Maybe after she gets some rest—"

An animated discussion took place at the other end, none of which I could make out. Finally, the security manager came back on the line. "Ms. Newman, the police insist that we let them into her unit. I'd prefer to get her permission. Please stay where you are. We'll be right there." The line went dead.

"They're coming up, Brandy."

She pulled the sheet over her bosom, looked at me and hiccupped. My heart bent a little, to think that she could be a victim of circumstance, too.

I opened the dresser where I'd stashed my exercise clothes and pulled out the first thing I saw: a white sweatshirt, the one I'd worn the first time Carter Chapman invited me to his ranch. I hated to taint that memory with whatever ridiculous events would likely unfold in the next few minutes, but there was no time for multiple choice. I tugged a pair of gray cotton jersey shorts from the next drawer.

The doorbell rang. I tossed the clothes to Brandy. "They're here. Time to sober up."

Gertie beat me to the door. At the threshold stood The Wellbourne night security manager and a tall, grim-faced uniformed officer.

The security manager looked a little pale. "Sorry to bother you, but—"

The officer broke in. "Is there a Mr. or Mrs. Irwin Bayne here?" He was all business. I sensed another downhill slide for the morning that was just approaching sunrise. I nodded.

"We need to speak to one of them." He turned in the direction of the Bayne apartment and gestured for someone to join him.

I matched his tone with an attitude of my own. "She's getting dressed. What's this about?"

His jaw tightened. "And you are . . . who?"

"Her neighbor."

"Your name, ma'am?"

"Samantha. Newman."

The officer scribbled in his notebook and turned to Gertie, who froze.

"This is my friend, Gertrude Gold," I said. "What's the problem?"

He scribbled some more, then glared at me. "We're opening their apartment, with or without consent. If one of them is here, they need to show themselves. Immediately."

As if on cue, Brandy appeared. Although she was barefoot, she teetered like a pre-teen on four-inch stilettos. Her bra-less torso filled my sweatshirt more than mine ever had. The bottom of it hiked up, revealing her hourglass midriff. The officer's eyes popped, ever so subtly.

"I'm here, I'm here!" She flounced onto the living room sofa and stretched her legs along the seat cushions like the courtesan in that famous old painting. Those gray shorts were skimpier than I remembered.

The officer cleared his throat. "May we enter?" He didn't wait for an answer. A second officer—a pretty Latina with cropped hair—followed the men inside. She spoke in undertones to the other two.

The first officer turned to Brandy. "Mrs. Irwin, uh, Brenda Bayne?"

She blotted her eyes with a tissue. "Everyone calls me Brandy. It was my professional name."

"Mrs. Bayne, I'm Officer Ray Mather, with the Houston Police Department. This is my partner, Officer Ramirez. We were called here to investigate a situation involving your apartment. You live in 13F, next door?"

She nodded and fluttered her lashes.

"Mrs. Bayne, are you aware that your front door is smeared with blood?"

Brandy let out wail. Gertie paled and sank into a chair beside the sofa.

This was beginning to sound like more than a drunken spat. I was grateful I hadn't passed Brandy's door on my way in. "Are you sure it's blood?"

Mather did an eye-roll. "Can you tell me what happened, Mrs. Bayne?"

Brandy wailed again. "I didn't mean to, I didn't mean to, I didn't mean to!"

"Didn't mean to what?"

She continued her mantra.

Mather broke in. "Mrs. Bayne. Where is your husband?" When no answer came, he nodded to the security manager. "Let's open it. Ramirez, you stay here with Mrs. Bayne and her friends."

Brandy took up wailing again. Gertie sat beside her on the sofa and tried to comfort her.

As the morning skidded into unknown territory, I hustled to the kitchen for more coffee. Whatever had happened next door, it was sure to involve more energy than I could muster without a heavy infusion of caffeine.

I made a fresh mug. The warm earthy scent was almost enough to revive me. I took a sip and wondered what new joys lay ahead, as Day Two of my marathon dawned.

CHAPTER THREE

Crystal Blues

Officer Mather was back at my door. I could see the security manager, looking slightly green, over his shoulder. Mather motioned to me. "May I speak to you in the hallway?"

Something in his voice made the back of my neck prickle. I wanted to run downstairs, get back into the car and drive another seven hundred miles away. Too late. I joined Mather in the hall.

He kept his voice low. "I need you and your friend and Mrs. Bayne to stay put in your apartment."

I blew out a lungful of breath that I hadn't realized I'd been holding. Not that I would mind staying in the apartment. But this situation probably wouldn't include the hot shower and sleep I'd been craving since I left Nebraska.

"As I suspected," Mather said, "there's more blood inside 13F. And a deceased person. Your night security manager confirmed it was Mr. Bayne."

My knees turned to jelly. I slumped against the wall.

Mather's eyebrow arched. "Did you know the gentleman well?"

I was not about to go down that road. I willed my body vertical. "It's a shock, is all. And I've been up all night and—" I caught myself, remembering a friend's advice from the first mess I'd been involved in. Never offer extra information. Keep your answers brief.

Mather eyed me, but moved on. "Until homicide gets here, I have to keep Mrs. Bayne out of her apartment.

They'll want you and your friend to answer questions, too. Right now, I have to give Mrs. Bayne the bad news."

"No!" That came out a little too loudly. Ramirez opened the door and peered out.

Mather waved her off. He tried to take my arm.

I pulled away. "Can't you tell her the bad news somewhere else? She's already a basket case. She needs medical attention. My friend and I are just staying here temporarily. We don't know her all that well. We can't possibly help."

"I don't think you understand, Ms. Newman. You and your friend are involved in a suspicious death investigation. No one goes anywhere until we're through here."

A sound halfway between a laugh and a sob rumbled up from my gut. I tried to swallow it down, but it had already filled my mouth with an aftertaste of déjà vu.

I trailed Mather into the living room.

Gertie and Brandy were on the sofa where we'd left them. Brandy dabbed her eyes and struggled to a standing position. She managed a weak smile. "I'd like to go home. I'm sure my husband's cooled down by now."

Mather and the security manager exchanged a look before the officer held up a hand to stop her.

"Let's hold off on that a minute, Mrs. Bayne. I'd like you to sit down."

Brandy tipped backward, but somehow managed to stay upright. "I'm fine now, really. The two of us fight, you know, but it doesn't mean anything. We love each other too much."

"Sit down, please." Mather's tone froze Brandy in mid-teeter. The smile left her face. She backed up to the sofa and plopped next to Gertie, whose eyes searched mine for a clue to what was happening.

"Mrs. Bayne, I have some bad news," Mather began.

"When we entered your apartment, we discovered your husband unconscious on the floor in the bedroom."

"Well, he'd had . . . um . . . a lot to drink—"

"He's dead, Mrs. Bayne."

Gertie jumped up and nearly tumbled over the coffee table, her face a peculiar shade of putty.

Brandy looked strangely composed. "No, he's not dead. I just . . . he . . . his forehead was bleeding pretty bad, but you know how a head can bleed? It always looks worse than it is. I tried to put pressure on it to try to stop it, but he was, you know, kinda angry, and—"

"I'm sorry, Mrs. Bayne. He is not okay. He's dead."

Brandy froze. Only her eyelids moved, blinking her crystal blues like the indicator on a flash drive when it loads data. When the blinking stopped, she crumbled. And Gertie fainted.

CHAPTER FOUR

All the Fun

The rest of the morning was a blur of police and forensics. Gertie came to right away, but she was a shaky mess. She'd been a tower of strength for me when the rough stuff at the old company came down. Now I was the one holding her together.

A homicide detective, Buron Washington, arrived. He looked like a fresh-faced rookie, but he was all business. He dispatched Gertie and me to the kitchen and ordered us not to discuss the situation while he interrogated Brandy. He sent Officer Ramirez along to make sure we didn't.

It's hard to *not* talk about the thing that's currently occupying ninety-nine percent of your brain.

"How was Nebraska?" Gertie glanced at Ramirez to make sure she wasn't out of line.

"Sad. Only a half-dozen people at the memorial. I tried to explain to Lista's folks that her life wasn't a waste. I told them how she'd saved me after my family died in the fire, when I really needed a friend. Wish I could've done the same for her."

"You tried your best, dear."

I knew that, but it wasn't enough. It still felt like I'd failed Lista in some way.

As if reading my thoughts, Gertie added, "Some people are beyond saving."

She glanced at my right hand. I'd been twirling my Mom's ring, the one she'd worn forever until the fire took her and my Dad and my brother from me. I don't know when the habit started, but back when Gertie was my secretary, she claimed she could measure my stress level by how fast I spun the ring.

I poured the rest of my coffee down the drain. "Lista's parents asked me to stay one more night, but I just couldn't be there anymore. There wasn't much to stop for along the way, so I just kept driving."

Gertie peeked at Ramirez, who stood column straight by the door. "You probably should have stayed in Nebraska."

"What, and miss all the fun?"

By the time Detective Washington called me into the living room, Brandy was nowhere in sight.

"Has my neighbor returned to her apartment?"

The detective was writing what seemed like a book on his notepad. Without looking up, he answered. "She's been escorted downtown."

I sat on the sofa while he added another chapter. At long last, he looked at me. His eyes traveled to my hand, where I'd taken up spinning the ring again. I pulled my thumb away.

"How long have you known Mr. and Mrs. Bayne?"

I tried a shortcut. "You know, I haven't lived here very long, and I was out of town when everything happened. I'm probably not the best person to help you with this."

He looked directly at me and repeated the question. "How long have you known Mr. and Mrs. Bayne?"

He continued with a barrage of questions that I tried not to answer. In truth, I didn't know much about either one of them. I could have rambled on for hours saying close to nothing, if that's what he wanted.

Finally, he dismissed me, but not before forensics

swabbed me up and down, looking for what, I've no idea. Then he set on Gertie. Even though I desperately needed a shower, I wanted to be there for her when her interrogation finished. I made myself another cup of coffee and waited.

By noon I was nearly a zombie. Apparently, Officer Mather had not painted Gertie in a good light. Her nerves and lack of experience with this kind of situation must have led Washington to suspect her of something.

I was still in the kitchen with Ramirez an hour later when Washington called the officer to the living room. Nobody stopped me from following, so I did.

Gertie had that putty look again. Her body quivered.

Washington looked up from his notes and addressed Ramirez. "I'm taking Mrs. Gold to the station for further questioning."

"No!" escaped from my mouth before I could stop it.

Washington glowered. "Your friend could be an accessory to a homicide."

"You can't arrest her! She was only trying to help."

"Helping a possible murder suspect by tampering with evidence is a potential crime, Ms. Newman."

"But all she did was—"

His eyes bored into me. "Were you here to witness the entirety of Ms. Gold's actions in this matter?"

"No, but—"

"Are you trying to impede this investigation?"

I took a breath. If forensics had swabbed and scraped Gertie like they had me, they probably found blood from when she'd tried to clean Brandy up. I glimpsed a slight smear of brownish red across the front of her checkered robe that I hadn't noticed before.

"But she didn't know . . ."

Washington glared at me. "I am taking her to the

station as soon as we bag what she's wearing for lab testing. If you want to help, get her a change of clothes."

Gertie looked at me, trembling and mute. I reached in to hug her, but Washington stuck his arm between us.

"Don't worry," I told her. "They'll see how wrong they are. I'll come with you."

"No you will not, Ms. Newman. Go get her some clothes, or I'll put her in a jail-issue jumpsuit."

Gertie let out a tiny shriek.

I protested. "Do you have to scare her like that?"

Ramirez gave me an apologetic look.

Washington didn't blink. "Ramirez, escort Ms. Newman to find Ms. Gold something else to wear."

Odd, how a person can be totally exhausted and hopping with energy at the same time. Hours of forced wakefulness burrowed deep into my body, ached in my bones and fogged my thinking, but my nervous system sizzled.

Washington and Ramirez left with Gertie in tow. At least they hadn't cuffed her.

I was determined to follow them to the station, but my car-trip funk begged for a refresher. I hopped into the shower for a quick sponge-off, put on clean jeans and a long-sleeved tee, twisted my damp curls into a knot, and returned to the Ferret for a trip to the police station.

Halfway there, my mind cleared enough to realize that Gertie might need an attorney. I didn't know who to call, but I knew who would.

At a stoplight, I texted an S.O.S to Carter, even though I'd promised myself I wouldn't try to contact him. During my marathon drive back from Nebraska, I'd nearly decided to purge him from my life altogether.

We'd met only days before an explosion put me in the hospital, yet Carter had sat at my bedside like an old friend, day after day, while I recovered. And afterward, when I stubbornly ignored his warnings and marched back into the lion's den at my old job, he'd rescued me before I was nearly offed again. If ever there were a superhero in my life, it would be Carter Chapman.

I longed to feel the way I did when we were together—confident, safe, loved—before he'd left me like a sack of yesterday's lunch. He'd been gone for weeks, and in that time I realized how little I knew about him.

What I did know was that he was addicted to secrecy. He consulted on cyber security, which was probably what he was doing now. I preferred to think that's what he was doing, anyway.

Or, he could be quietly assassinating some baddie on the government hit list. But with his deep law enforcement connections—from local to Federal and probably beyond—Carter was the one person who might get Gertie released.

My last friend on earth was in trouble, and even though I hated myself for missing him as much as I did, this was not about me. I hoped my message would reach him, wherever he was in the world.

It took forever at the police station to find where they were keeping Gertie. Whiffs of sweaty desperation permeated the maze of sallow hallways. It gave me the heebie-jeebies just to be there.

Luckily, I spotted Gertie's nephew, Kevin Molton, outside a set of gray metal double doors that sported a forbidding No Entry sign. I was so relieved to see him I practically knocked him over.

"Kevin! How's Gertie? Where is she?"

He straightened his glasses. "Aunt Gertie is holding up well, I'd say, given the circumstances."

"You saw her?"

"I flashed my FBI badge." His shy smile held a hint of embarrassment. He was a newbie at the Bureau.

I wanted to see Gertie, but Kevin discouraged me. "I'm told she'll be out fairly soon. Go home and get some rest. I'll stay here for as long as it takes."

Despite my exhaustion, I needed to wait and see for myself that she was okay. I looked for somewhere to sit. Not a chair or a bench in sight. Ten minutes in, I reluctantly said goodbye to Kevin and attempted to retrace my steps toward the exit.

By the time I found the doors I'd entered through, I'd forgotten where in the lot I'd parked the Ferret. I pointed the key and clicked in a few directions until I heard the familiar beep.

I didn't remember driving home, only that I was, at last, under the bedcovers, falling blissfully away, until a noise on the balcony jolted me awake. My eyes flew open. Last thing I wanted was to have to go out there and risk a bad case of vertigo.

Until that moment, I hadn't considered how spooky it was to be living next door to a possible murder scene. And now, this weird noise outside on the balcony.

I waited a little longer. Nothing. I ran through the possibilities. Probably a wayward bird, confused in flight, I told myself.

Eventually, my pulse slowed. I summoned my sketchy meditation skills—gleaned from a couple of videos Lista had shared with me—and snuggled under the covers again.

CHAPTER FIVE

Message from Afar

Carter Chapman's toffee-brown eyes held me in his gaze. He leaned down to kiss me. My heart quickened. Then the phone rang, and he dissolved into the void.

I don't know how long I had slept, but it was dark outside, and inside as well. I stretched an arm out from under the covers to locate the speaker button.

"Hello?" I sounded like I'd just come off a respirator.

"Samantha, it's me. I'm home."

"Gertie! You're at your place?" I sat up and flipped on the bedside lamp. "Are you okay?"

"I'm fine, dear." She sounded remarkably upbeat. "The exterminator gave the house the all clear, so Kevin brought me here."

"It must have been awful."

"At first, I thought I'd die, mostly of embarrassment when they patted me down, which is an understatement for what they really . . . Anyway, that almost did me in. But once I saw my darling nephew's face, I knew I'd be all right."

"I'm glad Carter reached him." At least Mr. Elusive had responded to my S.O.S., even if he hadn't bothered to answer me personally.

"Mr. Chapman? No, I wouldn't want to bother him with my problems. He has enough on his plate. I used my one phone call for Kevin. I'm still a little shaky, but it seems kind of exciting, looking back anyway. Poor Brandy, though."

"Yes, poor Brandy." Widowed and jailed and sad as she was, she had my sympathy, but I was busy working on why Carter hadn't responded to my text, and what the heck was on his 'plate.'

Gertie chattered on. "Oh, I almost forgot, with everything else happening. I wanted to ask if you would come to a tea tomorrow for one of Mr. Chapman's charities. The one with the kids and the music. Two-thirty at The Women's Club. It's the first one I've arranged for him, and I'd love it if you were there."

I was confused. "So, you've heard from Carter?"

"Not directly. After De Theret International fell apart, I thought he'd hired me out of kindness for my age, and because I'd worked for you. But before he ran off with that New York fellow, he said he'd keep in touch. Ralph contacts me if Mr. Chapman needs anything. There hasn't been much, except the charities. But, God bless him, I've already gotten my first salary check. So will you come?"

Ralph was Carter's chauffeur, pilot, ranch manager, computer guy, and keeper of secrets. If Carter communicated with Ralph, and Ralph with Gertie, why not with me? I knew he'd made piles of money from his cyber work—at least, it's where he said the money came from. But his charities? I was clueless.

"Samantha?"

I halted the snit that was brewing in the limbic center of my brain. "Two-thirty? I have a job interview at the TV station in the morning, but it shouldn't last past noon. Sure, I'll come."

I hung up and looked at the time: almost eight. I was still exhausted, but my stomach wanted food. Plenty of time to raid the fridge and check my messages before I turned in again. I peeled myself off the bed, snagged my laptop and padded barefoot into the kitchen.

Peanut-butter-and-jelly sandwiches were pretty much what I lived on these days. But when I opened the refrigerator, a potential feast revealed itself: roasted chicken, mandarin oranges, fresh milk, loaf of bread, a dozen eggs, and, glistening gaily under their clear plastic wrapping, four of the most delectable-looking muffins in muffin history.

Gertie. Always the nurturer, she'd stocked the fridge while I was gone.

I ditched the PB&J idea and opted for the muffins. They were the chunky chocolate ones Gertie made for special occasions. I plated one and stuck it into the microwave for a quick zap, just enough to get the chocolate warm and oozy. The aroma wrapped me in a blanket of happy. Maybe I'd have two.

I poured a tall glass of milk and booted up my laptop for one last chance to research KHTS.

I'd been on-camera at the station several times as the spokesperson for De Theret International. I prayed no one there would hold my past employer against me. I needed this job. Working in promotions was lower-rung, but my savings were dwindling, and I was determined not to mooch off Carter much longer.

My laptop screen flashed with phone messages: one from the station, confirming my interview at 10:00 a.m. tomorrow; one from Detective Washington, asking for a follow-up meeting; and one from a blocked number.

The voice-to-text program had made a hash of the last message, so I clicked to listen. In his unmistakable Brooklyn accent, Roland Dabney began to speak. My heart flipped.

Dabney was the man Gertie had called "that New York fellow" who had swooped in like a long lost friend and snatched Carter away from the ranch to who-knows-where with no time for goodbyes.

Supposedly, Dabney was a network news television producer. I didn't know much about the relationship between the two men, except that they seemed bonded by their past—something more than their resumes revealed. I'd put money on it, if I had any.

The message ended before I could catch my breath and open my ears. I hadn't heard a word after, "This is Roland Dabney . . ."

I played it again.

" . . . with an update on the story in Houston. My man will be there as soon as he clears his schedule."

That was the entire message, but it was enough to restart my heart. Dabney's message wasn't about a news story. It was about his 'man.'

Carter Chapman was coming home.

CHAPTER SIX

Games

My alarm shattered the only good sleep I'd had all week. Heavy-eyed, I pulled my face from the pillow, dragged out of bed and willed myself into the shower.

I tried to focus on the job interview, but thoughts of Carter kept popping in. Mostly they were replays of the questions I'd been asking myself over and over again: Why did he leave so fast? Where did he go? What was he up to?

That little reverie had eaten up precious primping time. So much for the extra care I'd planned for my makeup and hair. Quick swoops of mascara and lip-gloss were all there was time for. I pulled my jade suit off its hanger and slipped it on. "It makes your eyes even greener," Gertie had said the first time she saw me in it.

In the full-length bathroom mirror, I looked remarkably together. But a last-minute glance in the magnifier made me gasp. My hasty dab and gloss had missed the new facial feature I'd acquired overnight: a three-inch imprint of a wrinkled pillowcase slashed diagonally upward from my right cheek to my eyebrow, like a pirate scar. I could only hope it would disappear in time for my interview.

I silently vowed to wear the mark like a badge of honor, and grabbed the key to Carter's Tesla. No Ferret for me today, not when I needed all the help I could get to feel awesome. I made a mental note to return the little red rental car soon, before they charged me with grand theft auto.

On my way out, I almost walked over a neon yellow envelope just inside the front door. Someone must have shoved it under after I'd returned from the police station. I picked it up and rushed out.

I was about to open the envelope in the hallway when a set of forensics officers appeared around the corner. The way they were eyeing me made me think twice, so I dropped the envelope into my bag. It seemed like forever until the elevator arrived.

Elevators are perverse machines. If you're leaving to run errands and have all day to kill, you push a button, the doors open immediately, you board and are delivered to your destination in seconds. But it doesn't work that way when you're running late for something important—like a job interview. The claustrophobic cubicle takes eons to arrive, and when the doors finally open, it is jammed with other people, each of whom has pressed an exit floor before yours.

It's like being trapped in Sartre's version of Hell. And that's only one of many high-rise elevator games.

My playmates this morning were Pansy and Hubert Gump, who looked to be octogenarians. Her face was round and concave as a satellite dish, and powdered a shade or two lighter than her skin. Black olive eyes, thin vermillion lips, and tomato-red circles on her sunken cheekbones reminded me of the funny-faced pizzas my Mom used to make for my brother and me on Sunday nights.

Hubert was slightly shorter than she, with a pear-shaped, florid face and bulbous nose that hinted at more than one daily tumbler of spirits.

Behind the Gumps stood a valet next to a cart full of shopping bags stuffed with what looked like random pieces of clothing headed for a charity shop.

I could feel Pansy's flinty eyes study me as the doors closed.

"You're that new young woman, aren't you?" She tended to sound like the Duchess of Kent, though she'd previously bragged to me that she was 'one of the very rare' Houston natives among the city's diverse population. "What's your name again?"

"Samantha Newman." This was the third time we'd had this exchange.

"Ah, yes," she said. "Thirteen. Isn't that where the commotion was last night?"

Word traveled fast. I caught a glimpse of the bright yellow envelope glowing from the depths of my bag. Dying to know what was inside and seriously worried about being late for my interview, I was ready to bolt as soon as the elevator freed me.

But the doors opened onto the next floor, where two young residents waited to board. From their similar attire—dirty baseball caps (hers, on backward), holey tees and ragged shorts—they appeared to be brother and sister. The boy, about fifteen I'd guess, hung back. The little girl, his junior by at least five years, bounded in.

She turned to him in disgust. "C'mon!"

He reluctantly complied, eyes cast downward as he slouched toward us. He pivoted his skinny body—his arms and legs, all knobs and sticks—and faced into the corner. We all rode together in silence, though my brain was screaming *Let me out!* at the top of its lungs.

Pansy, Hubert and the valet exited at the top garage level. "We must speak," she said on her way out. I figured she was talking to me, but with her deadpan face and even tone, I wasn't sure.

The kids and I rode to two, where the Tesla was parked. I made eye contact with the little girl as I stepped out. I thought she was about to say something, but she glanced at her brother, then concentrated on the floor. I'd noticed the same behavior once before, in the gym. I wondered what that was about.

At last I was free. Before I backed the Tesla out of its parking spot, I took a precious minute to dig the envelope out of my bag. It didn't take long to read the message inside, scrawled in red ballpoint on a torn piece of newsprint.

She didn't do it.

That was all it said.

The interview at KHTS took longer than I expected. Even though I was there for a promotions department job, they wanted to put me through an on-camera test as well. The Grand Canyon on my face must not have bothered them.

Before I could think of a reason to say no, they sat me at the news desk, facing a camera and a barrage of studio lights so bright they made my eyes water. The words on the teleprompter swam through the blur, some old news copy about a dead body that had been found by a neighbor. The wife was accused. Like Brandy. I could hardly get through it without choking.

"You okay?" Jay Patel, the station manager, had popped in to watch. He seemed concerned. From my teary eyes and strangled sentences, I suppose he thought I was having some kind of breakdown.

"Fine," I lied. "I'm not used to the bright lights."

"Want to try again?"

"No thanks."

He looked at me like he'd never known anyone to turn down a chance to be on TV. I kicked myself for seeming disinterested.

"I'd love a rain check if the promotions job doesn't happen." I tried to sound sincere. At least I'd hedged my bet. The job I applied for was way down the ladder from my former executive position, but after that disaster, I wasn't eager for much responsibility, or visibility.

I left the station hoping that my on-camera performance hadn't erased what I thought had been a good interview. There was plenty of time to meet Gertie at the charity tea.

A check of my phone revealed a new message from Detective Washington, demanding that I return his call immediately, and another from a number I didn't recognize.

I wasn't in the mood to deal with Washington yet, especially with the note inside the yellow envelope still working through my brain. I opened the second message, and a West Texas twang began to speak in what sounded like a series of short declarations.

"Samantha Newman! Rufus Kingsbury here! Brandy Bayne's attorney! Need to talk to you ASAP! Call as soon as you get this!"

I'd heard of Kingsbury. If you lived in Texas, you'd have to be a cave dweller not to know his name. He was the bombastic, colorful and highly effective defense attorney whose image was regularly splashed across the screen on the late local news. If he represented you, it was assumed that you had money, that you were guilty, and you would beat the rap. He was legendary, and Brandy had him in her corner.

I hit Call. To my surprise, he answered right away— no receptionist, no assistant, just him. He must have seen my caller ID, because he started right up.

"Howdy! Gotta see ya! Right away! Your place! Half an hour!"

I hadn't even said hello. "Sorry, I'm not there, and I

won't be for the rest of the day."

"Okay! Have it your way!" He hung up.

I wasn't sure what that meant, but I let it stand. Given his reputation, I was pretty sure he'd catch up to me, sooner or later, if he wanted to.

CHAPTER SEVEN

Scherzo

The Women's Club building, a red brick neo-Colonial, sprawled under a canopy of loblolly pines and hundred-year oaks near Memorial Park. Back in my pre-Apocalypse career, I'd hosted dozens of luncheons and breakfasts there for clients of De Theret International. The members catered the meals themselves, Southern-style. Their sticky buns were a city favorite.

I parked the Tesla and stepped out into the shade. It always seemed ten degrees cooler and a couple of centuries earlier there. On a movie set, it wouldn't have looked odd to see a slave greeting a guest at the door with a mint julep. Thank goodness we were past all that in real life, mostly.

Inside, the pre-tea hubbub was going strong. Empty fruit punch glasses littered the side tables. People crowded around the doors to the dining room, waiting to be let in. I was just in time.

I found the sign-in desk and registered. The poster behind the desk announced the official title of the affair: Let the Children Play, sponsored by The Maggie & Mike Foundation.

That's when it hit me. Maggie and Mike—Margaret and Michael—those were the names of Carter Chapman's twins who, along with his wife Katherine, had been killed by a drunk driver. The foundation sponsoring the tea was a memorial to Carter's children. I'd had no clue.

Something else fell into place. The first time I had seen the children's names was on their gravestone at Serenity, Carter's ranch in the rolling hills of Central Texas. I hadn't been back there since the day he left me.

To his credit, he'd written a sweet note of apology, including what I'd thought was either a hint to where he'd gone, or the key code to enter his mysterious third-floor office. But when I mounted the winding staircase and tried the combination, the door wouldn't budge.

Ralph, Carter's aide in all things secret, must have seen me through a hidden camera. He'd opened the forbidden portal and waved me in. "Mr. Chapman said you'd probably try to get in. But you can't stay long."

The room was what I'd expected for a cyber-guru's lair. A couple of workspaces, banks of computers and walls of monitors, all of the screens blank, no doubt turned off for my visit.

On the only wall not plastered with screens hung several violins of various sizes, arranged in pairs. The tiniest—one pink, one blue—were barely a foot long, like something a four-year-old could handle. The next pair looked larger by half, but still smaller than full size, their deep amber wood glossy in the muted light. The last two were full-size.

"They're Mr. Chapman's kid's instru—"

I raised my hand to stop Ralph's explanation. It was obvious what they were. They took my breath away. The twins were not quite eleven when Carter lost them and their mother.

Beneath the violins sat a cello and a stand with sheet music on it. It didn't take much imagination to guess that they had been Katharine's. A lonely guitar rested on the floor in the corner. It looked like it had just been set down.

"Miss? It's about to start." The young woman's voice from behind the registration desk brought me back to the charity tea. I blotted a tear away, found my nametag and pasted it to the shoulder of my suit.

In the dining room, I saw Gertie waving at me from a table near the stage. She beamed as I approached.

"You made it! Sit here, next to me, and meet these lovely people."

To her right was a striking long-necked woman, the Executive Director of The Maggie & Mike Foundation. Next to her sat the principal of the city's arts magnet high school. Seated beside him were two people from the Symphony League. I didn't quite catch the name of the woman next to them, or the man next to her. The chair beside mine was empty.

The Chairperson had begun speaking into an echoing sound system. " . . . giving children the opportunity to incorporate music into their lives. I want to thank everyone for coming today, and . . ." I stopped listening at that point, not because I didn't want to know more about the charity that Carter had poured his money—and probably his heart—into. Someone had pulled out the chair next to me. I turned to greet the new arrival.

"Rufus Kingsbury!" he announced as he sat his very tall and substantial frame down.

The woman at the podium stopped mid-sentence. All eyes turned to our table. The room buzz swelled, then dipped again as the speaker returned to her speech. I stared at Kingsbury, and he stared back. I couldn't think of a thing to say, out loud, anyway.

In person, he appeared younger and much better looking than he did on TV. His eyes were small and slightly too close together, but they twinkled blue with alarming liveliness. He had a large head and a slightly florid face, framed by hair most women would kill for: natural strawberry-blonde in a sunny corona, as if it were lit from above.

"Rufus Kingsbury," he repeated in a loud whisper. He stuck his hand out to shake mine.

I kept my hands in my lap, but I did manage a word. "Obviously."

He tipped his head toward me. "I love these charity things, don't you, Ms. Newman?" His eyes peered directly into mine, and I began to understand the reason for his celebrity. He was a force to be reckoned with.

I donned my invisible armor. "Are you stalking me?"

"Me? Goodness no. I pay other people to do that." Twinkle-twinkle. His laugh shook his whole body in a jolly-Santa kind of spasm.

Applause rose from the attendees. Speeches were over and we were free to chitchat. Servers passed platters of crustless tea sandwiches, garden salad, fresh fruit and pastries around the table.

While Kingsbury introduced himself to our tablemates, I shifted my attention to Gertie. She appeared to be mesmerized by the person sitting on the other side of Kingsbury—a man about her age, with kind eyes and wavy gray hair. His gaze was fixed on her, too. Their silent exchange continued for what seemed to be an unhealthy length of time, so I purposefully interrupted. "Gertie?"

She jolted from her trance. "Oh! Samantha, let me introduce you to the rest of our table. First, the HISD Music Teacher of the Year." The woman and I nodded and smiled at one another.

As Gertie came to the next man, she broke into a silly grin. "And this is Louis Kleschevsky." Her eyes locked on his again.

He rose to shake my hand. "My granddaughter is on the program today," he said, completing the introduction. He sat and was immediately engaged in a conversation with the music teacher. I turned to Gertie to ask more about him. She was still transfixed.

I elbowed her. "What's the story here? You know him?"

"Well, yes and no," she said. "We've met before, but I had no idea what he looked like until today."

That made no sense to me, but I couldn't ask more because Kingsbury was trying to re-engage. He offered me a small pitcher of salad dressing. "French?"

"No thanks."

He poured a gallon of the pink stuff over his greens and passed it the other way. I tried to pick up the conversation with Gertie, but she was trading eyeballs with Kleschevsky again.

"Did you know that French dressing's not really French?"

I pretended I hadn't heard Kingsbury's question, but he repeated it, and added an elbow nudge of his own. "Did you know that French dressing—"

"I know." He reminded me of Bobby Olson, the twerp who sat behind me in fourth grade and pulled on my ponytail relentlessly until I had to turn around and admire his goofy face. "Okay, you win. You have my attention. What do you want?"

Kingsbury's grin softened. "I need to talk to you about my client's case, and I have to do it soon. Sorry if I came on too strong. It's a bad habit. Could we talk after lunch?"

Random chance had pulled me into the Brandy Bayne mess. Much as I wanted to remove myself, I couldn't. She'd seemed so vulnerable that night, and alone. "Okay."

That was all it took to get him to ignore me for the rest of the meal. I tried to engage Gertie again. No luck. She and Kleschevsky were still in an eye-lock.

The entertainment portion of the program began. A group of middle-schoolers trouped onstage to perform in a string quartet. They were remarkably polished for their age. The next chamber group, high schoolers this time, was even better.

There was a short break while a grand piano was rolled onstage. When it was set, Kleschevsky's granddaughter, Zoe, appeared in a fluffy pink dress with a ruffled skirt.

She was a tiny thing, barely four feet tall, with a dark brown ponytail that trailed to her waist. Perched on the piano bench, she stretched the toes of her black patent Mary Janes down to the pedals. Once set, she bowed her head, raised her delicate arms and launched into a Chopin scherzo with such ferocity I thought I saw the keyboard bounce.

I pulled my eyes away to peek at her grandfather. Head nodding in rhythm, he was deep into the music with her, smiling as her small hands attacked the keys with the power of a man three times her size. She managed the quiet parts as delicately as a seasoned professional. When she finished, the room exploded with applause. Clapping like a maniac, Gertie led a standing ovation.

The chairperson returned to the podium for her final remarks and encouraged everyone to drop a pledge card into the box by the exit door. An excited murmur filled the room as everyone rose on cue and began to file out.

I offered congratulations to Kleschevsky on Zoe's remarkable performance. "She was amazing. I've never seen a child her age play with such confidence."

"And artistry." Gertie had joined us, her face aglow. "A prodigy, for sure."

"Thank you." Kleschevsky accepted the praise, though he seemed almost embarrassed by it. "She works very hard."

Someone tapped my shoulder. Kingsbury.

"Ready, darlin'?"

I bristled. "No, I'm not ready." I wanted to ask Kleschevsky more about his granddaughter, and get the scoop on him and Gertie. "I'm talking to my friends."

"Them?" He waggled his thumb in their direction. They were leaning into one another, laughing and smiling, deep in conversation. "Looks to me like you'd just be interrupting."

He grinned and gave me another eye twinkle. "How 'bout we meet back at your place. I could use another gander at the crime scene."

I hadn't decided how I felt about Brandy's situation. Whatever she'd done, after a glimpse into what the Bayne's marriage was like, I couldn't help but think of her as the victim. Still, she wasn't the one who had ended up dead.

And now there was the note I'd found this morning. *She didn't do it.* Did someone witness the murder and know she was innocent? Or was it a guilt-driven statement from the real killer? I had to tell someone about it. The logical person was Kingsbury.

I could have invented a forgotten appointment, but he'd likely be lying in wait for me back at the condo no matter what the hour. Might as well surrender to the inevitable.

"Okay, meet me at the condo."

I could feel his eyes following me as I walked outside. When I reached the Tesla, I turned and saw him standing on the steps waving at me, golden-haired and smiling.

Before I left the parking lot, I checked my phone for a sign of life from Carter. None.

The charity tea reminded me why I'd fallen for him in the first place. Not once had he mentioned his charitable endeavors, or bragged about his money. I longed to see him and ask him more about the foundation and those tiny violins.

Secretive as he was, the visible fragments of his life seemed to bend toward expressions of love. If he couldn't share anything about his work, maybe I would get used to it.

Then again, if he truly cared for me, why would he leave me in the dark, unless he was an emotionally remote jerk?

CHAPTER EIGHT

Red

Under The Wellbourne porte-cochère, Kingsbury leaned against his Torch Red Stingray, arms crossed. I stopped and lowered my window.

He smiled and twinkled down at me. "What took you so long, darlin'?"

Normally, if a man I hardly know calls me honey, sweetie, or anything like it, I bristle like an old-school feminist. But Kingsbury's easy charm was engaging, from his Western-cut suit to his custom cowboy boots. He was worming his way into my good graces. Not that I'd let him know it.

"Hello." That was all he got from me. I pulled the car in front of his, got out and strode into the lobby.

While he stopped at the concierge desk to register, I scouted for a spot in the lobby that would give us some privacy. At an out-of-the-way nook opposite the elevators, I sat in a leather chair and waited for him to catch up.

He made a face as he approached. "Can't talk here, darlin'. Too public. Let's go to your place." He offered his hand to help me up, blue eyes a-twinkle.

I ignored the gesture and stood on my own. "I'm not in the mood to entertain. Fifteen minutes and you're out."

I spied Pansy and Hubert Gump ahead of us. Another perverse elevator game loomed: If you've had one elevator encounter that day with an annoying neighbor, you are destined to endure their company again before the next day dawns.

The doors slid apart. Pansy held them for Hubert, who trundled in. Much as I tried to slow our progress, she patiently kept them open for us too. I considered waving her off and waiting for another elevator, but Kingsbury barged ahead.

Pansy X-rayed the two of us as we rode up together, lingering on Kingsbury's face. I don't know if she recognized him, but she kept staring at him, then me, then him, and back to me again like she was trying to figure out where in her mind to file us.

She settled on me. "Tell me your name again?"

"Samantha Newman." I refrained from adding, *for the hundredth time*. She was too busy sizing up Kingsbury again to notice the snip in my voice.

The doors opened onto a garage level, revealing the same two kids from this morning. They acted out their usual routine: the little girl boarded; her brother held back; she coaxed him in. He glumly turned his body to face the corner. We rode up in silence until they reached their floor and got out.

"Weird kids." Kingsbury's comment renewed Pansy's curiosity, but she was thwarted by our exit on the next floor.

As the doors closed behind us, Pansy called out. "We must speak." Same as this morning. I figured it was her way of saying tootle-oo.

Kingsbury chuckled. "That was a cast of characters." His penchant for finding humor in the oddest things was disarming. I found myself smiling, too.

The moment I unlocked the door, he strode past me into the apartment, stopping in the entry to survey the place. "Kinda masculine for a looker like you. Where's the boyfriend?"

Before I could answer, he had marched into the living room. "I am in dire need of coffee! That affair was way too stingy on refills. Where's the kitchen?"

With that, he conducted a walk-through of the entire apartment. I barely kept up until he found his destination.

"Where d'ya keep the stuff?" He opened and closed the cupboards until he found the right one. By then, I'd realized there was method to his madness. He was checking the place out.

"I think you missed a few places," I snarked. "What about the medicine cabinet?"

"Nah, you're not on anything interesting. Too healthy." He plucked the coffee container from the shelf. "Where's your machine?"

I pointed to the French press next to where the coffee had sat. He chuckled. "If it'd been a snake, it woulda bit me."

He removed his suit jacket and draped it over the back of a barstool before returning to the coffee. It was easy to see that he stayed in shape. No muscles bulging under his shirt, but a trim waist rose up in a V and out to exceptionally broad shoulders.

He turned and faced me. "Instant hot?" He pointed to the extra chrome spigot on the sink.

I nodded. He smiled. "Why don't you get us some mugs? I'll take the biggest one you got."

His brand of pushy seemed to be a natural extension of his down-home demeanor. He was comfortable in his own skin, here, at the charity tea, and I'm guessing, just about anywhere he went.

He returned to the coffee and pressed the sieve's post slowly downward until the grounds packed against the bottom of the carafe and dense dark liquid bubbled up, ready to pour. I set two mugs on the counter—a small green one for me and the biggest one I could find for him, shiny black with a big red question mark on it.

He filled the small mug, poured the rest of the coffee into the big black one and shifted his attention to the cabinets again. "Sugar?"

I opened the cupboard behind me. The sugar bowl was on a high shelf. I stretched on my tiptoes to reach it.

"I'll get it, darlin'."

As he stretched over my head to pluck the bowl from the shelf, the press of his body pushed me off balance. I managed to twist around and grab his shoulder to keep from falling. His other arm caught me, and for a weird second, his eyes locked onto mine. He smelled like pumpkin pie.

Everything in me froze, except my heart, which pounded a gazillion times a minute. His baby blues twinkled as he dipped his face closer to mine.

I don't know what might have happened next, because, out of the corner of my eye, I glimpsed the presence of another person in the kitchen with us.

Carter Chapman was standing in the doorway with a bouquet of flowers in his hand and a question on his face. "Samantha?"

I tried to say something, but all that came out was a strangled, "Mmmpph!"

Kingsbury jerked his head around. When he saw Carter, he set the sugar bowl down and backed away from the counter, and me.

Carter's eyes bored into mine. Then he glared at Kingsbury. The three of us stood speechless, blinking at each other for what seemed like half an hour. I needed something to happen so I could start breathing again.

Kingsbury stuck his hand out and strode toward

Carter. "Hey, fella, Rufus Kingsbury here! Nice to meet ya!"

Carter didn't offer his hand in return. He just stood there and locked me in a stare-down.

Kingsbury tried again. "Hey, guy, this isn't what it looks like."

"Get out." I'd never heard the frigid North in Carter's voice before. It chilled my heart, and for a moment, I wondered if he was talking to me. Another two centuries went by, until his glare took a sweep toward Kingsbury. "Get out. Now."

Kingsbury seemed to be reviewing his options. He shot a look my way. "We still need to talk."

"Get out!" I'd never heard Carter raise his voice above room level before, either. His words were still bouncing off the kitchen walls when Kingsbury took one more glance my way, grabbed his jacket and left.

"Carter, I . . . he . . . he was just helping me get the sugar, and then I fell, and—"

"I will give him time to get out of the building, Samantha, and then I'm leaving too."

"No! I don't know what you think you saw, but . . . I don't even know him!"

I silently prayed that the gentle, loving, patient man I knew him to be, the one who had nursed me back to wholeness and saved my life, that man would hear me out. "I just met him today. He's Brandy's attorney, you know Brandy, from next door, who's . . . well, it's a long story and—"

I stopped babbling, took a deep breath and started over. "He came to talk to me about her case and he wanted coffee and I couldn't reach the sugar and I . . . and he . . ."

It was no use. Carter's eyes filled with a familiar sadness, and something else: anger, or disappointment.

"I'm headed to the ranch, Samantha. I'd thought you'd be coming with me. But not now. I need some time to get the image of you and that . . . whoever he was . . . out of my system, alone." He dropped the flowers next to the sink and walked out.

I slumped against the counter. The moment I'd been yearning for, when I'd see him again and forgive him for leaving and tell him how much I missed him and let him hold me and tell me he missed me too: that moment was dust.

I wanted to run after him, but my body would not cooperate. My lungs filled with a huge gulp of "No!" until the pressure was unbearable and it burst from me in an inarticulate sob. I didn't want us to end like that, it couldn't end like that, with me blubbering and him thinking the worst. I willed myself to move. I didn't know what I was going to say, but I sped out to stop him.

Too late. As suddenly as he'd appeared in the kitchen, he had disappeared from the apartment. I ran out the door and down the hallway, hoping to catch him.

Third Perverse Elevator Game: When you need the blasted crate to slow down and wait, it is long gone.

CHAPTER NINE

Grilling

In my panic to stop Carter from leaving, I'd locked myself out of the apartment. Now I had to go downstairs and ask security to unlock the door. But first, I had to stop crying.

I wiped my eyes and paced the hall until I was sure they would stay dry. Police tape festooned the entrance to Brandy's apartment, but the door had been cleaned, thank goodness. A vision of Detective Washington crossed my brain. I wondered how much longer I could avoid him. I pushed the elevator button. Mercifully, it arrived empty.

By the time I got inside the apartment, I was exhausted and angry and sad and ready to call it a day. The sun had moved to the other side of the building, muting the living room in shadow. I made my way into the bedroom to change into my jams.

As I pulled the top over my head, I thought I saw something move outside on the balcony. I'd only caught a flutter of shadow and a faint unidentifiable sound, like the noise that had wakened me last night. Probably another bird, or the same one, I told myself. Even so, the back of my neck prickled.

When I first moved into the high rise, I'd kept the drapes shut in an attempt to ignore how high up the apartment was. But that left me feeling claustrophobic. Little by little I got used to the view. As long as I didn't have to venture all the way out to the balcony railing, I was okay.

Occasionally a bird would bounce off the window, take a moment to collect itself and fly away. If it was a bird out there now, it could be wounded. I had to check.

I baby-stepped toward the sliding glass door. Halfway there, I glimpsed something moving beside me. Heart pounding, I jerked backwards, only to discover my wide-eyed reflection staring back at me from the mirror. I'd nearly scared myself to death.

I swallowed the lump in my throat, continued toward the door and slid it open. Only the cool evening air and the muffled whirr of street traffic greeted me. I exhaled, closed the door and locked it.

Much as I wanted to fall into bed, I figured I'd better check my messages to see if anyone from KHTS had called with a job offer. My phone was in my bag, which was still in the kitchen where Kingsbury, Carter and I had played our little comedy.

I wandered back to the scene and flicked on the light. Evidence of the mini-drama was everywhere. Untouched mugs of coffee sat on the counter. Beside them, the inglorious sugar bowl perched precariously, half on and half off the edge.

Everything in me wanted to shove it all the way off and savor the bang when it shattered on the floor and sent plumes of white crystal exploding all over the place. What difference would one more sticky mess make?

But then I'd have to clean it up. Too many messes already. I stifled the impulse and pushed it out of harm's way.

The flowers taunted me from the counter where Carter had left them. Peonies, my favorite, though I can't imagine how he knew that. They were almost white, with a creamy pink blush like the softest feathers of a nestling spoonbill. I raised one to my face, let its petals tickle my cheeks and breathed in the tender fragrance.

Through a teary blur, I found a vase and filled it with water, pared the stems and stuck them in. No point trying to arrange them into some sort of symmetry. Not tonight.

I stifled a new round of tears and busied myself with the coffee things. I rinsed them and shoved them into the dishwasher, out of sight.

I needed something to ease my soul. I opened the fridge. Gertie's chocolate muffins beckoned.

Once I'd poured a glass of milk and gently zapped a muffin, I retrieved the phone. Nothing from the TV station, but Detective Washington had called, twice.

His last message needed no interpretation. "If you do not return this call today, I will have you brought downtown in the morning."

I called him back. Since it was already evening, I expected voice mail to answer. A faulty assumption.

"Buron Washington." His voice was as passionless as I remembered.

"Hello, Detective," I sputtered. This is Samantha Newm—"

"I will see you here, in my office at eight a.m. sharp tomorrow morning. Do not be late." He hung up.

No other messages. Not that I expected any, especially from Carter. I wondered if he would call, ever again.

I returned the phone to my bag. The neon-yellow envelope with the scrawl proclaiming Brandy's innocence caught my eye. I'd missed the chance to give it to Kingsbury. I didn't want it burning a hole in my brain while Washington was interrogating me, but I wasn't keen on seeing Golden Boy again, either.

I took a bite of muffin and a swig of milk. As my mind slowly cleared, I figured out how to pass off the envelope and avoid seeing Kingsbury before I met with Washington. That was a load off.

Fixing things with Carter would be more of a challenge. I downed the rest of the muffin and milk, turned out the kitchen light, and found my way back to the bedroom in the dark.

Tomorrow would be a better day, I told myself. No more crying. But when my head hit the pillow, I realized I was wrong. Oceans of tears had been waiting in queue, ready to flow.

The next morning, I unglued my face from the mascara-smeared pillow, took a quick shower and headed out for the police station. On the way, I stopped downstairs to drop off the yellow envelope, carefully camouflaging it inside a larger manila one. I messaged Kingsbury that "something important" was at the concierge desk for him to pick up.

That was a weight off. Now I had to steel myself for another face-to-face grilling by Washington.

He barely looked up from his desk to greet me. "Follow me."

He grabbed a file and led me to a room with sweat-beige walls and a small conference table and chairs in the center. He gestured to a chair facing a mirrored window. "Sit."

Treating me like a perp in an episode of Law&Order must have been his plan to pry the tiniest details from me about Brandy's relationship with her husband. I wasn't inclined to help him build a case against her, so I gave him as little as possible to work with, which only made him more determined.

"Tell me again about your relationship with Mr. Bayne."

For the third time, I droned out an answer. "I hardly knew him. I've only lived there a few weeks."

"The officer at the scene reported your reaction to Mr. Bayne's death as . . ." he checked his notes, " . . . emotional."

"The officer was mistaken."

"He says here that you almost fainted when told Mr. Bayne was deceased."

"Listen, I'd just found out there was a body next door. It was kind of a shock. I'd driven all night from Nebraska. I was exhausted, and when I got home all hell broke loose."

He probably thought I was a cold bitch, but I couldn't let him poke into my still-raw wounds. No use explaining that I'd buried my two best friends in the past few months and I was at my limit for mourning. "Look, I'm sorry Irwin Bayne is dead. I'm sorry that Brandy lost her husband. I didn't know them that well. What do you want me to do, make something up?"

That little roadblock sent him back to his notes. He spent a long time turning pages back and forth. It gave me hope that he'd run out of questions, until he stopped on a page and tapped it with his finger. Without looking up, he let fly a doozy.

"So, the apartment next to the Bayne unit, where you live. My records show you do not own it. Who does?"

My heart sank to my knees. I didn't want to be the one to drag Carter into this. "What does that have to do with anything?"

"We are investigating all possibilities here, Ms. Newman. You said you haven't lived there long. Who owns the apartment?"

"A friend."

He raised his eyes in a challenge. "Your boyfriend, Carter Chapman?"

The question hit like an electric shock. I must have registered the jolt. His eyes shifted to my right hand where I was furiously twirling my mother's ring round and round my finger. I stopped twirling.

"It's complicated." If he asked me anything more about Carter, he'd see what constituted emotional.

He studied his notes again. "And the night of the incident—"

"I wasn't around!"

"But you were, Ms. Newman. At the very least, you harbored the accused in your apartment after the fact, where evidence, important evidence, was destroyed. We will go over this as many times as I say we will, until I get everything I need."

If I was ever going to get out of there, I had to give him something. Something that didn't involve Carter. "Okay. Here's the only thing that comes to mind. But it's only my opinion."

"Go on."

"Brandy and Irwin. I could hear them yelling a lot, and I got the impression that they drank a lot, too, and that he was hot-tempered. Brandy always seemed defensive. She's sweet, but a little dim. And I noticed she had a little bit of a black eye that night."

"Was Mr. Bayne ever aggressive toward you?"

I'd had an encounter with Irwin the week before, when the creep had suggested that the two of us should get to know one another better while his wife was out getting a pedicure.

I hadn't wanted to mention it before, but maybe it would get Washington off my back. "He made a pass at me once, but I shot him down."

"And?"

"He stayed down."

There was a tiny break in Washington's face. I think it was a smile, but I couldn't say for sure. In the end, he didn't get anything else, except more frustrated. He dismissed me with a warning.

"We are not finished here."

CHAPTER TEN

An Offer

I'd learned a long time ago that anxiety was not my friend. Better to take action than stew my insides to mush. As I drove away from the police station, I attempted to address the issues the way I'd done it back when I was working: itemize, prioritize and apply the best solution.

I tackled the easiest thing first, called the car rental place and re-upped the Ferret for another week. I could have kept driving Carter's Tesla, but it didn't feel right.

With the car issue postponed, I had one problem down, four to go. My brain swam through an endless mind-loop of murder, job, apartment, Carter. Something in me knew I needed a friend. I turned the car toward Gertie's house.

"Samantha, what a nice surprise! Come in."

For a second, I thought I'd knocked on the wrong door. The aroma of fresh baked sweets was familiar, but the sight of Gertie threw me into an alternate universe. Her kinky gray curls were tamed into wavy swoops, and she had traded her usual roomy blazer and skirt for a silky wrap dress that took years and pounds off her. I couldn't remember if I'd ever seen her wear eye shadow, but there she was, totally primped and polished.

She read my surprise. "I spent the morning at Neiman's. Did you know they have private shoppers who can engineer an entire new look in a matter of hours? They even worked me into the schedule at the salon!" She performed slow three-sixty, arms akimbo. "How do you like the new me?"

The woman who'd been my faithful, efficient, and decidedly frumpy secretary, now passed for a River Oaks matron, minus the mansion, of course. I was speechless.

She saw my face and deflated. "You don't approve?"

"You look great. It's just that I expected to visit an old friend, and I'm looking at a young chick instead."

Her smile returned. "Thanks. I don't know about the 'chick' part, but I definitely feel young again. Imagine that!"

"Does this have something to do with that man at the tea yesterday? The one whose granddaughter—?"

"Oh, Samantha, I'm in love! I want to tell you so much. Let's go to the kitchen and talk. I have some lemon squares cooling on the counter, and I'm packing up the brownies right now. Louis is having a big dinner party tonight to introduce me to his friends, and I want to make a good impression. Even if they don't like me, I hope they'll like my cooking."

I didn't care anymore if Gertie was my only friend in the world. She was the one I needed. I could feel my spirit lift, even if the joy was borrowed.

She started a pot of coffee in an old percolator—the kind where you dump the grounds into a metal basket on top, and boiling water rises through a narrow tube in the center, then burps out and down and cycles up and over again until the liquid at the bottom is drinkable. I had a feeling that the percolator, like those frumpy old blazers of hers, would soon be traded for a whiz-bang upscale model.

She plated a couple of brownies, set them on the pink and lime plaid oilcloth that covered her kitchen table and gestured for me to sit. The percolator gurgled to life.

She watched as I bit into a brownie. "What do you think?"

I closed my eyes and let the moist, chewy morsel fill my mouth with deliciousness. I didn't have to answer her; my face said it all.

"I hope Louis's friends like them, too." She hummed to herself while she set out two cups with pink roses on them. The percolator burbled furiously. She took it off the burner, filled the cups and joined me at the table.

I took a cup and added milk from a creamer shaped like a cow. "Okay, who is this man, and how did he sweep you off your feet so fast? Or have you been hiding him from me?"

"Hiding him? Gracious no. I just met him. No, that's not exactly true." A cloud replaced the sunshine on her face. "In a strange way, you brought us together. He was in the hospital where you . . . uh, after the car bomb."

"Where they took me after the explosion?"

She nodded. In all that horror, Gertie had apparently met the source of her present joy.

I took a sip of coffee. "He's a doctor?"

"No, a patient. After they sent you home, Mr. Chapman wanted to meet me there and—"

"Wait a minute. Carter asked you to come to my hospital room after I left?"

"I thought you'd been sent back. I got there as fast as I could, and when I walked into your old room, there he was!"

"Carter?"

"No, Louis. Only I didn't know who he was then. All I saw was a poor soul encased head to toe in a body cast. I'd bought some lilies for you at the hospital flower shop and they were making me sneeze. He looked terribly pitiful, so I set them on his lunch tray and walked out."

Gertie's story was hard for me to follow, especially after she'd mentioned Carter. "Why did Carter want to meet with you?"

"He was looking for someone inside De Theret to work with, and he thought I could help."

"So that's how he recruited—?"

"Exactly."

I was beginning to think that I needed someone to interpret Carter, past and present, for me. I shook off my bewilderment and tried to focus on Gertie's story. "That still doesn't explain Louis."

"Here's the funny part. When I dropped off the flowers, I noticed his name by the door of his hospital room. It was so unusual, hard to forget. At the affair yesterday, lo and behold, the man introduced himself. Louis Kleschevsky!" She said his name as if it were a magic charm like *Abracadabra*.

"He brought his granddaughter to The Women's Club early, so she could run through her piano piece. When he told me his name, I nearly fainted. I confessed that I'd been the crazy woman with the flowers and, well . . . we had a good laugh. We started talking and didn't stop until early this morning." She blushed.

I wanted to ask more, but I couldn't get my mouth to work.

Gertie's forehead creased. "Samantha? What's wrong? Why are you crying?"

I hadn't realized it, but while I was listening to her joyful story, the dam had broken. Tears fell onto my brownie. Why was I crying? Pick a reason.

She produced a box of Kleenex from somewhere and sat patiently waiting for me to recompose.

My cellphone chirped from inside my bag. I reached

for a tissue with one hand and fished for the phone with the other. It was the TV station.

I fought to control my heaving chest and connected. "Hello?"

A series of hiccups shook me as Jay Patel spoke. He was offering me a job, but I'd missed whether it was for the promotions department or an on-camera gig.

I risked sounding like an idiot. "I'm sorry, could you repeat that?"

He sounded rushed. "I said we'd love to have you work here. Can you come in today to get things started with HR?"

"Today?" *Not today*, the voice in my head pleaded. "Oh, I uh, I'd love to, but I can't. Car trouble, unfortunately."

"Tomorrow then. Say, nine a.m.?"

"Sure," I said, although I wasn't at all sure what I'd agreed to. "Thanks."

Gertie was refilling our cups. "Car trouble?"

I set the phone down and stared at it, as if that would clarify things. "KHTS just offered me a job."

Another item on my worry-list removed. I should have been over the moon. But all I could muster was mild relief. "I just couldn't go there today."

Gertie offered another brownie. "I knew it wouldn't take long for you to get back on your feet. No reason to be sad now, Samantha."

My face cracked again. I reached for another tissue, but instead of tears, words flew out of me at breakneck speed. Most of them were *Carter* and *why*.

After I'd blown through a few tissues, Gertie reached for my hand. "You matter to him very much, Samantha. I knew it the first time I saw him sitting with you in the hospital. He cares deeply for you, I'm certain of it."

"I'm not so sure."

"If you knew what had kept him away, you would understand."

"That's the problem. I don't know. Do you?"

"I only know its important."

I shook my head. "Even if he were James Bond, it wouldn't excuse the way he acted yesterday."

I recounted the whole disgusting drama with Kingsbury and how Carter had walked in on us.

"If he'd only told me when he would be there, I'd have been waiting for him, just him alone and . . ." I yanked another tissue from the box, anticipating tears, but I was empty.

Gertie tried to convince me that I couldn't ask for a better man to love. I needed more than her assurance. I needed Carter to open up and let me in.

I wished her good luck on her debut with Kleschevsky's friends and hit the road back to the condo. Halfway there, a construction detour caught me inside a traffic jam of epic Houston proportions. Traffic was going nowhere, and neither was I.

Something had to knock the pitiful wimp I'd become back to normal. I should call Carter, I thought, and have it out. Up or Down, In or Out, Forever or Never.

I was ready for a showdown, but before I could scroll to Carter's number, the phone came to life. I connected.

"Ms. Newman! Rufus Kingsbury! About the envelope you left for me. We need to talk, ASAP!"

"Not today. I'm beat. I'll call you tomorrow."

"No! Must see you imme—"

I hung up and shut the phone off. I'd wait to contact Carter when I got to the condo.

CHAPTER ELEVEN

Romeo?

The little girl with the strange older brother was waiting alone at the garage elevator. Her right knee sported a fresh, oozy scrape. A remnant of a tear hung from the corner of her eye.

I couldn't help but engage. "Looks like you took a tumble."

She glanced down at her knee. "Nah, it's nothing."

"Nice skateboard," I said, though it looked a lot like she did: ragged, scraped and peeling.

"It's my brother's, but he doesn't want it anymore. He says skateboarding is for losers, but I don't care. I'm gonna be a champ some day, soon as I learn how to ride. He gave me this, too."

She took a coin out of her pocket and thrust it toward me. It looked like a Mardi Gras doubloon, shiny blue with the words Krav Maga on one side and what looked like Hebrew letters on the other.

"Krav Maga. I've never heard of it. Are you Jewish?" It seemed a reasonable question to me, but she screwed up her face.

"What's Jewish?"

Hmmm. "Maybe you should ask your parents."

"They never tell me anything, except clean up my room and stuff."

The elevator arrived and we boarded. We rode the first couple of floors in silence, but she kept looking up at me. I tried another tack. "What is Krav Maga?"

Her face lit. "It's the awesomest! My brother saw it

on YouTube and now he practices every day. He says he could kill anybody with one blow." She punched the air between us with her fist.

"Really?"

"He's into that and Parker now, so he doesn't have time for the skateboard anymore." The doors opened on her floor. "Bye." She hefted the skateboard under one arm and limped toward her apartment.

When I reached my floor, relief poured through me. Despite the good smells from Gertie's kitchen, my clothes still held a police department clamminess. I couldn't wait to rip them off. Then I'd call Carter. I fairly flew down the hallway.

Kingsbury was leaning on my front door. "Hey, darlin'." He smiled down at me, blue eyes a-twinkle.

"Can you *not* take no for an answer?"

"We need to talk."

"Not today, Mr. Kingsbury." I turned the key and pushed the door open.

He followed me inside. "I promise it won't take long. I gotta figure something out, and I need your help to do it. By the way, my friends call me Rufus."

I turned to stop him from getting past the entry hall. "I'll remember that, in the unlikelihood that we become friends."

"I think we will, if you give me a chance." He smiled and took another step toward me. "Brandy's innocent, and she could use a friend, too."

My glare was sub-zero. "Friends know when to back off, which you clearly don't."

"Just a coupl'a minutes. For Brandy."

Geez, he was hard to get rid of. "Shut the door and wait for me in the kitchen." Not even Kingsbury would stop me from changing into something loose and clean smelling. I made for the bedroom.

Afternoon shadows and an imminent storm rendered the room almost completely dark. I peeled off my clothes and turned on the closet light to look for my warm-ups. As it clicked on, I heard a faint clatter behind me. It sounded like it had come from the balcony. I turned to look, but all I could see was my reflection on the glass.

I slipped into warm-ups and crossed the room to check the noise. No sign of a bird out there, but a small plant had been knocked over, perhaps from the wind that was kicking up ahead of the storm. Still, the back of my neck prickled. I checked the lock and headed to the kitchen.

Kingsbury had all the coffee fixings out on the counter. "Want some java?"

I flashed on the last time the two of us were in here. "No coffee."

He shrugged. "I noticed a nice red in the wine cooler. Any objection to opening it? I could use a little smoothing off. You?"

Wine, after the day I'd had? Definitely. But wine with Kingsbury?

He must have sensed my hesitation. "C'mon, darlin.' I just need you to be on my side, on Brandy's side right now. I don't want anything else from you. Honest. Can we just relax and have a little chat? For Brandy?"

I grabbed wineglasses from the shelf above the wine rack and set them on the counter. He retrieved the bottle, found the cork pull and opened it while I rummaged in the fridge for food. Gertie's brownies had been delicious, but the lack of a real lunch gnawed at my tummy.

The roasted chicken seemed a likely candidate. I grabbed it, the mandarin oranges, and the last two chocolate muffins while Kingsbury poured the wine.

I set the food on the breakfast counter and added plates and forks. He brought the wine glasses and sat opposite me. "You look kinda fried."

"Thanks."

"No, I mean, you're drop-dead gorgeous and all, but you look like you've seen a ghost, or something."

"Long day." I took a gulp of wine and tore a leg off the chicken. I didn't care if Kingsbury thought I was a Bolshevik slob. "And I just got spooked by a bird or something out on the balcony. So, no, not a ghost."

He looked at me with a question in his eyes that I took for disapproval of my table manners. "What? I'm hungry."

"Hell, darlin,' I don't care if you rip the thing apart with your teeth. But what you just said, about the balcony . . ." He took a sip of wine and drummed his fingers on the counter. "I wonder . . ."

While he ruminated, I finished the drumstick. He was still drumming and thinking, so I gulped another mouthful of wine, grabbed a knife and started sawing on the thigh.

"Let's go to your bedroom. I want to see this for myself." He was out of the kitchen before I could protest.

I found him on the balcony, leaning over the railing. A stiff wind blew his hair into a golden halo. He had turned the balcony light on and was scanning the space, peering up under the balcony above, down to the one below, and the ones to each side. He waved at me to join him.

As soon as I braved the first step outside, my hair lifted off my shoulders and into my face. I held it down with one hand and knelt to pick up the plant that had toppled.

"No! Don't touch anything!"

It was already in my hands. I returned it to the wrought iron shelf, beside its mate.

Kingsbury looked perturbed. "You don't follow instructions very well. Anybody ever tell you that?"

"You're one to talk."

He took another eye-sweep of the balcony before stepping inside. I nudged some dirt off the deck with my foot and brushed past him to get a broom and dustpan for the rest.

When I returned, Kingsbury had turned the light off and was opening and closing the sliding door, locking it, testing the lock, and unlocking it again. "Do you always set this bolt?"

"Sometimes."

"It was set when I tried to get out, just now."

"A couple of nights ago I thought I saw something out there, and again last night. It spooked me a little, so I locked the door. Ridiculous, really. Probably a pigeon."

"A couple of nights ago? You mean this isn't the first time you heard something?" He looked like he was about to levitate. "This could be important!"

"Important, how?"

"Don't know! C'mon, let's finish the wine and try to figure this thing out." He strode out of the room. "And don't use that broom!"

CHAPTER TWELVE

The Envelope, Please

Kingsbury was chewing a mouthful of chocolate muffin when I caught up to him in the kitchen. He looked like he was about to say something, but he bit off another chunk of muffin and worked it over for a while. I could almost see the wheels turning in his head.

I took advantage of the break and continued sawing on the thigh. He polished off the muffin and pointed to the one remaining. "You gonna eat that one?"

Well, yes, that was my plan, but the chicken was probably enough to fill me up. "It's yours if you want it."

The muffin was gone before you could say Rufus Kingsbury. He finished it off with vigorous tooth-sucking noises and the last of the wine in his glass.

He grabbed the bottle for a refill, topped my glass off, too, and leaned across, lowering his face just inches from mine and bathing me in the chocolate-wineyness of his breath. "Think very carefully. Exactly when did you hear the noise on your balcony the first time?"

I tried, but I honestly couldn't remember. How long had I been back from Nebraska? How many nights after that did I hear the noise? My head spun. I shook it, hoping to reconnect the circuits. "Sorry. The past few days have been a rollercoaster. It all jumbles together."

He sat down and looked at me for what seemed like a long time. "No matter. We'll clear that up later. Main thing is, don't tell anybody else about this, for now. And don't touch anything on the balcony until I can get my person here to study it."

"Are you saying a bird on my balcony has something to do with Brandy's case?"

"I've gotta think it through." He reached inside his jacket and retrieved a small plastic zip bag containing the yellow envelope. "Let's talk about this." He set it on the table between us. "Where'd you find it?"

"In the entry. Like it was slid under the door."

"Interesting." He drummed his fingers. "When?"

I made another attempt to access my internal calendar. Miraculously, it came to me. It was the day of my job interview at KHTS, the day of the charity tea.

"Why didn't you give it to me then?"

"I didn't know you'd be there. And then, when we came back here and you . . . I, and then Carter . . ."

"Ah!" He nodded. "Enough said! I was grievously out of line, by the way. Hope you managed to sort everything out with lover-boy."

"The jury's still out on that one." I emptied the wine in my glass.

"Sorry to hear that. If there's anything I can do—"

"Let's just talk about whatever you came to talk about. About Brandy."

"Brandy. Yes. Well, here's the thing. She's innocent. Poor thing's been buffeted by the slings and arrows of fortune, and—"

I held up my hand to stop him before he launched into what sounded like the first draft of his opening statement to the jury. "I'm really beat. Can we get to what you wanted to discuss, specifically?"

"Of course." He looked straight into me and gave me another twinkle. "I hope you'll be on our team. I need—"

He suddenly popped up from the barstool and hit his forehead with his big mitt of a hand. "Wait a minute!"

He paced the kitchen twice, coming to a stop across

from me, his hands splayed out on the countertop. "You found this envelope in your entry?"

I nodded.

"But it couldn't have been shoved under your door!" He started pacing again. A full minute went by before his attention returned to me. "This is important!"

"What makes you think it wasn't slipped under—?"

"Ms. Newman, I didn't come to The Wellbourne today to see you. My goal was to look over Brandy's place and get the lay of the land. I was hoping to catch you, too, but you weren't here, so I tried to shove my card under your door. The thing's tight as a drum! Even a thin business card couldn't get through, much less a note inside an envelope!"

"But the envelope was right inside the door."

"It couldn't have come from the hall."

"So, you're saying what exactly?"

His face flushed as he broke into a huge grin. "Ms. Newman, I believe you have given me the key to Brandy's defense!"

The wine must have been messing with my head, because I had a hard time following him.

"Here's the deal." He sat across from me again, picked up the envelope and waved it in the air.

"You find this note that says Brandy didn't do it. Because it was by your front door, you assume it was shoved under. But as I said, nothing can pass through."

I started to speak. He held up his hand and continued. "Also, you hear noises coming from your bedroom balcony!"

It began to gel in my brain. "Are you saying—?"

He nodded. "I'm saying it's possible the note was put there by someone who came from your balcony!"

"From the balcony? Thirteen floors up? How . . .?"

"That's what we have to figure out! It could help

Brandy's case. Hell, it could damn well point to the real killer!"

All the times I'd heard a noise on the balcony, had the passing shadow been something other than a bird? I filled my wineglass with water and gulped it down.

Kingsbury laid his hand on my shoulder. "Hey, darlin', I didn't mean to scare you."

"I'm not scared," I lied.

I tried to move my mind back to the first night I'd noticed the shadow. Had it been before I found the envelope, or after? Could someone have entered when I was in the apartment, in the kitchen, or even sleeping in the bed right next to the balcony? Goosebumps pimpled my arms.

"Tell you what," he said. "Why don't we check all the balconies in this apartment together before I skedaddle? We'll lock 'em up tight, just in case. Tomorrow, I'll send someone to recheck, and we'll take a look at the ones over at Brandy's place, too."

I wasn't too keen on going near a balcony at the moment, but I figured it would be better if I didn't have to do it alone. "Okay."

He returned the envelope to his jacket pocket and followed me to the living room. We inspected that balcony first. It was as broad across as the room. Wind gusts teased at the tips of fig ivy that clung to the side walls. A low glass-topped iron table sat in the middle, flanked by matching chaises. It looked pretty sterile out there. Beyond the railing, downtown Houston spread its sparkling girth beneath a churning shelf of black clouds.

Kingsbury stepped out and emitted a high-pitched whistle, which sent my already-thumping heart into overdrive. "That view's a stunner!"

I baby-stepped over the threshold into the humid

dusk. The open space made me woozy. A tang of ozone and clap of thunder announced the official arrival of the storm. I flinched. "Can we go in now?"

"Okay." He slid the door shut and tested the lock a couple of times. Once he was satisfied, we moved to the guest rooms. Only two of them had balconies: the one where Gertie had stayed, and the one she'd put Brandy in after the commotion. He checked both balconies and locked them up tight. "And?"

"That's it. The other bedroom doesn't have a balcony. It's more like a study. Just a high window that doesn't open."

"Okay then. You'll be snug as a bug tonight. Nothing to worry about." He breezed out.

I caught up to him at the front door. "Just for the record, I wasn't worried."

"'Course you weren't. Better to be safe than sorry, right?"

"No way someone could get to the thirteenth floor from the outside," I countered, "unless it was Spider-Man, and he's a good guy."

Kingsbury smiled and patted me on the shoulder like a big brother. "Hate to run out on you, even though you're not scared and all, but I need to let this little idea of mine percolate some." He twisted the front doorknob. "What say we meet tomorrow and finish the conversation?"

Before I could answer, he opened the door and was gone.

I returned to the kitchen to put what was left of the chicken and the mandarins in the fridge. While I rinsed the wineglasses, my mind replayed the locking of doors. Had we locked the balcony door in the master bedroom?

We'd been out there only a few minutes ago, but I

didn't remember how we'd left it. I couldn't sleep in there tonight without knowing. I'd have to check the darned door myself.

The wineglasses chattered against one another in my hand. I set them down, took a deep breath and headed to the bedroom, hoping I wasn't walking to my doom.

It was easier to see the balcony without the inside lights on, but that left the room in darkness. Halfway to the sliding door, something moved beside me. I jumped and turned to look, only to see my reflection staring back at me from the mirror. I'd spooked myself, again.

Stupid. And for that matter, so was Kingsbury, for concocting his ridiculous idea of a balcony intruder in the first place. Obviously, he was grasping at straws, looking for a way to get Brandy off. Well, he could have his silly theory, but I wasn't buying it.

My heartbeat smoothed to normal rhythm. The balcony was exactly as we'd left it, except for the huge drops of rain that pounded the railing. The remaining dirt from the overturned pot had been washed away.

I checked the door. Locked. I closed the drapes, which probably violated Kingsbury's don't-touch-anything rule, but I didn't care. I didn't want to see or think about that balcony for a while. The storm had probably obliterated evidence already—if there was any to start with—and a human wasn't likely to risk it out there in such weather.

I turned on a lamp and considered my reflection in the mirror. "Get a grip," I said to my scaredy-faced double before I turned on my heels and made for the kitchen to finish cleaning up. A few sips remained in the wine bottle. I put it to my lips and chugged.

The doorbell rang, which sent my heart pumping again. I talked myself down. A bad guy wouldn't ring the doorbell and politely wait to be let in. It was probably Kingsbury, back with another scary thought.

I opened the door. Pansy Gump stood before me in a flowing paisley caftan and matching velvet slippers monogrammed in gold thread.

"We must speak." She swept past me into the living room. By the time I shut the door and turned around, she had draped herself over half of the sofa.

"This simply cannot wait any longer. I have important information, and no one has seen fit to take an interest. Unconscionable."

I plopped into a chair, a little harder than I'd planned. Must have been the wine.

She fanned the edges of her caftan outward until it covered almost the entire sofa. "I'm certain you are in touch with the police. You must convey my thoughts to them."

"What thoughts?" My words gurgled out like I had swallowed soapsuds. I cleared my throat, sat up a little straighter and tried to look like I cared.

"Young woman, I have observed your neighbor, the one who killed her husband, in the company of certain people, males who are not her husband, in—dare I say—compromising situations."

I wanted to lie down, but I knew she wouldn't leave until she'd had her say. "Like who?"

"Well, for one, that valet, the one from Namibia, or somewhere African, the handsome one with the big muscles." She looked at me as if that said it all. I stared back.

"I'm sure you've seen him. My husband, Hubert, goes to the gym downstairs every afternoon to ride that bicycle contraption, and I always go with him to make sure he doesn't hurt himself. Not an athlete, Hubert. Never was. The only person I know who could fall over backward and bump his nose."

I briefly tried to work out that image and gave up.

"And often, *she* is there with that valet, and he's helping her with the machines, showing her how to position her arms and legs and such. *Touching* her. And they laugh together." She spread her arms along the back of the sofa and waited for a reaction.

When I didn't respond, she started up again.

"She flirts with everyone, even Hubert. He's oblivious, of course. I've seen the way she wraps men around her finger. She even has that strange boy, the one with the ragamuffin sister, mooning over her. I don't know why we let people like that take up residence at The Wellbourne."

I had the feeling she would say the same about me, if I wasn't within hearing distance. She was clearly not on Brandy's team, as Kingsbury would say. I tried to form a coherent reaction, but words swam inside my head.

She came to the end of her diatribe and scanned the living room. "This unit shares the same layout as mine. It could use a more personal touch, if you ask me."

Well, I hadn't asked her. I wanted her to go away so I could lay my head on something soft.

"Do you have a roach problem? They're simply crawling in my apartment. Hubert, of course, is terrified of them. Last week I discovered one, feet up, in the hallway, and I left it there just to see what he would do. It lay there for two days. Two days! Then he comes into my bedroom and says, 'There's a roach in the hall.' And I said, 'I know. Its name is Sheridan Whiteside and apparently he's come to stay.' Well, that roach was gone in no time. You have to train these husbands, you know . . . Ms. Newman?"

I must have dozed off. A spot of drool had formed in

the corner of my mouth. I cleared my throat. "Sorry, I'm really tired."

"Have you heard a word I've said?"

Too many, actually. I wobbled to a standing position. "I'll share your thoughts with the people working on the case. I have to get some sleep. Goodnight, Mrs. Gump."

Her black-olive eyes grew wide. "Well! I'm not certain you understand the importance of my views on this murder business. I will have to contact the authorities myself." Pouty-faced, she stood and swept out the door without another word.

An urge to recheck all the locks came over me. I worked my way backwards this time, from the guest wing balconies to the living room and finally, the master bedroom. I peeked through the drapes. Even though everything seemed okay, I knew I wouldn't be able to sleep in there.

I tugged the comforter and a pillow off the bed and dragged them across the apartment to the guestroom without a balcony. The room was bare except for a mattress, lamp and dresser. I was so beat, I wouldn't have cared if it had been decked out like Versailles.

Between Kingsbury and Pansy, I'd had no chance to call Carter, and now I had zero energy for a confrontation. Maybe tomorrow. I tossed the comforter onto the bed, locked the bedroom door—just in case— and turned out the light.

CHAPTER THIRTEEN

The Platform

Damn Kingsbury for putting thoughts of an intruder into my head. Fresh fear startled me awake. The sky was bright outside a high window. Heartbeats later, I remembered where I was, and why. And my nine a.m. meeting at the TV station. There was no clock in the room, and I'd left my cellphone . . . where?

I sped out to check the time. The kitchen clock read 7:40. Just enough.

Thanking the gods of every heaven, I chugged a glass of water and headed to the master bedroom. I hesitated at the doorway before I braved it through and opened the drapes to scan the balcony. It looked normal. Safe enough to risk a shower.

The moment the water hit my body, my mind conjured the bathroom scene from Psycho. Was a Norman Bates copycat poised to slash me with a butcher knife? I shook the thought away. If I were chopped to pieces, being late for work wouldn't matter. If I survived the shower intact, I'd better be on time.

"Here you go, Ms. Newman." The receptionist handed a visitor's badge to me. "They want you in make-up first."

I looped the maroon lavaliere over my head. "Make-up?" After my first on-camera disaster, why would they put me through it again?

She checked the schedule. "Yes ma'am. It's through those double doors, past the soundstage. Ask for Jojo."

The hallway pulsed red from a flashing *On Air* sign above the soundstage door. The morning show was starting its two-hour run. I tiptoed past.

"You don't have to be quiet out here. Just don't bust in screaming bloody murder." A familiar sultry voice spoke behind me. I turned.

The voice belonged to Alicia Sultana, the raven-haired evening news anchor. The blinking light launched her high-collared red silk suit into maximum diva overdrive. My average-size frame felt puny beside her basketball-worthy height.

When she smiled, the only facial feature that moved was her mouth. Her teeth were big, perfectly straight choppers, whiter than white against her dark chocolate skin. "Are you lost?"

"I'm looking for Jojo in makeup."

Her expression tightened, ever so slightly. "Jojo?" Her eyes scraped over me like a body scan. "I'm going that way myself."

She had a full-on paint job already, but who was I to argue? I followed in her Shalimar wake to the next door, which opened into the makeup area.

"Alicia! Good-morning-you-look-gorgeous-as-ever." The makeup guy, an anorexic platinum-haired, tattooed thirty-something with a serious overbite, double-kissed Alicia and circled her appreciatively. "What are you doing here so early, Miss Thang?"

"It's the Holiday Wishes spot. Don't know why it couldn't wait 'til this afternoon. It's still September, for chrissakes."

"Did your own makeup dear? I'm hurt, but you do look fabulous." Before Alicia could respond, the punker noticed me. "Who's your friend?" Both of them looked me up and down as if I were a new piece of furniture.

It was cold as a meat locker in there. A gofer handed

Alicia a mug with steam curling upward from the top. I wondered if there was more where that came from.

"Samantha Newman." I offered my hand to Alicia, who kept both manicured hands around her coffee. "I thought I'd be meeting with HR, but when I picked up my badge, I was sent here."

A frown threatened her forehead. "What for?"

"I'm not sure. I interviewed here a couple of days ago for a promotions job, and I was invited back today."

She seemed to relax a bit. "Well, if that's all you're here for, you don't need Jojo."

We eyed one another, she in her royal crimson, me in my all-business gray. "Nice suit," she said. "Bad on camera, though. Much too dull."

"Too butch," Jojo added. "But that dark auburn mane and those green eyes . . ."

"She's here for me." Jay Patel extended his hand as he approached. "Sorry I'm a bit late." His smile warmed the room ten degrees.

Alicia cooled it down again. "Jay. Good to see you."

"Alicia. Nice of you to make it in. We'll do your promo in Studio B right after we take another look at Ms. Newman."

Patel must have seen me wince. "It won't take long. I want Jojo to see what he can do with that scar on your cheek."

"Scar?" I pulled my hair back. No pirate face today. I stifled a smile.

Jojo peered at my skin like a dermatology intern. "Flawless, boss."

Patel shook his head. "Must've been something on one of the lights. Just tan her up and send her to Studio B. I'll be waiting."

Alicia stiffened. "I'll be in my office." She whirled

and followed Patel out the door.

As I hopped onto Jojo's makeup chair, my phone chirped. I stole a peek: Kingsbury. I connected and preempted his exhortations. "I don't have time now."

"I need permission to enter your unit. My investigator will be there at ten to check the balcony situation."

"Okay." I disconnected and called The Wellbourne security desk. "Sorry," I said to Jojo.

"That's okay, sweetie, we don't have much to do. Your face is a natural for the camera, I can tell. So could Alicia, poor old hussy."

The on-camera tryout went better this time. I read copy about an oil refinery employee who had reported the plant's poor safety oversight months before an explosion that killed two people.

Jay Patel seemed pleased when we met in his office afterwards. "That was pretty good. Next time, you'll be even better."

Next time. I held my breath and crossed my fingers.

"Here's what I want to do, Ms. Newman. I think you'd be a great on-air asset. I know it's not the job you applied for, but as soon as I saw your name, I remembered who you were, and the segments you'd done with us. I believe you'd be a great addition to our team, given your reputation."

My face heated. "My reputation?"

"Let's be frank. Your last employer imploded in rather spectacular fashion. We ran stories on De Theret International and your role in its downfall for weeks. People know who you are. Your whistle-blowing history is your best asset. It's a strong platform for reporting on public malfeasance."

In his words, I sounded like a different person: noble, courageous, someone to be taken seriously. I'd once felt close to that, when I was building De Theret's sterling public image. But after everything blew up, something inside me collapsed, too.

"I'm not a whistle-blower. I was just trying to find my friend."

"That's not how the public saw it."

"You mean that's not how you reported it." By the look on his face, my smart mouth had just sunk any chance of a job at the station. I wracked my brain for a way to take it back.

"I know your reporters were just doing their job. Their stories were legitimate, but they made me sound like a crusader, and that's not what I was.

"My friend disappeared. I set out to find her. If I'd known the whole company would crumble and wreck so many innocent people's lives . . ." I shook my head. "Calling me a whistle-blower doesn't make me proud. It makes me sadder than sad."

The words tumbled from my mouth in a voice I barely remembered. I sounded like Samantha Newman V.P. again, someone passionate, polished, confidant. Where had that come from? And why had I spewed it at a man I needed on my side?

He shoved papers around on his desk like it was his way of cursing. "Here's how I see it, Ms. Newman. At great personal risk, you exposed a deeply corrupt and criminal operation. That's the bigger picture. Our viewers will come to see you as their voice against powerful institutions. You have real potential there."

He leaned his elbows on his desk and spread his hands. "I'm asking you to be open to the possibility of using your history as a platform to do good."

I'd never thought of myself as having a "platform." I was struggling just to get my feet on the ground again. A voice for the people?

Patel sat back. "Sorry if I blind-sided you. I tend to be very direct when I want something. Don't worry, we'll give you all the support you need. Shall we give it a go?"

I wasn't sure I bought his elevated opinion of me, but truth was, he could have asked me to be open to the possibility of a root canal and I would have said yes. I'd work out the platform stuff later.

I sailed out of there. This job meant a car of my own. A place of my own. I could finally return to something resembling a life.

I wanted to call my Mom and Dad to tell them the news. Or my brother. Or Lista. Even Derek. But all of them were gone from this world. Suddenly my happiest moment in years plummeted to the loneliest. I sat in the car and cried.

The station's security guard knocked on the window. "You okay?"

I waved him off and fished a tissue from my bag. In the visor mirror, Jojo's makeup job held firm. I gave myself a happy face, like the one I'd managed in front of the camera, and then I called Gertie.

No answer. Last night had been her coming out party with Kleschevsky's friends. The possibility that she could be doing the walk of shame this morning made me smile. Without her, my list was down to the only other person in the world who would understand what this job meant to me: Carter.

Between Kingsbury and Pansy, my plan to have it out with him yesterday had evaporated. I took it as a sign. I was still hurt and angry, but if there was a chance we could find our way back to where we were a month ago, I was willing to take it.

Problem was, how to begin? I couldn't just blithely announce my new job and ignore his sudden condo appearance and rude exit.

Me, happily: I have a job!

Carter, frigidly: Why should I care?

The whole thing could backfire.

One scenario after another played in my head, until I hit on a reasonably comfortable solution. I cleared my throat and tested my vocal chords. When the syllables stopped wobbling, I cleared my throat again and tapped his number.

He picked up on the first ring. "Sam. I'm so glad you called. I can't stop thinking about . . . what happened the other day."

His voice hit my eardrum like warm honey, obliterating the cool attitude I'd rehearsed. I couldn't trust myself to recite any of the speech I'd planned. Thank goodness he kept talking.

"I should have called you, Samantha. I should have been the one to call. When can I see you?"

A tear slipped down my cheek. "I'll be at the condo."

CHAPTER FOURTEEN

The White

The little girl that Pansy Gump called a ragamuffin waited beside me at the garage elevator. I remembered how forlorn she had seemed last time, like she could use a friend.

"Since we keep seeing each other like this, I think we ought to know each other's name. I'm Samantha." I stuck my hand out to shake. She grabbed my fingertips in an attempt to reciprocate. "And your name is?"

She mumbled something.

"Elizabeth?"

A glum nod. "I hate my name."

"Well, what do your friends call you?"

"My parents call me that name. My brother calls me Lizard, but I hate that even worse."

"What do you like to be called?"

"Lizzie's okay."

"Well, Lizzie, it's nice to see you again."

"Thanks."

We boarded the elevator together. She squinted up at me. "Are you a model or something?"

Must have been Jojo's airbrush work. "No, I'm a . . . I work at a TV station." It felt good to say that out loud. "Where's your skateboard?"

She screwed up her face. "Totaled."

"Sorry to hear that."

"It's okay, 'cuz now I can do Krav Maga more." She chopped the air with her fist and kicked her leg out. "My brother's a green belt, but I'm gonna be a black someday." The doors opened onto her floor. "Bye."

On the short ride one floor up, I let out a whoop. I had a job! I floated out and down the hallway toward the condo.

A band of light spilled out from the apartment. The door was slightly ajar. Carter had said he'd meet me there, but I assumed he'd been at Serenity when I called. I didn't expect him until later.

I nudged the door open wider. "Hello?"

No answer. I pushed it fully open. On the floor, not two feet from the threshold, was another envelope. A white one this time. I snatched it.

A whooshing sound came from the master bedroom, like someone was opening or closing the balcony door. "Carter?"

Still no answer. If it had been Carter, he would have answered. I backtracked down the hallway toward the elevator and pushed the down button. Nothing. I pushed it three times more.

Fourth Elevator Game: When you are about to be attacked by a cat-burglar-slash-axe murderer, don't rely on the perverse metal box to save you. It's too busy transporting others downstairs to check their mail.

I reversed direction. As I neared the apartment again, another noise came from inside.

"Carter?" My voice sounded puny. If only I knew some Krav Maga moves like my new friend Lizzie. She wouldn't fear noises in the middle of the day. I shook it off and marched toward the door.

A voice called into the hallway. "Hallo?"

Kingsbury. I'd forgotten that he'd be checking the balcony again today. My pulse returned to normal.

He poked his head out and grinned at me. "Hey, darlin'. You playin' hide and seek?"

I had no patience for the Mr. Charm act. I walked past him into the entry. "Find anything?"

He shook his head. "Not what I was looking for. But my investigator says it's possible that a person could have been out there."

I held up the white envelope. "Then why would they leave a note at the front door?"

"That wasn't here when I came in." He snatched it from my hand.

"It's mine." I gave him the stink-eye. "You have the other one. I need this one for the police. It could be important evidence."

"The cops will just bury it, 'cuz it doesn't fit their case against my client."

"How do you know? You haven't read it."

I tried to take it from him, but the harder I tugged, the tighter he gripped. I was afraid the paper would tear, so I eased up.

He yanked it away. I grabbed for it again, but he was too quick.

I shouted in his face. "It's mine. Give it back. Now!"

Another voice spoke behind me. "Give what back?"

No need to turn around to know who it was. "The envelope in his hand belongs to me."

Kingsbury looked from me to Carter to the envelope and back again. He seemed to be considering his next move.

"Okay, it's yours." He handed it over. "Promise you won't give it to the cops until we talk it over."

I glared at him. He nodded at Carter and sidled past us into the hallway.

Carter's eyes narrowed as he followed Kingsbury's backside down the hall. "Didn't expect to see him here again." He followed me inside and shut the door.

"Neither did I."

"So we're clear on that."

"Clear?"

When I'd played it in my mind, this conversation hadn't begun in anger. Damn Kingsbury. He'd primed my flash point and set me on torpedo launch.

I wheeled around. "You've made nothing clear to me, Carter, not one thing! What am I to think, after you make me feel like the most special person in the world and then leave me like a crumpled piece of garbage? Then you reappear from nowhere and storm out again!"

He backed toward the door, stunned. My words buzzed around us. When they settled, he spoke.

"I'm sorry. For everything."

"Everything?"

"I never should have left you the way I did that day at the ranch. I should have taken the time to explain. I don't blame you for being angry. Not even for what I saw between you and that jackass in the kitchen."

I pounced. "What you saw? You saw nothing! The guy was reaching over me and I slipped, and he caught me."

"It looked like more than that."

It had felt like more than that, but that was beside the point. "Do you even know who he is?"

"I do now." He shook his head. "I suppose I overreacted."

"Big time."

He met my glare with those sad brown eyes that could melt me like butter on a sizzling griddle. I had to cool down.

The envelope in my hand felt like it weighed a hundred pounds, and my oh-so-professional business suit squeezed and pinched. I unbuttoned the jacket.

"You look nice."

"Thanks."

"What was the occasion?"

My new job. Without knowing it, he'd circled around to the reason I'd called him in the first place. But now there was Kingsbury and the envelope to deal with. A puff of compressed air escaped my lungs. "Let's sit somewhere. There's a lot to talk about."

Despite being the backdrop of our last bad karma moment, the kitchen seemed a relatively neutral place. I set the white envelope on the breakfast island and poked my head into the fridge. I grabbed the carton of orange juice and waved it at Carter. "Want some?"

He nodded and tapped the envelope. "What's so special about this? Who's it from?"

"That's a good question. I think it has something to do with the mess next door." I pulled two glasses off the shelf and set them next to the envelope.

"Aren't you going to open it?"

There seemed to be no way around the seemingly ordinary yet potentially explosive object in front of us. I extracted the note. Like the first one, it was short on words.

She's innocent.

Printed in black ballpoint, the message was hard to ignore. A tinge of guilt wiggled in. Innocent or not, Brandy was in trouble, and somebody wanted me to help her.

"So? What does it say?"

Much as I wanted to focus on my new job and try to navigate a détente with Carter, I needed to bring him up to speed. After all, the Baynes were his neighbors.

I set the note in front of him. "Might as well start here and work our way back. But first, I'd like to get out of this suit."

He lifted his attention from the note and looked at me through the dark fringe of his eyelashes. "Need help?"

Our eyes locked. Nothing moved from my brain to my mouth.

He frowned. "Too soon?"

Wa-a-a-yy too soon. I tore my eyes away, shook my head and escaped down the hall.

CHAPTER FIFTEEN

Sonata

Kingsbury's aura lingered in the bedroom, but everything else seemed normal. I made a quick change into my camo warm-ups. In the mirror, my TV face looked garish, so I stopped by the bathroom to take it off. A passel of soaps and cleansers later, it finally felt clean.

Carter's eyes lit when I returned to the kitchen. "There you are."

"Sorry it took so long."

"No, I mean there you are. I love your face."

A chunk of armor fell away. My cheek muscles spasmed in a loop of smiling, frowning, smiling, frowning. I managed to rein in a shaky smile. "Let's forget this envelope for a minute and start with why I called you."

"Lay it on me."

My face started spazzing again. "I have a job."

He popped off of the bar stool. "Hey! I knew it wouldn't be long before somebody snatched you up. Who's the lucky company?"

"KHTS, the television station. I start tomorrow."

He clinked my glass of juice with his. Before he took a sip, he frowned at his glass and shook his head. "This news deserves something special. Is it okay to celebrate, for real?"

I was ready. I let my grin break free. "There's a bottle of champagne in the wine fridge. Shall we uncork it?"

"Perfect." Carter turned to retrieve the icy bottle.

"Can you get the flutes?"

I stretched up to grab the glasses from a high shelf. He reached over me to help, but I bumped him away with my hip. "I don't want to give my boyfriend the wrong idea."

My eyes dared him to say something.

"Touché." He peeled the foil off the top of the champagne bottle, then wrapped its frosty girth in a thin towel. Holding the cork in place, he turned the bottle until it made a little pop. Delicate foam surged to the rim.

I swiped a bit of foam onto my finger and touched it to my tongue. "I feel like we need silly party hats or something."

"Hats? Really? What if we just move somewhere more comfortable, like the music room? You can tell me about your new job and everything else that's happened since I . . ."

"Ran off again?"

Before he could react, I spun and headed out of the kitchen. The little devil inside me was out of the bottle too.

I hadn't spent much time in the music room. Carter was gone before I had access to the apartment, and without him the media system was a mystery. It would have been a perfect refuge from intruders last night: no windows. It had a manly leather vibe, and lots of books lining the wood-paneled walls—similar to his library at Serenity, only cozier.

He produced a champagne bucket from somewhere and filled it with chunks out of a built-in icemaker under one of the bookshelves. He filled our glasses, rewrapped the bottle and set it into the bucket.

I found a comfy spot on the suede sofa while he set up some music. A delicate piano sonata floated through the room. He joined me on the sofa me and held up his glass. "To you and your new career."

We clinked and took a sip. Foam tingled my upper lip. He leaned in and smoothed it away with his fingertip. His hand hovered near my cheek. We locked eyes. I pulled mine away. My body sizzled with the aftershock of his touch. Still too soon, I told myself.

He cleared his throat. "What will you be working on at the station?"

I couldn't risk eye contact. I spoke to my champagne flute. "They want me to be a commentator, kind of watchdog against corporate and institutional evildoers. A whistleblower, I guess."

"That makes sense."

"Why does it make sense to everyone but me? I'm no crusader."

"Says who?" He covered my hand with his. "You've been fighting for justice for a long time, Sam. You risked everything to bring your corrupt boss down. If someone wants to pay you for what you do by nature, I say wear the cape proudly. Sounds like a heck of a new career."

I studied the bubbles floating upward in my glass. "I'm not sure it rises to the level of a career yet. At least I won't have to keep mooching off you. I can afford my own apartment now."

"For Pete's sake, you're not mooching. I'm happy to—"

I held up a hand to stop him. "I want to stand on my own feet again."

"But—"

"You've been more than generous to me, but I need to separate that part of you from the part that I . . . that I . . . you know what I mean."

"Not really."

I turned to face him. "I have to feel like me again, Carter. Like I'm making decisions for the right reasons. And frankly, you should do the same."

"I know how I feel."

"Do you? What if it's only leftover endorphins from when you rescued me from De Theret? I'm not a damsel in distress anymore. I can take care of myself now."

He rolled his eyes. "You're too stubborn for your own good. I only had to rescue you because you ignored my warnings and tried to bring those bastards to justice by yourself. It almost got you killed."

"True, but . . . "

"Life's hard enough as it is, Sam. I don't see the harm in letting me try to make it easier for you. Why fight me on this?"

"I hate not being in control."

That sent him off the sofa. He stood directly in front of me. "You are in control, Samantha. You're in the driver's seat, especially when it comes to us. You have been from the moment we met. I'm not trying to buy you, if that's what you're afraid of. I'm the one begging, seems to me." He paced the room a few times before he sank into the sofa again.

He was probably right. My stubborn streak had caused heartache before, and now we were battling again. The first movement of the sonata ended, leaving us to fill the silence before the next one began.

I turned to Carter. "Let's change the subject."

"To what?"

"To what's going on around here. That envelope in the kitchen, it's not the first one."

"I'm not ready to give up on us, Samantha."

I drained my glass and swallowed hard. "Me either."

He reached for my hand. That crazy electric tingle in his touch: that was all it took to pivot the subject back to us. Our eyes locked.

He leaned in and kissed me, and every ounce of my resistance dissolved. He may have felt like he was the only one begging, but in truth, I needed him. Just him, loving me.

The music dipped and peaked, then dipped and peaked again, and then swooped and soared to a climax. Before the last movement ended, we lost ourselves in celebration.

CHAPTER SIXTEEN

Krump, or Something

Mid-afternoon light sifted into the bedroom from the shaded balcony. Carter propped himself on an elbow and beamed down at me. "Hi."

"Mmm." I closed my eyes, breathed him in, and opened them again. It wasn't a dream this time.

"You're really here."

"You noticed."

"We never talked about—"

He put a finger to my lips. "I know. We have time."

"Unless you get a call and run off again."

"Ouch." He sat up and grabbed his khakis.

I'd managed to kill the mood. "Sorry."

"I'm going to make coffee."

By the time I got to the kitchen, Carter was filling his mug. "Want some?"

I nodded. He poured another mugful, passed it to me and sat on a barstool. I sat opposite and took a sip. It burned my stomach. The clock read 4:10 p.m. I needed food.

I opened the fridge and silently cursed Kingsbury for polishing off the last of Gertie's muffins. I settled for bread and a jar of peanut butter.

Just as I popped a slice into the toaster, my phone buzzed. By the time I'd fished it out of my bag, the call had quit. The voicemail icon lit up. Detective Washington. His message was short and to the point.

I turned to Carter. "It's the homicide detective on the case next door. He's in the building and wants to speak to me again. I should probably call him back."

The white envelope lay between us. We both stared. "Leave it," Carter said. "Let's find out why he's here before we do anything." He gave me an apologetic look. "We should've talked about this first, like you wanted."

"Priorities." I smiled. "Anyway, you should know he likes to play the tough guy. He's the one who had Gertie hauled off."

Carter frowned. "He's called me at the ranch with questions, but we haven't met in person."

The doorbell rang. He rose to get it, his eyes glinting with the same icy steel he'd shot at Kingsbury. "I'm looking forward to this."

The surprise on Washington's face was priceless. His eyes fixed on Carter, but he spoke to me. "I didn't know you had company, Ms. Newman."

Carter bristled. "I'm not company. This is my place."

"Mr. Chapman?"

Carter opened the door wider and led him into the living room. We sat on the sofa. Washington took a side chair. He looked from me to Carter and back.

I wondered if he could tell we'd just rolled out of bed. Carter had slipped on his white tee, but it hung loose and rumpled over his wrinkled khakis. I was pretty sure my bed-head and warm-ups betrayed more than a hint of afternoon delight. I didn't care.

The detective rubbed his knees, cleared his throat and pulled out his notebook. He cleared his throat again. "Actually, I need to speak to Ms. Newman alone."

"That's not going to happen." Carter kept his eyes steadily on Washington.

"Sir, I—"

"That was my secretary you hauled downtown, Detective. It's obvious you don't know the first thing about—"

I jumped in. "Wait a minute. I'm sure we can have a conversation without arresting anyone today."

Washington broke free from Carter's stare and turned to me. "Ms. Newman, is Mr. Chapman your attorney?"

I shook my head.

"Well then, you and I, we either speak alone here or downtown."

Carter stood. "Samantha, I don't think this is a good idea."

"I'll be fine," I said. "Besides, I have something to give you, Detective. I'll be right back."

Carter tailed me into the kitchen. "Are you out of your mind? You don't even know what he came here for."

"He came to talk. And I want to give him the note."

He looked like he was about to burst.

"I'll see if I can get him to let you sit in. Promise not to say a word. Okay?" I took the envelope from the bar and walked out.

I returned to the sofa and conjured the sweetest tone in my arsenal. "Detective, Mr. Chapman doesn't know everything that's happened here in the last few days. I was about to fill him in when you showed up. I think you should let him stay. This is his condo, after all." I waved the envelope above his head.

Furrows spread across his forehead. "What's that?"

"Well, it could contain my grocery list. Or, it may be an important piece of evidence. I was about to give it to you and let you decide, but I'd like Mr. Chapman to be here when I do."

"Ms. Newman, if you are withholding evidence . . ."

"He'll behave, I promise. He won't say a word."

"I cannot allow . . ."

I raised my voice to top his. "I will not be bullied, sir. If you want to speak to me, Mr. Chapman sits in. Unless you want to haul me downtown."

Carter must have heard me. He rushed into the room. "What's happening?"

I glared at Washington and waggled the envelope in front of him. He returned my glare with one of his own before he gave in and motioned for Carter to join us.

"Ms. Newman has promised that you will remain silent, sir, unless I ask you a direct question. Agreed?"

Carter nodded, barely, and sat next to me.

I handed the envelope to Washington and waited while he read the note. "Interesting, isn't it?"

He inspected the envelope and studied both sides of the sheet of paper. "Where did you get this?"

"I found it on the floor of the entry, just inside the door, like it had been shoved under, only I've learned that it's impossible to shove anything under there.

"This is the second one, by the way. And there may have been an intruder from the balcony."

"What?" Carter's face turned red. I put a finger to my lips.

Washington pretended he hadn't heard Carter's outburst. He screwed up his face, set the paper aside and checked his notebook. "Tell me again about your relationship with the deceased, Irwin Bayne."

That was it? No 'thank you' for handing over the envelope, no 'attagirl' for finding such a provocative clue? What was he looking for, anyway?

"What about the envelope?"

"We'll come to that. What was your relationship with the deceased, Irwin Bayne?"

"I told you before. There was no relationship."

He checked his notebook again. "And your

relationship with Mrs. Bayne?"

"Brandy? Not much there, either."

"Has she ever done anything to make you suspect her of cheating on Mr. Bayne?"

My mind flashed to Pansy Gump's theory of Brandy the man-killer, but I didn't want to spread her gossip. "Not to my knowledge."

"So, you've never seen her flirting, or suspected her of flirting with anyone other than her husband?" His eyes darted toward Carter. "With someone close to you, for example?"

His question made my stomach hurt. "Where is this going? I don't understand."

He leaned over until he was practically in my face. "Ms. Newman, did you know Mrs. Bayne was seen flirting with Mr. Chapman on more than one occasion?"

Carter levitated off the sofa. "Stop right there!"

Washington snickered. "I'm sorry, Mr. Chapman, did you speak?"

Carter glared back. He started pacing the room.

I couldn't form words. Carter and Brandy? I searched his face for a clue. It was a mask of bottled rage.

Washington returned his focus to me. "You know what I think, Ms. Newman? I think you know more than you're saying."

I rocketed up. "I've told you everything! And that message says she didn't do it."

"This?" He waved the note over his head, mocking me. "It's clear that this—and your balcony intruder idea—is an attempt to throw us off. Brandy Bayne killed her husband. Period. Someone is trying to muddle the facts. Is it you?"

"Me? Why on earth . . .?" My laugh sounded more like a cackle than a ha-ha-ha. Tears spilled down my cheeks. "You're making up some kind of soap opera. I can't even follow what you're talking about."

Carter ceased pacing and turned to me, eyes ablaze. "I'm going to the kitchen for a minute, Samantha. Please don't say another word until I return."

My pulse raced ninety miles an hour. I wanted to follow Carter, but the Brandy comment from Washington had me stuck in place. I dropped onto the sofa again and initiated a careful inspection of my fingernails while my heart searched for its place inside my chest.

Washington marched to the living room balcony door and walked out, shutting it behind him. He seemed to be assessing the distances to each side, above and below. It looked like he might be opening his mind to the possibility of an intruder scenario. Even so, I fought an urge to get up and push him over the edge.

Before I could contemplate the idea further, Carter returned. "Where is he?"

I pointed toward the balcony.

"He doesn't know it yet, but he'll be exiting soon. Promise you'll stay quiet and let it happen." He rapped on the glass and gestured for Washington to come in.

I'd seen this play before. Carter had powerful contacts. If they could get this loony detective to back off, I was happy to let them.

"Have a seat, Detective." Carter joined me on the sofa. His voice was low and calm. "In a moment or two, you will get a phone call. Please take it."

Before he could sit, Washington's pocket erupted. He and I both looked at Carter, who sat mute as a rock.

The detective checked the caller ID and put the phone to his ear. "Sir? Yes, sir, but . . ." He noticed the two of us trying to follow the conversation and turned his back to us. "Yes, sir. But, sir, but . . . I was just . . . yes sir, but . . ." His shoulders sagged. He walked out onto the balcony and slid the door shut, still pleading his case. After a few more exchanges, he ended the call, passed a hand over his forehead, and deflated like a two-day-old party balloon.

When he reentered the living room, he glowered at Carter. "I guess I'm done here, for now."

Carter's face showed nothing. "Goodbye, Detective."

Washington gave me one last look, snatched the white envelope, and slunk out.

Carter grabbed my hand and gave me quick kiss. "You probably hate that I interfered. Couldn't help myself."

"Who'd you call?"

A sadness I'd first noticed when I met him played across his face. "The lead investigator into the hit-and-run drunk who killed my wife and kids. He's pretty high up in the department now. Did some rank-pulling for me."

My stomach growled like an angry puma.

Carter's passing cloud evaporated. He smiled. "Hungry?"

He stood and pulled me with him. But when he started for the kitchen, I pulled back. Another question needed answering. "You know Brandy Bayne?"

He let go of my hand. "What he said was ridiculous. I was going to argue, but I'd already broken my stupid oath of silence and I didn't want to start another debate about whether I should be in the room."

He hadn't answered my question. Total guy move. "Do you know her?"

"We met in the gym downstairs a couple of times. She was having a problem operating the elliptical, and I offered to help."

"Of course you did." That came out way cattier than I'd planned.

"Wait a minute! You can't think that I was attracted to her. Please tell me you don't believe what Washington said."

It's so darned hard for me to think when Carter's eyes meet mine, but I pushed through. "When you were in the gym with her, was anyone else there?"

He backed away. "You need witness verification before you believe me?"

"It's just a question."

He put his hands on his hips and dove into the memory. "Yes, there were people there. A guy on the free weights I'd never seen before or since, and an elderly couple. The man was pedaling a stationary bike about a half-mile and hour, and she was sitting in a chair barking instructions to him. I think their name is Krump or something."

"Gump?" I started laughing as Pansy Gump's vision of Brandy the Flirt came rolling back. "Hubert and Pansy Gump. That's who saw you with Brandy."

I threw my arms around him. "You weren't flirting with anybody."

Carter's breath tickled my ear. "I feel like I just said the magic word, only I don't know which one it was."

"Doesn't matter. Let's eat."

CHAPTER SEVENTEEN

Valet Service

The toast I'd attempted to make before Washington's visit was dry as an old loofah by the time we returned to the kitchen. I was chomping on a chicken thigh when the phone rang. I waved my greasy fingers at Carter. He'd been peeling a mandarin that misted orangey aroma over the table. He set the fruit down and answered.

"Hello? Yes, I'm here."

My radar ratcheted up as fast as my heart fell into my stomach. It sounded like another stupid I'm-outta-here call to duty.

I knew it. The minute I started to think I was the most important thing in the world to him, he'd get snatched away again by some omnipotent master. When this call ended, he'd be gone in minutes, off to who knows where, or for how long. I glared at him.

He didn't seem fazed. "Yes, she's here too." He tapped the speaker button. "It's for you."

"Hello, dear." Gertie's voice filled the kitchen. "I saw that you had called. Is everything all right?"

I swallowed the big gob of fury that had lodged in my throat. "Better, now."

"Mr. Chapman is there."

"Yes." Even though Carter seemed to be focused on peeling his orange, it was awkward to talk about him in his presence. "I'd called to tell you I got the job. Actually, an even better one than I'd applied for."

"Oh my! That's wonderful, just wonderful. I can't

wait to hear more about it. I have some news, too."

I'd almost forgotten about her coming-out party with Kleschevsky's friends. "How was the party?"

"Well, it isn't exactly over yet."

I read between the lines. "Is Louis with you now?"

Her voice lowered to a whisper, but I could hear the glee bubbling through. "Yes."

I grinned. "Gertie, have you been home yet?"

A silence. "I am home. I had a little too much wine last night to drive safely, so, well, Louis brought me back and, uh, we uh . . ." She cleared her throat.

"He made sure you got home safely. Nice to know he's a gentleman."

"Oh, yes, he's . . . well, yes."

"You can tell me more about it when it's just the two of us."

She sounded relieved. "That would be good. I'm happy for you, for the new job and all. We'll talk soon?"

We said goodbye, but not half a minute later the phone rang and Gertie's voice piped through the kitchen again. "Louis wants to take me to Brennan's for dinner tonight. Would you and Mr. Chapman join us? I'd love for you to get to know one another."

Carter and I exchanged a silent conversation of head bobs and hand charades. He left it up to me.

It was almost six o'clock. Something other than cold chicken was starting to appeal, especially when that something could come from the Brennan's kitchen. Plus, it seemed important to Gertie.

"Okay. We'll meet you there." I rewrapped the chicken and put it away.

Carter scarfed his mandarin. "Who's Louis?"

"Can we save that for the car ride to the restaurant? You and I still have some issues to get through."

"Agreed." He dumped the orange rind into the sink

and ran the disposal, which sent another whiff of orange zest through the kitchen. "There's not much time for talking before we leave, though."

I checked the clock again. "Shoot. I'd better get in the shower."

He grinned. "Me too?"

When the elevator arrived to take us downstairs, the valet I'd seen the morning I returned from Nebraska was aboard. As we rode together, I scrolled through that memory.

Why had he been in a rush so early? Was he the one Pansy Gump had seen in the gym with Brandy? Might as well seize the moment.

I checked his nametag. "Harland. I've been meaning to ask: Are you the one who helps people work out in the gym?"

His eyes acquired a deer-in-the-headlights quality. "Ma'am?"

"Someone told me you've been helping Mrs. Bayne with the machines. I just wondered if you would work with me too."

Carter looked at me like I had just arrived from Mars.

Harland lowered his eyes and hung his head. He seemed to be struggling with a reply.

I tried again. "Were you the one?"

He spoke to the floor. "I guess so."

The doors opened onto Lizzie and her brother. While the kids shoved in, Harland jumped out. The siblings took their usual places, the boy facing into the corner, the girl flanking him like a bodyguard. She stared straight ahead.

I tried to break the ice. "Hi, Lizzie."

She barely mumbled her reply. "Hi."

It seemed forever until the doors opened on the ground floor. The kids bolted.

Carter took my hand and squeezed it as we headed to the porte-cochere where the Tesla waited. "Interesting ride."

"Lizzie's kind of an elevator buddy. Her brother, not so much."

He raised an eyebrow. "What was that about Brandy and the valet?"

"I ran into him, literally, the morning I got back from Nebraska, before they found Irwin's body. He'd nearly knocked me over, barreling out of the elevator as I was boarding. Pansy had told me that she'd seen a valet helping Brandy in the gym. I took a guess and asked if he was the one."

"Gump? The person who set Washington on me?"

I smiled. "Yup."

Carter winced. "Well, she got Brandy and me all wrong."

I believed him, but something in his expression reminded me of the valet's face when I'd mentioned Brandy to him. It made me wonder if there was more to the story than Carter admitted.

I had hosted many a business dinner for my old employer—may he rot in prison—at Brennan's, but it had been years since the last one. After a fire broke out during a hurricane and decimated the place, the restaurant closed for a year and a half to rebuild. While it rose from the ashes, my career slowly sank. I didn't know how I'd feel about walking in again.

I needn't have worried. Everything looked nearly the same, only brighter, airier, refreshed. Carter took my hand as we followed the maître d' through the golden-hued dining room to our table.

Gertie and Louis were already halfway through their cocktails. She beamed. "Sit next to me, dear, so the men can get to know one another. I've told Louis all about you two. Oh, and I already ordered for us, I hope you don't mind. Would you like a drink to start?"

Carter and I took our assigned seats, and it wasn't long before he and Louis were locked in conversation.

Gertie leaned in. "What do you think of him?"

"He's certainly a fast worker. But how much do you know about each other?"

"I've seen his house, met his friends and, of course, his darling granddaughter. We've spent almost every minute together since we met. It doesn't take much more to know you like a person."

"Does he know they tried to tie you to Irwin Bayne's murder?"

"He thinks it's hilarious."

I studied the two men. "Liking is the easy part. But then you realize how much you don't know. That's my experience, anyway."

"You haven't patched things with Mr. Chapman?"

"We're working on it, sort of."

She patted my hand. "You certainly looked like lovebirds when you walked in, dear."

"Between our personal issues and the murder next door, there's a lot to wade through."

Gertie frowned. "What's going on with the investigation? I'm out of the loop, thank goodness, and I hope it stays that way. I can't stop wondering, though, if Brandy really did kill her husband.

Not wanting to spoil dinner with talk about the case, I didn't mention the two peculiar messages that had me wondering the same thing.

CHAPTER EIGHTEEN

Bring Ice!

After dinner, Carter wanted to drive to Serenity for the weekend. With Irwin Bayne's unsolved death and Kingsbury's stupid intruder theory rattling around in my head, I wasn't keen on spending the night at the condo anyway. We stopped there just long enough for me to pack some clothes before heading out for the ranch.

As the city retreated behind us, my mind returned to Brennan's. "Gertie's head-over-heels."

Carter glanced at me. "Louis, too. Seems like a good guy."

My thoughts remained on the happy couple for a few miles. Gertie had taken a big leap of faith, falling for a man she'd known for only a fraction of the time I'd known Carter. Why couldn't it be that easy with us?

Carter had moved on. "We have an hour ahead of us. Let's talk about the murder next door. The sooner you fill me in, the better."

"Might as well." I resettled myself in the Tesla's leather cocoon and began to rewind the events from my point of view, starting with my marathon drive back from Nebraska and the urgent call from Gertie. I tried to give a blow by blow of everything that came afterward, including the envelopes and Kingsbury's crazy balcony intruder scenario.

Carter took a moment to process what I'd said. "Tell me more about the first message. The one you gave to the attorney."

I called it up in my mind's eye. "A neon yellow envelope, about five or six inches wide, a little less tall, like the ones you get with greeting cards, only smaller."

"And the message inside?"

"Red ballpoint ink on a torn scrap of newspaper."

"Written?"

"Printed. Scrawled, really, like from a left-handed person with really bad penmanship."

Carter cogitated for a moment. "The one you gave Washington today was on plain white paper in a white business envelope. What else was different about it?"

I wracked my brain. "Black ink, not red."

"Anything else?" His eyes bored into me.

"The print looked a little neater?"

"Hmmm. Okay, let's move on. That valet. You left him out of the story this time."

"I did?"

"Was there anyone else up and about before dawn that morning?"

"Let's see . . . I drove up to the door, talked to the EMTs, passed the concierge desk—no one was there, by the way—then I ran into Harland at the elevator. I rode up alone, and—wait! The paperboy! When I got off the elevator, I heard a door shut down the hall. The paperboy was in the hallway making deliveries. Do you think he had something to do with it?"

"You never know. Anything else?"

I shook my head. "Nothing registers. I think that's it."

We lapsed into our separate thoughts again. Mine went to that funny look on Carter's face the last time I'd mentioned Brandy. I wanted to ask him about it, but I was talked out for the night. He was content to ruminate in silence, too, until we made the final turn onto the winding drive that led up to the great house at Serenity.

I don't think my body moved from the time my head hit the pillow until the next morning, when the aroma of French roast tickled my consciousness and teased me downstairs to the big country kitchen where Carter was scrambling eggs.

"Morning, sleepyhead."

I dumped myself into a chair at the long farmhouse table. It seemed like ages since I'd been in this kitchen. Low morning rays passed through the window over the wide porcelain sink and glinted off the shiny copper pots hanging above the cooking island. I covered my face to shield my eyes until Carter set the eggs in front of me.

He added a platter of his "famous" Texas waffles and a bowl of blueberries before he sat kitty-corner to me and poured the coffee. "Anything else come to mind from our talk last night?"

My thought processor was still in sleep mode. I squinted at the waffles and forked one onto my plate. After spilling out the entire saga last night, the last thing I wanted was more talk about the murder next door.

Carter passed the syrup and served himself some eggs. "Tell you what. When we're finished here, I'll ask Dottie to clean up. Then we can take a walk. And talk."

Dottie, a countrified version of Gertie, was Ralph's mother. She lived with Ralph and his two children in a ranch house on the property and took care of Carter's home and most of the cooking.

I jumped at the chance. "Can I choose the topic?"

"Sure, but I thought we'd—"

"We're not finished talking about us, Carter."

"Okay." He gave me a cautious glance before returning to his eggs. "I want to show you some property out toward the river. We can talk about anything you want on the way, deal?"

"Deal."

An hour later, we were crossing over a footbridge that spanned the lap pool. The first time I'd seen it, I'd taken the pool for a natural creek that wound around three sides of the mansion, until Carter explained how he'd had it designed to look that way, with a gentle current flowing against its rocky edges. We broke free of the line of trees behind the house and stepped out among the rolling hills. The sun blazed in a bluebird sky.

My first visit to Serenity was last spring. Back then, I couldn't imagine a more picturesque landscape, with its bounty of bluebonnets, paintbrush, buttercups and countless other wildflowers blanketing the new-green fields.

The autumn palette that spread around us now had a different beauty. Clusters of milkweed and coreopsis peeped from a sea of tawny grasses that covered the meadows.

Instead of heading east toward the stables, or up the well-worn path to the little cemetery where Carter's wife and twins were buried, we took a narrow trail I hadn't come across before. "Where are we going?"

He squeezed my hand. "You'll see."

As we crossed into a high swath of prairie, I was glad I'd brought a tee and shorts. The equinox may have indicated fall, but in this part of Texas, summer lingered.

I spotted something I'd seen on a walk from another direction. It was almost hidden under a giant tangle of desiccated dewberry brambles. "Is that the old well?"

Carter smiled. "It isn't our final destination. But this is as good a place as any to get something off my chest." He turned in the direction of the well. I followed him to the shade of a solitary oak. The temperature drop was noticeable, but that's not what brought goose bumps to my arms and legs. Careful what you wish for.

He faced me and took my hand again. "Couple of things. First, I may not have told you everything about my encounters with Brandy."

I hate my intuition. The muscles in my neck tensed.

"I don't want this to upset you. It's nothing, really. I just feel like I'd be hiding it if I didn't tell you."

"Just say it. You and Brandy . . ."

"There's no me and Brandy. Never was. Last time I saw her was late one night when I heard someone sobbing and banging on my door. I opened it, and there she was."

I took at guess at what he wasn't saying. "Naked?"

"Yes. And drunk. And she didn't want to go back to her place. Said her husband was out of control and she wanted to wait until he cooled off."

I let this sink in. "So, you let her stay?"

He nodded.

"The whole night?"

"It was either that or take her home by force and risk a confrontation with her drunk husband, too. I gave her a pair of my pajamas and put her in a guest room. Then I took some work to bed and locked myself in. She was gone when I checked on her in the morning."

I smiled at the mental image of Carter protecting himself from a drunken Brandy by locking himself in his bedroom. No way a man would admit to that if it weren't true.

He took my hand again. "Case closed?"

I leaned my back against the broad trunk of the oak. "Case almost closed. One more question. How did she look, naked?"

I knew the answer to this one. He'd better not fudge.

He looked into my eyes and nailed it. "She's pretty voluptuous. Not my type, though. Too ditsy."

I pulled him toward me, gave him a quick kiss and whispered in his ear. "Case closed."

"That's a load off. I would've told you earlier, when we were talking about the Gump woman and what she thought she saw in the gym, but the subject changed, and later, I didn't know how you'd react, and—"

I kissed him to a stop. "Case closed. Over. Finished. So, what's your other grand confession?"

"It's not on the scale of the Brandy thing. Only that I have to leave sooner than I'd planned."

"Again?" I backed away.

"Just a couple of days, I promise."

"Where to?"

He hesitated.

Old anger bubbled. "Here we go again."

"No we're not, Sam. Things are different."

"So tell me. Where?" I crossed my arms and dared him to answer.

"I want to tell you as much as I can, but . . ." He shaded his eyes and looked out over the sunlit field. "There's a nice spot to sit on the other side of this meadow. Do you mind?"

"Must be another long story."

"A long time coming, I guess. When it's over, you'll know everything that's worth knowing about me."

The last part of our hike took us over some rocky outcroppings. Trees were sparse until we reached a row of cottonwoods that curved along a creek below. We sat in the shade on the fallen limb of a sweetgum tree.

I toed the dirt with my sneaker. "Is this part of your property too?"

"It stops at the water, but I'm thinking about buying the other side."

I surveyed the opposite bluff. "That looks like a lot of land. What will you do with it?"

He tossed a twig into the stream, then picked up another one and threw it in, and another after that. I hadn't thought the question would be so hard to answer.

Tears gathered in the corners of his eyes and clung to his lashes. "I've had plans for this place for a long time. But after that drunken bastard killed my family, the only thing I wanted was to put him away."

I shuddered. "Mission accomplished."

He set his elbows on his knees and gazed off into space. "Everything stopped, except the rage. I took on every project, did anything I was asked to do. I couldn't be here. That's when I bought the condo in Houston."

He turned his eyes to focus on mine. "Meeting you was a miracle, Samantha. I see what a future might look like. If I lose you now because I've been a total jerk, I probably deserve it."

My eyes welled up. I plucked a shard of limestone from the dirt, brushed it off and tossed it toward the water. We both followed its trajectory until it plopped in and disappeared.

I wanted to tell him I understood, but before I could speak, something pricked my leg.

I reached down to brush it off. As soon as I touched my skin, there were more pricks, then burning pain.

My foot and ankle swarmed with ants. It looked like hundreds of them scrambling in and out of the top of my shoe and all around my leg. I flew upright and stomped around, trying to shake them off.

It took Carter a nanosecond to react. He tugged me away from the log, yanked my shoe off and knelt to swipe the buggers to the ground. "Fire ants!"

As a city girl, I'm familiar with urban varieties of vermin like cockroaches and spiders. I've endured bites from ants of the urban variety. If you'd told me a rattlesnake had just injected me with its venom, it might have explained the searing pain from the pricks of hell attacking me.

Red dots flared around my ankle. They didn't look like much, but they burned like acid eating into my flesh.

Carter retrieved my shoe, shook it out and inspected it for strays before he handed back. "Fire ants can be deadly. Let's get you to the house."

I couldn't argue for staying out there, not with my ankle burning like hellfire. He anchored his arm around my waist to lift weight off the foot. We hobbled back toward the house like last-place losers in a sack race.

When we reached the back steps, Carter hoisted me up and into the kitchen.

Dottie was at the sink washing dishes. "You're late for lunch. It's only tuna salad sandwiches and some . . . Good gracious, what happened?"

Carter sped through the room with me in his arms. "Fire ants. Bring ice. And some antihistamine. And an epi-injector!"

CHAPTER NINETEEN

Hard Case

Carter left Dottie to gather the medical supplies and hustled toward the library with me bouncing in his arms. He deposited me onto the soft leather sofa and inspected my foot, then scanned my face and ran his fingers over each side of my neck.

"No signs yet of allergic reaction. Are you nauseous? Dizzy?"

"I just feel kind of weird."

Dottie was there in no time with an ice wrap and the meds. Carter knelt and looped the cold pack around my ankle. "Take two pills with lots of water. Still feel okay?"

"The ice helps."

"Fire ants are serious business, especially if you're allergic to the venom." He must have seen a flicker of terror cross my face. "I think you'll be fine."

I eyed the syringe. I was familiar with epi-injectors, the safety net for life-threatening allergic reactions. "So, I won't need that?"

"Probably not. But you might want to stay quiet for a bit."

Dottie took the empty glass from me. "I'll be in the kitchen if you need anything. Lunch is in the fridge."

Carter spread a light blanket over me and sat on the floor. "Still okay?"

I nodded.

"Are you up to hearing the rest of the story, or do you want to rest?"

It wasn't the ideal situation for continuing our

conversation, but I didn't want to postpone it again. "Talk to me."

He laid his hand over mine. "Let's start with your question about that phone call I took out by the creek, and where I'm off to."

"M'kay." I shut my eyes. "Ready."

"Here's the thing about my travel plans. My security clients are people or entities that need an extra level of protection. Talking about where I go, and when, can risk a serious breach, even compromise public safety."

"I can't be trusted?"

"I hate to burst your bubble, but contrary to what I said back at the creek, not everything is about you."

"So, I can never know where in the world you are, or what you're doing?"

"I wouldn't say never. It's not all classified work, but generally, it's safer if you don't know. Most of the time it's pretty boring, really."

I wasn't convinced about the 'boring' part. Safer? That's what nagged at me.

A mist descended, blunting a bit of my pain. I tried to open my eyes, but the effort wasn't worth it. My thoughts free-floated from what he'd just said to something else he'd said at the creek.

My words slurred out. "Have you ever done other undercover stuff, like, kill people?"

The warmth from his hand on mine cooled. I heard him stand up and mumble something.

I strained to open my eyes against the first volley of antihistamine. "Carter?"

He had left the room.

When I woke, the morning was gone. I squinted into the early afternoon sun pouring in through the library's floor-to-ceiling windows.

The ice pack on my ankle had thawed. I unwound it and struggled to a standing position, still groggy and slightly lame. Pain had subsided, but when I whipped the blanket around my shoulders, its hem brushed against the stings, and the fire flared again. I hiked the blanket away from my feet and limped out of the library in search of Carter.

He wasn't in the kitchen, though someone had been there recently, judging by a tall stewpot burbling on the stove. If I stayed there, a human would probably come to check on it soon. I took a chair at the table and rested my foot on the one next to it.

Sure enough, Dottie appeared. "Feeling better?"

"I think I'll live."

She smiled. "I'm making soup. Fresh vegetables from the garden, plus a few secret ingredients that oughta help with the swelling."

"Smells good. Have you seen Carter?"

"Upstairs somewhere, I reckon."

I weighed the challenge of dragging a bum foot up the grand winding staircase versus my desire to find Carter, then said goodbye to Dottie and headed for the stairs. I limped upward, past the enormous framed maps that depicted Texas in its various historical allegiances: first Spain, then France, then Mexico. I stopped for a breather beside The Republic of Texas before I could make it to the vintage U.S.A. map at the top.

I hoped Carter was on the second floor so I wouldn't have to face another flight up. On the landing, I heard someone whistling from the direction of his bedroom. Thanking the gods of mobility for small favors, I headed that way.

He was tossing some clothes into a travel bag. "Hey! You're up!"

I leaned on the doorjamb to catch my breath. "You're leaving now?"

"Not yet. I wanted to get this out of the way while you were asleep so I could spend more time with your conscious self." He looked at my foot. "How is it?"

"Less like a blowtorch. More like a five-gallon wasp's nest."

He laughed. "Good news, you'll survive. Bad news, you may be in only slightly less agony for a few days. Those little suckers don't heal overnight."

I hobbled in his direction and landed my backside on the bed beside his travel bag. My heart twisted just looking at it. "What time will you go?"

"I'd planned to stay here another night, but I don't think you'll be up to doing much around the ranch for another day or so. Now that we know you're okay, we might as well get back to the condo." He zipped the case. "Dottie's making soup for you. Ready to eat?"

"Maybe later."

One thing was clear: Like it or not, his work was a call of duty, and I wouldn't be allowed to know where or why he was going. Or exactly when. Our talk hadn't so much opened him up as it had shut me down.

One of us had to give in, and the arrow pointed to me. A gaping hole took up residence somewhere near my heart.

He grabbed the case and started for the door. "I'll have Dottie pack the soup to take with us."

"Carter, wait." I popped off the bed a little too quickly and had to brace myself on a bedpost.

"I'll come back and help you downstairs. I need to catch Dottie before she leaves."

I fought the burning in my ankle and attempted to stand straight. "I can make it down by myself."

He rolled his eyes. "I know you can, Samantha, but you don't have to, as long as I'm here. Just wait a sec."

"Before we go, I want to say something."

He set the bag down, walked back to me and took my hand. "All ears."

I think I was still a little funny in the head, because the words *please don't go* threatened to gush from my mouth. It took all I could muster to replace them.

I lowered my eyes and blinked away a tear. "Thanks for saving me from those stupid ants today."

"You're welcome. Least I could do for dragging you into the wilderness."

More mental ramblings bubbled up. What if I never saw him again? "I know you can't share everything, and I'm sorry if I—"

He raised my chin and stopped me with a kiss, and then another. His breath tickled my neck.

"It's okay, tough girl. I'm used to hard cases."

CHAPTER TWENTY

Pool Party

I must have conked out in the car soon after we left Serenity. It felt like I'd barely blinked before we pulled under The Wellbourne porte-cochère.

Carter held the car door open. "Can you walk, or should I load you onto the luggage cart and wheel you upstairs?"

I ignored the hand he offered and hoisted myself out of the car, determined not to hobble as I pushed past him toward the entrance.

The concierge stopped me at the front desk. "Will you be attending the residents' pool party this afternoon?" I had no idea what he was talking about.

Carter had caught up. "Party?"

"Good afternoon, Mr. Chapman. I was reminding Ms. Newman about the pool party. Last one of the year. It's just started."

Carter answered for me. "Sounds like fun." He headed for the elevators.

I limped after him with a new snit brewing. "It's been kind of a long day, don't you think? I'm not really dressed for a party, and my leg . . ."

"It's a pool party, Sam. Everyone will be in bathing suits or shorts. If you don't want to come, fine, but I want to scope out the balconies from the terrace."

So much for spending our last few hours alone together.

When the elevator reached pool level, I hobbled out. Carter continued up to drop our bags at the apartment.

In truth, the sooner the questions of the balcony phantom and the mess next door were answered, the sooner we could get on with life. I donned my sunglasses and resolved to seek out a clue or two myself.

Afternoon sun bleached the terrace partygoers in a lemony haze. A young couple played in the pool with two toddlers who joyfully squealed every time their dad splashed them. A few older couples hovered around the buffet spread, loading their plates with tamales, nachos and guacamole.

I managed to snag a lounge chair in the shade so I could keep my foot elevated. A waiter came by with a tray of frozen margaritas. I wondered if it would be too much to ask him to tape one to my throbbing foot. I grabbed a frosty glass and took a sip instead.

Pansy and Hubert Gump appeared at the pool gate. Her brightly spangled silk caftan fanned in the breeze, nearly obscuring Hubert, who wore his usual dress shirt buttoned to the top, with suspenders hiking his slacks higher than any human waist could possibly be. They each balanced a margarita and a plate of food.

She spotted me and made a beeline for the empty chairs next to my chaise. On approach, her bejeweled sandals glinted in the sun. She sat in the chair nearest me, set her food atop a small teak table and directed Hubert to sit beside her.

She lowered her Chanel sunglasses and glared across the pool. "How dare those people think they can reserve the best tables, just because they own the penthouse. New money. I simply cannot abide pretentiousness!"

I sipped my margarita and hoped Carter would arrive soon to rescue me. Scanning the façade of the building, I counted floors in an attempt to locate his condo. He was out on the balcony, looking down at the party. I waved.

Something caught my eye. I had to look twice to

make sure I was seeing right. A man—at least, the figure looked masculine—was sitting atop another balcony railing, dangling his feet over the edge. My first instinct was to shout and point, but with Pansy nearby, I didn't want to start a kerfuffle. Whoever the person was, he didn't look suicidal. He seemed as relaxed as Huck Finn on a fence, swinging his legs as if he were merely two feet off the ground.

My eyes traveled back to Carter's balcony to see if he had noticed the figure. He wasn't there anymore. I surveyed the gathering to check if anyone else had noticed. No one seemed to be looking in that direction. I returned to the person on the railing. It made me queasy to look up at him.

"That pitiful woman." Pansy was pointing toward the end of the pool. "I have never laid eyes on her before. Does she live here?"

I followed the direction of her finger to a woman, fortyish, in a wheelchair. She wore sunglasses, a floppy hat and a loose, flowered dress that covered her legs. Something about the way she was hunched in the chair seemed off-kilter. Sitting beside her on the ground was Lizzie, busily scraping guacamole onto a tortilla.

I spotted an empty chaise beside the wheelchair, mumbled an excuse and made for it. Like Pansy, I'm not too keen on pretentiousness either.

Lizzie squinted up at me. "Hey." She saw me eye the chaise. "You can sit there, if you want. Nobody likes to sit next to us. This is my Mom."

"Pleased to meet you." I lowered into the chaise and stretched my legs out. My ankle started up again.

Lizzie scooped another lump of guacamole off her plate. ""She can't talk. She had a stroke, and now she can't do anything."

"She can hear us, don't you think? And I'm very glad to meet her." I raised my voice slightly. "My name is Samantha." There was no response.

Lizzie shrugged. "Hers is Elizabeth. Like me."

The waiter came around with more margaritas. I'd left mine at the table next to Pansy, and there was no way I'd be returning for it. As I grabbed a fresh one off the tray, I caught a glimpse of Carter across the pool. I waved.

Lizzie swept the last of the guacamole onto her index finger and licked it clean. "I want a Dr Pepper. I'm not supposed to leave Mom alone. Can you watch her for me?" She was gone before I could reply.

Carter arrived and crouched down on the other side of my chaise. "That took longer than I expected. I wanted to check out the balconies."

"Did you see the person sitting on the railing?"

"Person? Where?"

I craned my neck toward the spot where I'd seen the figure. The sun had moved and was casting sharp shadows, which made it hard to pinpoint the exact balcony. "Somewhere up near your place. He was just sitting there, casually swinging his feet."

Carter scanned the building. I wondered what kind of calculations were sparking in his brain.

Lizzie came back with her drink. She noticed my ankle. "What's that stuff on your leg?"

"Ant bites. Ugly, aren't they?" I turned to Carter. "My foot's really throbbing. I ought to get upstairs and ice it."

He picked up my hint and pulled his eyes from the balconies. "I'm ready." He hoisted me onto my feet.

"Good to see you, Lizzie, and to meet you, Elizabeth." I smiled at the woman. She hadn't moved since I'd sat down. If there was a response behind her dark glasses, I couldn't see it.

When we got upstairs, Carter went straight out to the balcony. I lay on top of the bed, icing my ankle.

The glass door slid open. "I don't see anyone out there. Are you certain you saw a person?"

"It had two arms, two legs and was wearing a tee shirt and shorts. Yep, pretty sure. Any theories?"

He scratched his head. "Gotta let things percolate a bit until they make sense. I'll figure it out by the time I get back. How's the ankle?"

"Better with ice. At least it will heal, eventually." My thoughts drifted back downstairs. "That poor woman in the wheelchair . . . "

"Is she that girl's mother?"

"Yes. Just met her. Now I understand why Lizzie seems so lost, like an orphan. If she has a father, I've never seen him."

"Sad."

I nodded. "She's been trying to teach herself to skateboard on one of her brother's hand-me-downs, and now she's hoping to beat him at Krav Maga some day."

"Pretty serious stuff for a little girl."

"What is it, exactly? All Lizzie could tell me was that it's the 'awesomest.' Is it some kind of martial art?"

Carter sat beside me on the bed. "Kind of like jiu-jitsu. The Israeli Defense Forces developed it for close combat, and now most police departments use a version of it. I know a few moves myself." He playfully jabbed my shoulder, then lowered himself, pressing my arms against the mattress.

My fingers found the corner of a pillow. I yanked it and bonked his head.

He raised up and straddled me. "So that's how it's gonna be." He grabbed another pillow and dropped it on my face.

I pushed it back at him and rolled free. "Ha!"

He took the pillow and conked me on my behind. I tried to get away, but he was too fast. He attacked with the pillow again, then grabbed my hands in a wristlock over my head. I tried to break his grip. It was no use, even though I knew he was being extra gentle. His face was inches from mine.

I was breathing hard. "Is this Krav Maga?"

"Lover's version." He leaned down and kissed me.

My ankle burned like blazes, but I wasn't going to let it spoil the fun. He'd be gone soon. No telling when we'd have another moment like this. I kissed him back, and pretended everything would be all right.

CHAPTER TWENTY-ONE

Vortex

I wouldn't hate mornings as much if they didn't come so darned early, especially on a Sunday. Carter left before sunrise. Just as well, I suppose. I had a lot of preparation to do before my job started, and only one day to do it.

First order of business: clear my head from the antihistamine fog. The ant bites still drove me crazy, but I needed to get my thoughts on paper before I showed up at the TV station. I was determined to spend the day drug-free, except for aspirin. And caffeine, lots of caffeine.

I padded into the kitchen, made coffee and poured my first cup. My phone chirped. I followed the sound to the counter where Carter had left my purse. Battery dangerously low, it warned. I plugged it into its cradle, and the screen lit, full of messages: Kingsbury, Kingsbury, Kingsbury and—the icing on the cake— Detective Washington.

I wasn't ready to swim in that swamp. I let the phone simmer while I stuck bread into the toaster. As the slices browned, I pondered why both had called me on a Sunday.

I kicked the question to the back of my mind. Priority number one was to organize my thoughts for the new job. No way I'd let that duo of dunces interfere until I was finished.

I spread almond butter on the toast and sat at the breakfast island with my coffee and a notepad and pen.

Jay Patel had assured me that I was in the driver's seat when it came to positioning my platform. "You have good instincts," he'd said, and left it up to me.

Ten Objectives, I wrote at the top of the page, then I skipped to the next line and scribbled: *Number 1.*

I took a sip of coffee and a bite of toast. I drank more coffee. I retraced the *Number 1* until the paper threatened to shred under the ballpoint's pressure. I took another bite of toast and another sip.

"Number One," I said aloud, hoping to conjure invisible forces for support. When no aid came, I scratched out *Number 1* and decided to start with a list of random thoughts that I could prioritize later.

I'm not sure what had inspired Patel's faith in my ability. I wasn't a journalist. My previous on-air appearances as the spokesperson for De Theret had focused only on what I knew about the employment market. I wasn't an expert in anything else. And despite Carter's encouragement, I didn't feel like a natural-born crusader, much less a holier-than-thou TV pundit.

I tore off the sheet, wadded it up and sailed it into the sink, then wrote on a clean piece: *Five Objectives.* I drank more coffee.

Merde. Hard to say if it was the drugs still lurking in my bloodstream or the blasted messages from Kingsbury and Washington waiting to pounce, but I was way too distracted to concentrate. I finished the toast and returned to the bedroom, put on my workout clothes and headed for the gym. If I couldn't wake my brain with caffeine, I'd do it with exercise.

I didn't expect anyone to be in the elevator at the crack of dawn, but there was Harland the valet, just like he'd been on the morning of the murder. It occurred to me that he must work the overnight shift.

He lowered his eyes and mumbled a greeting.

I took the chance to open him up a little. "I didn't mean to startle you the other day, when I asked if you'd helped Mrs. Bayne in the gym."

He wouldn't look at me. "Yes ma'am."

"It's just that, I'd like some help on my workouts, too." That wasn't exactly true, but I thought it might be a way to see if he knew Brandy better than he should have, as the ever-vigilant Pansy had posited.

He studied the floor. "I only did it a few times. When I'd be in there making rounds, sometimes she'd ask me to help her set the elliptical program or something."

It didn't feel like he was telling me everything. The elevator doors opened and a man and woman got on— attorneys, by the look of their expensive suits and rolling file cases. We rode in silence until they exited at the top garage level.

As soon as the doors closed, Harland came undone. "Please, Ms. Newman, I don't want to get in trouble."

"It's okay. I understand. It's just that Mrs. Bayne is my neighbor, and she's in serious trouble. I wondered if you knew anything that might be important."

He shoved his hands into his pants pockets and closed his eyes. "If I tell you something, can you keep it a secret, like, who you got it from, and all?"

I nodded. When the doors opened to the lobby, I pressed the button for the top floor. The doors closed, and we were alone again, riding up. "What is it?"

Harland opened his eyes and stared ahead. "Okay, here goes. About a month ago, when I was doing my night rounds, I was coming out of the elevator on their floor and I heard somebody crying. It was Mrs. Bayne. She was locked out and she said it was Mr. Bayne who did it, and he wouldn't let her back in. She was crying real bad. She asked me to get the valet key to open the door so she could get some clothes."

"She wasn't wearing any?"

He lowered his eyes to the floor again. "No ma'am."

"Go on."

"I went downstairs and got the key and opened the door for her. I asked if she wanted me to wait outside, in case Mr. Bayne, you know, pushed her out again, but she said no. It was quiet inside, so I figured it was okay and I left."

"That's it?"

"Here's the thing. I didn't write it up. I'm supposed to report anything unusual that happens on rounds, but I didn't. And we're supposed to log a key in and out whenever we use it, but I didn't do that either. I could get fired for not reporting it." He raised teary eyes to mine. "I have a wife and a baby, and my school tuition, and . . . Do you think I have to tell somebody now?"

We reached the penthouse level. I pushed the hold button so we could finish our conversation.

His story didn't add anything new, except one more witness to Brandy's naked middle-of-the-night humiliations, but that base was covered by Gertie and Carter. No need to involve Harland. "Don't worry, your story is safe with me."

The relief on his face almost brought me to tears.

I'd been down to the gym infrequently since I'd moved to The Wellbourne. I knew that some Type A's in the building took regular pre-dawn workouts, but I was surprised to see the lights on so early on a Sunday. The whine of a lone machine greeted me from across a long row of ellipticals, rowers, and other apparatuses.

Lizzie's brother was on a treadmill at the far wall. When he saw me, he picked up his pace and pounded away at a punishing rate, his footfalls so fast and heavy that the machine squealed and groaned under the strain.

There was an unoccupied treadmill next to him. Though an elliptical would have been easier on my ankle, I decided to see if, one on one, the boy might not be as painfully shy.

"Hi," I offered as I made my approach. He ignored me and kept thrashing away, his face red. Sweat poured from his hairline into his eyes and dripped from his chin onto his sodden shirt.

I hopped onto the treadmill and set the program to beginner. The minute mine started up, he jumped off of his in mid-stride, which sent him lurching into me. His sopping shirt made a wet circle on my tee that instantly soaked through to my skin. He bounced off awkwardly, and without a word, he ran from the gym.

The treadmill he'd been on was still groaning. I turned it off, and mine too, and got some paper towels from the restroom. I blotted the wet spot on my shirt and swabbed the puddles of sweat he'd left on both our machines.

The encounter left me rattled. My ant bites started prickling. I took a steadying breath, moved to an elliptical and set the program to an easy level. A slow, rhythmic pace was enough while I concentrated on the outline for my TV platform. I vowed not to speak to anyone else for the rest of the day.

After a shower, I pulled on a comfy tee and some baggy pajama bottoms. Drying my hair in front of the mirror, I did a double-take at the hand that was holding the brush. Mom's ring was not on my finger.

Had I lost it in the gym? The shower? I cursed myself for never having had it resized to fit better.

I mentally retraced my steps. I couldn't remember wearing it since yesterday. The ant bites had caused some general body swelling, making the ring uncomfortably tight. The first thing I'd done when Carter and I returned to the condo was soap it off and set it on the nightstand.

I glanced across the bed to where I'd left the ring. It wasn't there. I looked under the lamp and searched inside the drawer. I stripped the sheets. No ring.

As a last resort, I dropped to all fours and looked under the nightstand, then under the bed. Through the murky light, I spotted it amid a checkerboard of dust bunnies. Our pillow fight had likely sent it sailing under there last night.

The ring was just beyond my reach. I got up and took a wire hanger from the closet to tease it out. Kneeling again, I swept the hanger under the bed. As I drew it toward me, Mom's ring appeared, along with a few dust bunnies, and something else.

I tested the ring on my finger. It fit. Before I swept away the clumps of dust, I inspected the other object. It was some kind of metal or hard plastic and seemed to be a decorative zipper pull with a strange design, M-shaped, or maybe it was a W, with a P or B or D looped on one side.

I didn't think it was from anything of mine. I put it on the nightstand in case it had come off of something of Carter's.

I headed to the kitchen to revisit my alleged TV platform. I made a tall glass of iced coffee with sugar and milk for support and sat at the breakfast bar where the pen and pad were waiting.

The Five Objectives I'd never listed mocked me from the page. I tore the sheet off, wadded it into the tightest ball possible and tossed it out of eyesight.

Take a deep breath, raise pen, and begin: those were my silent instructions to the left side of my brain, which was poised to commit thoughts to paper. But my right brain interrupted, and all I could think was, what did Kingsbury want that was so urgent? And why was Washington calling?

The answers lay tantalizingly nearby on my phone, which was still in its cradle on the counter, directly across the bar from me.

I caught myself spinning Mom's ring like a tiny mala around my finger. I pulled my thumb away and forced the pen onto the top of a fresh page and wrote: *Ideas.*

I thought I'd been concentrating on a list, but by the time my mind returned from another round of Kingsbury and Washington wanderings, I had punched another hole in the paper. I gave up and retrieved my phone.

Kingsbury first. Message number one: "Urgent! Call me." Message two: "Call as soon as you get this!" Three: "Situation serious. Where the devil are you?" The last message was time-stamped about an hour ago. If he hadn't exploded already, he could wait a little longer.

No telling what Washington's message was about. As I opened his voicemail, my heart ticked a little faster.

His tough-cop tone was gone. "Ms. Newman, I want to apologize if I insulted you at our last encounter. Some new developments have surfaced. Please call as soon as you can."

Please? I hadn't seen that one coming. Carter's detective friend must have read Washington the riot act, because the person who'd left this message sounded like Mr. Congeniality. I was intrigued.

"Washington." It took me a second to realize his voice wasn't a recording. "Ms. Newman?"

Darned Caller ID: so useful when you're screening calls; so inconvenient when you want to leave a message and hang up. Oh well. "You called?"

"Yes. There've been some new developments, and I'd like to get your input."

"My input." I maneuvered my thoughts around the one-eighty in his attitude. "About what?"

"It's a little complicated. I'd rather do this in person. Could you come to the station first thing tomorrow?"

"Tomorrow's my first day at a new job."

"Oh." He sounded disappointed. "This is really important."

I don't know why, but I offered an alternative. "How about lunchtime?"

"That works for me."

"I'm not sure how much time I'll have, or when, but I'll try to call you as soon as I know."

"I'll be waiting. Thank you very, very much."

The call left me wondering if Washington's "new developments" had anything to do with Kingsbury's urgent messages. I chugged the rest of my coffee and tapped his number.

He picked up immediately. "About damn time!"

"I have a life, Mr. Kingsbury."

"Got no time for your life, darlin'. Somebody else is a little more important right now."

"Is Brandy okay?"

"Brandy? Oh, yeah, she's fine. Not her I'm talkin' about. I'm on my way to your place now. Be there in two shakes of a lamb's tail." He hung up.

I should have known Kingsbury would suck me back into his vortex. I eyed the woefully incomplete list on my notepad. No way I could concentrate until the ginger-headed clown crawled back into his hole.

CHAPTER TWENTY-TWO

Pineapple Pizza

Kingsbury stood in the hallway in deck shoes, baggy shorts and an orange polo shirt, with a Star Pizza box in one hand and a chilled six-pack of Lone Star in the other.

"I was on the way to my boat with this. Had the whole durned day planned. But business trumps pleasure in the big city!"

He marched in and went straight to the kitchen, leaving a bracing whiff of Eau de Pepperoni in his wake. By the time I caught up, he had taken a seat, opened the box and was about to dig in. "Hope you like deep dish."

I tried not to gag at the sight of the gargantuan heap of cheese, hamburger, sausage, onions and pineapple.

"I'll pass."

"Suit yourself." He twisted off a bottle cap and offered the beer to me.

"Can we just get to why you had to see me?"

Whatever had been urgent was apparently not as important as downing a mouthful of pizza and a swig of beer first, then chasing the beer with another gloppy chunk of cholesterol on an alarmingly unstable crust. I grabbed a knife and fork and set them in front of him.

He rolled his eyes and pulled another swig from the bottle. "I need that note and the envelope it came in."

"The white one?"

He nodded, and burped.

"I don't have it."

His eyes got big and round. "Where is it?"

"I gave it to the detective investigating the murder."

"What?" He shot off the barstool like a rocket. "No! Please, tell me you didn't."

"You have the other one, the first one in the yellow envelope."

He rubbed his forehead with his non-pizza-eating hand and paced the kitchen. "Why on Earth would you give it to the police?"

"I thought it would help."

He stopped pacing and shut his eyes. "What did the detective say when you gave it to him?"

"Not what I expected. For some reason, he thought it was bogus."

Kingsbury paled. "How could he tell?"

"I don't know. I think he was grasping at straws. He even accused me of . . ." Kingsbury's last question hit a neuron inside my skull. ". . . Wait! You said, 'How could he tell.' You think the second note was bogus, too?"

He lowered himself onto the barstool. His baby blues were not a-twinkle. "Let's just say, theoretically, it may or may not have been strictly authentic." He buried his head in his hands.

My neurons niggled again. Why would Kingsbury be so attached to the second note, unless . . . He was lying!

If it weren't for gravity, I would have shot through the ceiling. "You! You planted it in the entry and duped me into believing it was real!"

"Wait a minute here. Don't you go accusing me . . . " He took a breath and crossed his arms. "Look, real or not real, what difference does it make?"

He took another pull on the beer and drained it. "We all know Brandy's no killer and that's what counts. What may or may not have happened that night, she doesn't deserve to rot in jail, take my word for it."

"Like hell I will."

"So what if somebody tried to make sure you believed in Brandy's innocence? It's no big deal."

"You made me pass fabricated evidence to the police!"

"What are you talking about? I told you to give it to me, remember?"

I fought the urge to take the unused knife and fork and commit murder myself. "What do I do now? Detective Washington is meeting me at lunchtime tomorrow."

"What's he want with you again?"

"I don't know. He said something's come up and he wants my input."

"Ms. Newman, whatever you do, do not tell him what we suspect about the second note. Nothing good can come of it."

"Except get a sneaky lying attorney disbarred."

"For what? I haven't done anything wrong, other than try like blazes to keep my client out of prison. For the love of justice, do not betray poor Brandy."

Poor Brandy? So now this wasn't about him? The fork was begging me to poke him in the eye; the knife called for a jab to the jugular. I wrestled for control.

"Take your pizza and go." I marched out and waited for him at the front door.

He took his sweet time in the kitchen while I orbited the entry like a hound with a bee on its tail. He appeared at last, beer pack in one hand and sagging pizza box in the other. I held the door open. In the hallway, he turned back like he wanted to say something, but I slammed the door before he could utter a syllable.

The kitchen reeked of pepperoni, pineapple and cheese. I added ice to my coffee, grabbed the notepad and pen, and escaped to the music room.

When Carter got back, I'd get him to teach me how to operate the sound system. Until then, my earbuds would have to do. I stuck them in my ears, filled my head with Mozart and tried to put Kingsbury, Washington and my blasted itchy ankle out of mind.

Write something, anything, even if it's wrong, I told myself. I pressed the pen to the paper and wrote one word: *Whistleblower.*

The moniker was still too weighty to contemplate. I wasn't against calling out corporate malfeasance, but how was I supposed to feel confident enough to do it on television? Panic began to frazzle my thinking. I considered calling Patel to tell him his idea was crazy, that I couldn't do the job, and he was risking his own neck for thinking I could.

Or was I a fool for not trying? I took a sip of coffee, set the pen tip on the paper and wrote down my response to him that day: *I am not a whistleblower.* Maybe I could pivot from there toward a positive starting point.

No use. I couldn't shake the thought of Kingsbury and the possibility that the note in the white envelope I'd given to Washington, was—as the detective had first guessed—bogus. Was that the "new development" he wanted to ask me about? If so, what would I tell him?

It took a Herculean effort to redirect my thoughts to the new job and the words I'd just written. I read them aloud. "I am not a whistleblower."

The statement pierced through the earbuds and into my ears. I read the words again. And then I crossed them out.

CHAPTER TWENTY-THREE

Parking

The guard at the KHTS employee parking lot checked his roster. He handed me a card key. "Welcome, Ms. Newman. You'll be next to the fence. Number thirteen."

I'm not superstitious, but I couldn't help wondering if the number was an omen. I wasn't as prepared as I'd hoped. Even so, I walked through the staff entrance with nervous energy pumping like wildfire.

The receptionist handed me a packet full of employee forms and a printout with a schedule of introductions and meetings for the day. First was Jay Patel. I lowered the lavaliere with my shiny employee ID over my head and straightened it along the lapels of the royal blue suit I'd chosen as my first-day-at-work ensemble. It felt like an Olympic medal. I patted it for good luck.

Patel was in his office on the phone. He waved me in.

I sat and waited for him to finish the call. While he spoke, his eyes scanned a row of monitors on a side wall. "I'll take it in here in a minute or two. Call me when it's ready."

He hung up. "Samantha." The enthusiasm I'd expected in his voice wasn't there. He busied himself rearranging papers on his desk, shuffling and piling them into stacks. "Samantha."

Okay, his desk was neater and he knew my name, but there was clearly a problem getting past it.

"Samantha." Again. "Something's come to my

attention this morning." Judging by his tone, this was not going to be a go-get-'em welcome speech. I held my breath.

His phone buzzed. "Okay," he said to the caller. "Send it."

He disconnected and looked me in the eye. "We've just received some breaking news. They're forwarding the raw footage now. I think you should see it."

I figured I was about to get my first assignment. If I hit the ground running, that elusive platform I'd struggled with might work itself out naturally. I let myself exhale.

He pointed a remote toward one of the monitors. "Here it is."

I sat up to give it my full attention. The on-camera reporter's voice streamed through the speakers.

"A surprising development early this morning in the murder investigation into the death of Irwin Bayne comes from the coroner's office. A second autopsy that had been requested by the defense has determined a new cause of death. The D.A.'s office reports that Brandy Bayne, the dead man's common-law wife, will not face murder charges at this time. However, she remains a person of interest."

Patel paused the report and turned to me. "The next part is what I want you to see." He let it roll again.

The reporter kept talking while he walked up a few steps in front of the police department entrance. "I'm here with Rufus Kingsbury, Mrs. Bayne's attorney. Sir, what does this mean for your client?"

Kingsbury leaned into the microphone. "I've said all along my client didn't do it."

The reporter moved the microphone back and forth between himself and Kingsbury as the interview continued. "What happens now in the case?"

"First, they've got to decide if it's even worth pursuing as a murder case. Then they need to look at other possible suspects, and there's a slew of 'em with motive and opportunity. I've uncovered vital information from my client's next-door neighbor about a balcony intruder, and I've just handed the evidence over to the police. They should be following that lead instead of harassing Mrs. Bayne, who's only a poor, grieving widow."

The reporter turned away from Kingsbury, checked his notes and spoke straight into the camera. "That neighbor, by the way, according to Mr. Kingsbury, is Samantha Newman, former chief of media communications at De Theret International, the global staffing firm that made headlines recently in several murder and drug trafficking investigations."

Patel stopped the video and turned back to me. The room telescoped to a tiny pinprick, exploded to normal size, then tunneled and inflated again. I thought I was going blind.

"Samantha? Are you okay?" Patel's face swam in front of me.

"Water." I croaked like a dying toad. He sprinted out.

Gripping the arms of the chair, I dared a peek at the monitor. The reporter was frozen in mid-sentence. Kingsbury's face was half out of frame, but the glee in his twinkly blue eye was unmistakable.

Patel returned with a bottle of water in one hand and a mug of coffee in the other. He shrugged and offered both. I pointed to the water.

After a couple of swigs and a deep breath, I reached for the mug too. I took a bracing sip. "Thanks."

I was still croaky, but at least the room had settled back to normal.

Patel returned to his desk. "I didn't mean to blindside you. It's just that, we have a problem here. In this business, if an employee winds up in the news, we come smack up against conflict of interest issues when we report on it. We're not going to run the part with your name in it—for now—but before you start working here, we need to understand your role in this criminal investigation. Can you explain how you came to be involved in a murder case, again?"

I returned the card key to the parking lot guard on the way out. Patel had already politely confiscated my employee packet and my badge. As I was leaving, he'd offered a bone: "We need to let things cool down and sort themselves out. When all this clears, I'm sure we'll want you back." He'd looked at me with genuine regret. "Take care, Samantha."

I pulled away from the station not knowing what to do next. At a strip center down the block, I parked the car and tried to steady myself.

The lot was mostly empty, except at the far end, where early supermarket shoppers worked their bag-laden carts through the grid of parked cars. I watched their comings and goings for a while. Smaller stores flanking the market—a yogurt shop, shoe store, dressmaker, and half a dozen others—began to draw a few customers.

A plumbing company van backed into the space next to mine. The service guy got out and slammed his door shut. A brief but awkward eye exchange yanked me out of my mental paralysis.

Shock and desolation dissipated. Only rage was left. I called Kingsbury.

"Hello, darlin'."

"You bastard! You threw me under the bus!"

"Now, darlin'—"

"Shut up, you weasel. Your stunt just cost me my job!"

"Whoa, now. Understand that I'm only trying to do my legal duty. You gave me evidence that you should have shared with the cops in the first place. I simply completed the circle."

What? Had he really just spun my personal disaster into his own perverted ethical imperative? "You smug jerk!"

"Hey! I'm tryin' to do what's right to save my client. That's a damn sight more important, don't you think?"

"What are you talking about?"

"Here's the thing. After you tossed me out yesterday, I got a call from the medical examiner I'd hired to double check the coroner's report. She figures that, even though Irwin Bayne suffered a blow to the head— the one Brandy may or may not have inflicted—it might have been too slight to kill him. She concluded that Irwin was blind drunk that night, and that he likely passed out, threw up and choked on his own vomit. Suffocated. Ergo, not murdered by Brandy."

"Where'd she get her degree, Lyingfool University?

"She's certified."

"But all the blood . . ."

"Head wounds bleed like beer from a keg. Doesn't take much to make a messy scene, but it takes a lot more to make it murder."

"Why did you give my name to the reporter?"

"Sorry about that. It just slipped out."

"I'll bet."

"Look, it's one post mortem against another now. The cops don't give up that easy. Brandy's still on their radar, but now they're willing to look at other possibilities. That's why I gave them the first note today, the one in the yellow envelope."

"And you told them who it came from."

"Had to. It's evidence. Chain of custody is critical."

An urge to scream strangled me. I shut my eyes and took a breath.

Kingsbury chuckled. "I wouldn't worry, although they'll probably want to question you on it."

"What about the one I gave them, in the white envelope?"

"No one mentioned it."

If he'd been standing in front of the car just then, I'd have shifted to drive and gunned it.

He was on a roll. "Of course, if they ask about another envelope, I'd counsel you to tell them only what you know for a fact about it, which is—and I'm guessing now—that you found it in roughly the same place as the yellow one. You can't really say for sure how either one of 'em got there, or where they came from. Am I right?"

CHAPTER TWENTY-FOUR

Know-It-All

L *iar, liar, pants on fire.*
       I knew in my bones that Kingsbury had faked the second note. The trouble was, I couldn't prove it. Now he'd trumpeted his ridiculous balcony-intruder theory to the police. It hit me, how masterful he was at muddying the facts. Good news for Brandy, I suppose, but why did he have to drag me into it? I wanted with all my being to kick him where it hurt.

The parking lot was beginning to fill with early lunchtime activity. I sat in the Tesla, feeling exposed in a whole new way. My meeting with Detective Washington loomed. I had a decision to make: postpone, or get it over with. My day had already nosedived. How much worse could it get?

A cozy-looking coffee shop next to the dry cleaners beckoned. I joined the line at the counter, where my blue power suit attracted lots of eyeballs. That's the effect I'd wanted for my first day at work. Now I longed for the drab, anonymous gray. I grabbed a double-iced-latte, headed for the car, and locked myself in. As I sucked the drink down, my mind played through variations of how a conversation with Washington might go.

I slurped the last puddle of coffee from the tall plastic cup. The straw grumbled and hissed until all I sucked was air. I couldn't sit in the parking lot all day. Time to decide.

I pulled up Washington's number on my phone. My

thumb hesitated over the call prompt until the screen went black. Staring into the blankness, I noticed my reflection staring back. In the darkened image, my frown lines looked like the Twin Canyons of California. I tossed the phone into my bag. Enough punishment for now.

I was suddenly ravenous. A hipster restaurant I'd eaten at in my old expense-account days was just around the corner, but I didn't feel together enough to face the hostess's eyebrow-raised greeting: "Just *one*?" Yes, just one, you haughty twit, because I'm so totally, miserably alone. Thank you for announcing it to the world.

I could feel a meltdown coming on. I had to get back to the condo, pronto, but I was hungry and the cupboard there was getting thin. I moved the car to a spot nearer the supermarket, grabbed a grocery cart and steered it around the fresh produce while Eighties-era classics played. Everything looked shiny and nutritious and not remotely what I felt like eating.

An old Air Supply song my parents used to love started up. I don't know the title. I'd always called it the Know-It-All song, because it repeats "I know (you something something) and I know (you something else), and I know (another something) and I know (a bunch more stuff)" a jillion times. It hit my nerves like a dental drill.

I wanted to bolt the store. Luckily, I had progressed to the frozen desserts aisle. I yanked open the nearest glass door and raked random pints of ice cream into the cart. As the song whined on, I made a beeline for the cashier.

A bright display of potato chips flanked the checkout counter. I grabbed a jumbo bag of Classic Sea Salt and tossed it onto the conveyor belt behind the ice cream.

As the last chorus from that blasted song began, I added a handful of Snickers bars and some individual serving packages of Oreos from the candy rack.

Fifth Perverse Elevator Game: When all you want is to hide inside your bubble of self-pity and make it to your apartment unaccosted, a chatty person will be waiting to intercept you. The doors slid open onto the unlikeliest of pairs: Pansy, decked out like the Duchess of Windsor in a navy silk dress and multiple strands of pearls, and in the other corner, Lizzie, shrouded in a ragged hoodie that swallowed her arms and hung past her knees. I pinched my grocery bag shut and got on.

Pansy CAT-scanned my power suit. "I didn't see you at the Ladies' Garden Club breakfast this morning. Of course, I was seated among the honorees. Perhaps your table was too far to the back."

I took that for a rhetorical question, and shrugged.

Unperturbed, Pansy went on. "The flowers were simply inexcusable. Who on earth uses carnations in a centerpiece? So common. And smelly! They set me sneezing for the entire program." She opened her purse, retrieved an embroidered hanky and blotted her nose. "Horrid little weeds."

The doors opened onto Lizzie's floor, but she didn't get off. When it came to my floor, I hurried to escape, a little too quickly. The ice cream assortment shifted in the bag and threatened to spill.

Lizzie rushed out behind me and grabbed the bag of chips before they hit the ground. She handed me the chips and took the bag. "I'll carry it for you." She followed me to the apartment door.

Before she relinquished the bag, she peeked inside. "Ice cream! Are you having a party? Can I come?"

I shook my head and took the bag from her. She looked pathetic in her oversized raggedy jacket. I reached into the bag and grabbed a pint off the top. Chocolate Chip Cookie Dough. "Here, take this."

She looked from the carton to me. "Can't I come to your party?"

"No."

She stared down at her sneakers. My heart went out to her.

"Okay, you can come in for a second. Your Mom probably wouldn't like it if you stayed too long."

She followed me into the kitchen. "My Mom never knows where I am. She doesn't care, anyway." She hopped onto a barstool and tested the swivel seat, twisting left and right. "Cool!"

I emptied the bag and stowed the pints in the freezer, except for the Chocolate Chip Cookie Dough. As I scooped the ice cream into a plastic cup, Lizzie tried again.

"I could stay and help you with the party. There's no school because of some stupid holiday, and I don't have anything to do."

"No, Lizzie. I'm feeling really sad today. I need to be alone. Besides, I'm sure your Mom cares where you are. She just can't say it."

"So who's all the ice cream for?"

"Just me. It's a pity party, only for me." I stuck a spoon into the cup and handed it to her.

She set it on the bar and continued twisting right and left on the stool. "Can't you have a pity party with two people? I'll be sad with you, so you don't have to be by yourself."

Anyone but Lizzie would have annoyed me beyond endurance, but somehow, she and I vibrated at the same frequency. "Tell you what. You can eat your ice cream here while I change out of my suit."

"Okay." She stopped twisting, pushed the long sleeves of the hoodie up past her elbows and dug in. Her first scoop overpowered the spoon. Gooey ice cream tumbled onto her jacket in a big blob.

I grabbed a sponge and wiped it off. "You'll have to put this in the wash when you get home."

"It's okay. It isn't even mine. It's my brother's, but he threw it in the trash. I'll just toss it out again.

The jacket was pretty shabby, and ripe with old sweat. Throwing it out wouldn't be a loss. I rinsed the sponge and left her to finish her ice cream.

In the bedroom, I ditched my camera-ready duds and changed into a sweatshirt and PJ bottoms. The blue suit lay in a heap on the floor, a perfect metaphor for how my life was going. I wanted to stomp on it and rip it to shreds.

When I got back to the kitchen, Lizzie was licking her spoon. It wouldn't have been so bad to have her around a little longer, but it didn't feel right to keep her without parental permission.

"I'm sorry Lizzie, but I think you should go now. You can take the rest home with you." I held the half-empty pint out to her.

"I guess my Mom and I can have our own pity party." She took the ice cream, slipped off the barstool and followed me to the door. I watched as she made her way down the hall to the elevators.

The distant buzz of my phone reached my ears from the kitchen. By the time I got to it, the caller had disconnected. Detective Washington.

Just as well. He would have to wait. Everybody could wait. I had some serious thinking to do. I turned the phone off and stuck it in the pocket of my PJs.

From inside the freezer, the call of ice cream beckoned. I reached in.

Cookies 'N Cream? Not bad for a starter, but I wanted something meatier. Rocky Road? Pass. I'd had enough rocky roads lately, and I don't mean the ice cream. Banana Pudding? Hmmm. I grabbed the pint and got a spoon.

The first bite put me back inside my parent's house. My Mom used to make banana pudding— the real kind— for an after-school treat. I spooned another bite into my mouth. It tasted almost like Mom's. Another taste brought tears to my eyes. If only I could be back there, in the kitchen with her right now, or anywhere on this earth with her, and my Dad and little brother.

I heaped more Banana Pudding onto the spoon and shoveled it into my mouth. It froze my palate for a few seconds until the creamy deliciousness took over. I wanted to eat it all, yet it somehow didn't feel like enough. I remembered seeing a bottle of dark rum in the music room. That could be just what was needed to make a truly spectacular pity party.

I jammed the spoon into the pint and took it with me in search of the rum. I found it on the serving cart, among the other bottles of booze.

I poured rum into the ice cream carton and tested the combination. Nice. I ate a few more spoonfuls to make room for more and poured it in.

After a few bites, the pudding softened, but the vanilla wafers held firm. I added more rum, mixed it all together and tried it. The cookie chunks soaked up the rum and gave the concoction just the right chewy texture. It was the most delicious chunky milkshake ever.

I wanted to relax and savor the rest, but there were only a couple of bites left in the carton. I polished them off while I stood there. It felt really good going down.

There was still rum in the bottle, but I'd run out of ice cream. I inventoried the rest of the tray: a nice port from that winery in Bryan, some good vodka, scotch, bourbon, tequila, and a couple more. As I mulled the possibilities, I had a hard time remembering which ice cream flavors still waited in the freezer. The port wine looked good, so I stuck it under my arm with the rum. Just in case, I grabbed the vodka and returned to the kitchen.

I hadn't noticed how warm I'd become until the cold freezer air hit my face. I stuck my head deeper inside and kept it there until my ears practically froze. Eating more ice cream would help cool me down. This time I'd choose something soothing. Cherry Vanilla made sense.

I tossed the empty Banana Pudding carton into the sink, but I must've turned back to the refrigerator too quickly, because I was suddenly dizzy. I plunged my head inside the freezer again to let the coolness settle before I plucked out the Cherry Vanilla, then I swirled port wine into the carton and tasted it. Not bad, but a little sweet. I ate a little more off the top and added vodka. Perfect.

I needed to slow down. I figured I'd be more relaxed in the bedroom. I could watch TV.

I hooked the port wine bottle and the vodka under my arm, in case the Cherry Vanilla needed more oomph at the end. The potato chips called to me, so I grabbed them, added the bottle of rum to my stash and tucked the candy bars into my PJ's. There was still room for one pack of Oreos.

As I turned toward the hallway, I was light-headed again. I leaned against the doorjamb to recover before completing the trip to the bedroom.

I set the bottles and snacks on the nightstand, emptied my pockets and turned on the TV. The first round of *Jeopardy!* was half over, up to the part where the host spends a few minutes talking to the contestants.

I hadn't watched the show since high school. It had been one of my family's daily rituals. We usually watched it before dinner, then my folks would use the day's categories for mealtime discussions with my little brother and me.

The last time I'd laid eyes on that old television and dining room table, their shrunken remains were barely recognizable among the bitter, smoky ruins of the old house where we had once lived, and where I'd lost them all.

I plopped onto the edge of the bed with my Cherry Vanilla/port/vodka slush and scraped spoonfuls until I came to the bottom of the pint. A booze-soaked cherry made the last bite. I considered going to the kitchen for the Cookies 'N Cream, until the potato chips caught my eye.

I reached over to set the empty pint on the nightstand. Somehow, the spoon flipped out and landed on top of the blue suit I'd left crumpled on the floor next to the bed. A dime-sized puddle of ice cream spread to quarter-size on the jacket's lapel. As I watched it seep deeper into the fabric, an explosion of nuclear magnitude hit my brain. I screamed.

"Aaaaaack!!!" I flung the empty pint at the suit. The carton bounced once and landed upside-down next to the spoon. A dark ring began to emerge from its circumference, soaking a perfect circle of goop into the jacket's shoulder.

A sob threatened to heave itself up and out of me. I gulped it down, ripped open the bag of potato chips and spread it flat over the bed like a platter.

Starting with the broken ones, I made piles of six chips each. Sometimes it was hard to push a whole pile into my mouth, but I managed. Once they were gone, I moved on to the perfectly intact chips. The salty crunchiness was delicious.

Halfway through, I got thirsty. I unscrewed the rum bottle and took a couple of swigs. Then I tore open a Snickers bar. My ant bites fired up again.

I don't know when I started crying, only that I couldn't stop. I staggered to the bathroom for a box of tissues, stumbled back and threw myself onto the bed. *Final Jeopardy!* 'think' music was playing. The subject was Ancient History. I never heard the answer.

I awoke in semi-darkness, my face half-stuck to a damp pillow. I rolled up on one elbow. The pillow stayed attached for a second before gravity peeled it off. The room swam in the flickering light of the TV screen.

A celebrity prank show was on, spewing laughter all over the room. I fell into the pillow again and reattached. I tried to ignore the hoots and hollers, but the relentless cackling wouldn't let me sleep.

I patted the sheets around me, hoping to locate the remote without having to open my eyes, but the only thing I accomplished was to scatter potato chips all over the place. I struggled up to a sitting position and fumbled through the bedclothes until the little bugger revealed itself, all smug under the blanket.

I clicked the TV off and fell back onto the pillow in blissful silence, until a clatter pulled me from the fog.

I opened my eyes. The room seemed a little steadier, so I pushed myself up and looked around.

A shadow passed across the balcony. Probably another bird. I wiped some grit from my eyes and started to lie down again when the shadow grew larger. I decided to ignore it, puffed up my pillow and burrowed under the covers.

Another clatter. I pounded a fist into the mattress. My heart started pumping fast. I wanted that stupid bird gone.

I sat up, and the shadow moved again. That did it.

"Hey! Stop it out there!"

I ripped the sheets off of me and bolted toward the curtains. Without thinking, I tore them open, unlocked the sliding door and staggered out onto the balcony.

I stumbled and fell forward. The cool night air and the lights of the city rushed at me. At first, the railing caught me at the waist and held me back. Then momentum took over, and I was tumbling headlong into the void.

CHAPTER TWENTY-FIVE

Scout's Honor

Thunder in my head. Rough stone, hard and cold against my cheek. My eyelids blasted open. I shut them to quell the pressure between my ears.

It was nice here in the night air, calm and cool. After a while, the drone of high-rise air handlers overtook the roar in my head and soothed me like a lullaby.

It had been months since I'd felt this serene. Visions of Carter's ranch swam behind my eyelids, with the sun swooning toward the horizon beyond the ancient oaks, turning everything golden. I wanted to be there again.

I could hear his voice calling me from far away. There it was again, closer this time, and again, closer still. Then someone lifted me up from the stone.

Carter. I could feel him, breathe him in as he scooped me up and carried me inside. I bounced in his arms for what seemed like miles before he lowered me onto something soft. A light clicked on.

I cracked an eyelid. I wanted to tell him how happy I was to see him, but all I could manage was, "Hi."

He frowned. "What happened, Sam?"

"Happened?"

He laid his palm on my forehead, then pressed his fingers gently to my neck to check my pulse. His hand swept the hair away from my face. "Can you sit up?"

"I'm a little dizzy." My voice slushed and slurred. "Could I have some water, please?"

While he was gone, I worked at reconstructing the time. Images flickered in and out. They weren't pretty.

He returned with a tall glass of ice water and an ice pack. I finished the water in one gulp and handed the glass back to him. "More please."

He set the ice pack between the back of my neck and the pillow. "This should sober you up pretty quickly. Take it easy. I'm going to recheck the bedroom and shut the balcony door."

I hadn't realized until then that he had put me in the guest room where Brandy had been before the police came. I remembered how sad and alone—and drunk—she'd seemed. Here I was, reenacting a startlingly similar scene. That was enough to sober me a little.

He returned with another glass of water. "You did a real number on the bedroom back there."

I attempted to swing my legs to the floor. "I'll clean it up."

He eased me down and sat on the bed beside me. "I'm afraid that mess will need a Hazmat crew."

I winced. "That bad?"

"Worse." He plucked pieces of potato chip out of my hair. His brows furrowed. "What's going on?"

Tears threatened, but I beat them back. "I lost my job."

"Lost? But you only just started."

"Actually, I never had a chance to start."

"Why?"

"Kingsbury."

His face drained. "That guy again?"

I nodded. "There's a new development in Brandy's case."

"I know. Another autopsy. What does that have to do with your job?"

"When the station interviewed Kingsbury about it, he mentioned my name. Made it sound like I could be the murderer. That's all it took for them to put me on hold indefinitely."

His hand balled into a fist. "Rat bastard."

"Anyway, after that everything came to a head, and I fell apart. Never done anything like that before. Sorry."

Carter took my face in his hands. "Nothing to apologize for, Sam. You've been through a lot the past few months."

I touched his hand. "Thanks. At least it gave you another chance to save my life."

"All I did was pick you up off the floor."

"No, before that, when you grabbed me and kept me from falling over the railing. Can't believe I was that drunk."

"What are you talking about?"

"When I barreled out there and couldn't stop myself. I almost took a nose-dive over the rail, but you yanked me back." I nudged him in the ribs. "C'mon, don't be so modest. You saved me, again."

He looked straight at me. "No, I didn't."

"I may have been falling-down drunk, but I know you pulled me back from certain doom. Don't deny it, Superman."

He shook his head. "When I got here, you were flat out unconscious on the balcony."

For all his maddening secrecy and obfuscations, I'd never known Carter to lie. Why wouldn't he take credit for another act of courage?

I searched his face for a crack, a smile that might give him away, but he only looked bewildered.

"It wasn't you?"

He raised his hand in a Scout's Honor pledge. "Nope."

I shivered. "If not you, then who was it?"

CHAPTER TWENTY-SIX

Mama Bird

I was too freaked to stay in the apartment. Carter booked a suite at The Lancaster, the downtown hotel where we'd first met. Staggering into the gracious lobby, I must have looked a sight in all my post-binge glory.

When I woke the next morning, the hammer inside my head reminded me where I was, and why. I heard Carter's voice coming from the sitting room. He poked his head in the door. "Feeling better?"

I nodded, despite the rumble in my stomach.

"Room service just delivered breakfast. I got you something easy on a hangover. Are you up to it?"

"Could I have it in bed?"

"Yes ma'am." He wheeled the dining cart to the bed. I propped myself on a couple of pillows, downed a glass of apple juice and reached for a dry English muffin.

Watching me like a mama bird, he pulled up a chair, poured a cup of coffee for me and refilled his own. "We need to talk about what happened out on the balcony yesterday."

I nibbled at the muffin and searched my memory. Nothing emerged, except the feeling that I was falling again into the void. I dared a sip of coffee. The hot liquid scalded my throat.

"It's no use."

"Then we'll have to work it another way. Time to get the police involved."

"Why? I wasn't attacked. Somebody saved me."

"Someone who was trespassing, Sam, and who may

be involved in the death next door."

"Why would Irwin's killer bother to save me?"

"Lots of questions to be answered. Before we clear the mess you made in the apartment, I think you should alert the detective."

"Washington?" I groaned. "I was supposed to meet with him yesterday, but I blew it off. He's probably polishing a set of handcuffs for me right now."

Carter smiled. "His interviewing skills aside, I'm told he has good instincts."

"He must have ignored them when he questioned us."

"He's a creative thinker, I'll give him that, but you have to dial him in."

My head throbbed. I wanted to fly far, far away. I sipped more coffee and finished the muffin, even though it tasted like damp sawdust. I washed it down with the rest of the coffee and shut my eyes. "Okay."

I heard the scrape of Carter's chair. "I'll get your phone."

He quickly returned. Washington had left two messages since my no-show yesterday. Without listening to them, I selected the last one and connected.

Mercifully, the detective was brief and brusque as usual. We set the meeting for tomorrow at the condo, after forensics had time to assess the balcony and the cleanup crew was finished in the bedroom.

I shot Carter a dirty look. "Happy now?"

"Tell you what, Ms. Grouch. Let's stop waging war with the world for a while. It's time you got out of bed. Think you can make it to the sitting room on your own?"

He wrapped his arm around my waist and helped me to a standing position. My legs felt like they belonged to

Gumby. An unfamiliar tee hung past my knees. I hadn't been awake enough to notice it before. "Where are my clothes?"

"I sent them to be laundered. After I washed the chips and dirt and I'm not sure what else off of you last night, the only clean things to put you in were mine. Yours should be delivered soon."

My face heated as the memory floated in. Me, under the shower. Carter, washing my hair, tenderly lowering me to the tub, soaping my body, massaging my shoulders, gently patting dry. He had literally showered me with love, and I'd been too wasted to notice.

He took my face in his hands and looked deep into my eyes for the longest time before he spoke. "Sure you're okay?"

Yes, I wanted to say, I'm okay with you, no matter what.

The sitting room was spacious for such a small hotel. I stretched out on the sofa. Carter picked up the remote. "TV?"

"Too noisy. Could we just talk?"

"Sure. You pick the subject."

Foggy though I was, I knew what to chose. "Serenity. After the fire ants, you never finished telling me what you want to do with the land across the creek."

There was that brief flicker of sadness in his eyes again. He put down the remote and stood there, hands on hips, head bowed. By the set of his shoulders, that property held heavy meaning for him.

"Or we could watch TV, I guess."

He shook his head. "No, this is as good a time as any."

He sat beside me, wrapped an arm around my shoulders and pulled me to him. "Ready?"

I nestled closer and leaned my head on his shoulder.

The rhythm of his breathing and the warmth of his body was better than any hangover remedy. "Ready."

He cleared his throat. "As I was saying before your fire ant attack, I'm planning to acquire the property adjacent to Serenity. The people across the creek want to sell, and developers are circling. I put in a bid, and I'm waiting to see if they'll accept."

"What will you do with it?"

"Leave it as is, except for a hundred acres or so."

"And those?"

His breathing stilled. "When my kids were alive, I worried that they'd grow up spoiled by our good fortune. I wanted them to learn what it feels like to share. One day when I was there at the creek, it struck me—how I could teach them to give back."

He cleared his throat again. "My idea was to create a retreat for children and families in distress, a place to escape, at least temporarily, from whatever difficult circumstances they were in. A camp with a purpose: lots of recreation, programmed and otherwise, with access to therapists and social workers to help them work through their issues. Nobody would have to pay if they couldn't afford it.

"I wanted my kids involved, so they could learn how good it feels to help people who need a lucky break. Katharine loved the idea. I was about to start when . . ." He picked at a place on his khakis.

Tears pooled in my eyes. "It's a wonderful idea."

"Thanks." He unwrapped his arm from around me and leaned forward, elbows on knees. "I'm still going to buy the land, even though it's not the same without . . . " He struggled for words and gave up.

I conjured a picture of what his dream would look like. "You could make life better for so many—"

The drum in my head picked that moment to return with a vengeance. It merged with a subterranean vibration rising from my gut. I shut my eyes and rubbed my temples. Much as I wanted to hear the rest of Carter's idea, my stomach had a more urgent plan.

"I think I'm going to be sick." I stumbled into the bathroom.

Carter held my hair back while I hugged the toilet bowl and retched. Afterward, I mumbled a weak apology, fell into bed, and stayed there for the rest of the day, sleeping off and on.

Toward evening, he ordered broth and crackers for me before he went out. When he returned, he stayed in the in sitting room, possibly doubting his judgment in choosing to stick with me.

CHAPTER TWENTY-SEVEN

Recognize These?

I was glad to skip another visit to police headquarters to see Washington, but not so keen on returning to the scene of my latest nightmare at the condo. At least the detritus from my pity party had been cleared. The balcony, too. Everything looked sterile and a little spooky, like nothing, good or bad, had ever happened there. I wondered if Brandy's place looked the same

Carter did a walk-through to check things out while I changed into a clean pullover and jeans. The hotel laundry had done its best to wash my post-binge PJ's, but they went straight into the laundry hamper again. On second thought, I stuffed them into the trash.

Carter had asked Gertie to join us for our meeting with Washington. The two of them arrived at the same time, proving the point of the Sixth Perverse Elevator Game: If you are stuck in a long ride with only one other person, it's probably someone you never ever wanted to see again.

At the front door, Carter let Gertie in, but he kept Washington in the hallway for a private powwow. She and I had only enough time to exchange hugs before the men were back.

"I'm going out for a few minutes," Carter announced. "Detective Washington has assured me that this will be a friendly session with the two of you, so everybody just relax." He shot a serious glare at each of us. "I won't be long."

Gertie and I moved to the sofa. Washington took a

side chair, dropped a thick file folder on the coffee table in front of him and shuffled a few pages before he made eye contact. "Thank you, Mrs. Gold, and Ms. Newman, for taking the time to speak to me again."

Carter's friend at the police department must have leveled the riot act at Washington. "Please," he'd said on the phone, and now, "Thank you," although he immediately refocused his attention to the file, shifting things around like he was preparing for a major interrogation.

I decided to accept his gesture of détente. Might as well start on positive footing. "You're welcome." Gertie managed an almost-smile.

He thumbed through the papers again and stopped at a group that was stapled together. Upside-down, I could make out the word 'Coroner' on the cover. He tapped his finger on the second page and cleared his throat.

"As you may know, there are new findings that attempt to change our understanding of what happened to Irwin Bayne. However, they come from a consultant for the defense, and I believe those findings are false.

"Also, we have new physical evidence that deserves more scrutiny. And now there is the incident on the balcony with you, Ms. Newman, which may tie to the Bayne case. I'm trying to rethink everything, so bear with me."

When he returned the coroner's report to the rest of the papers, I caught sight of the neon yellow envelope. It was inside a clear plastic evidence bag, peeking out from the pile like a snake under a rock.

An idea struck. That note, or the white one, could be the key to exacting revenge on Kingsbury for tanking my job. I wish I'd thought of it sooner. Still, there might be a chance.

Washington drew the bag with the yellow envelope

out of the pile and set it in front of us. He retrieved another bag with the white one inside, placed it beside the yellow one and nudged the edges of each until they were in perfect alignment. The notes had been opened and were displayed so they could be read through the plastic.

He looked me straight in the eye. "Recognize these?"

My mind moved into high gear, racing to find a way to sink Kingsbury. I came up empty. "They look like the ones I found inside the front door of the apartment."

Gertie leaned in to get a better look. I'd never mentioned them to her. As she read the messages, her eyes widened.

Washington continued. "And when was it that you found them?"

I pointed to the yellow one. "That one came first, the day after you arrested Brandy and Gertie." I felt her stiffen beside me.

Washington shifted his attention to her. "I'm sorry to have put you through that, Mrs. Gold. Had to be done."

The memory of Gertie being marched off like a two-time offender sent my rage meter surging again. Since this was supposed to be a friendly chitchat, I squelched the urge to yell at him and squeezed her hand instead.

She squeezed back. "I wasn't actually arrested, dear." She turned to Washington. "All is forgiven, Detective."

I finished answering his question. "The white one came a couple of days later."

He tapped his finger on the bag with yellow envelope. "After you found this first one, what did you do with it?"

"I was in a hurry, so I dropped it into my bag to open later."

"And later . . .?"

"I opened it and found a newspaper scrap inside with a note written on it."

He pointed to the note. "This it?"

I nodded. He scribbled in his notebook, taking his slow, deliberate time before returning his attention to me. "After you saw what was in the note, did you call me, or anyone in my department and turn it in?"

He already knew what the answer was, since he'd gotten the envelope from Kingsbury. The detective must have been dialing back some hostility of his own.

"My schedule was really hectic that day. I meant to let you know about it as soon as I could."

"But you didn't."

"No." I caught myself twirling Mom's ring and grabbed the armrest to stop it. "I gave the envelope to Rufus Kingsbury, Mrs. Bayne's attorney."

While Washington made notes, I searched frantically for a way to insinuate Kingsbury's envelope flimflam into the conversation. No luck. The detective stopped writing and tapped his pen on the bag with the white envelope. "Tell me about that one."

This could be my chance. I sat up. "I found it in the same place as the other one. I'd been out that morning. It was there when I came back. Kingsbury was there, too. Perhaps there's a connection?"

Washington harrumphed. "If he was there, why not give it to him, like the yellow one?"

"He wanted it, but I did what I should have done with the first one and saved it for you." I hoped I'd get points for that, but the detective didn't seem interested. He returned to his notes.

My brain was screaming: *Say more about Kingsbury and his envelope trick! Tell him!*

I had a conversation with my pulse rate and cleared my throat. "About the yellow envelope. I think you should know that I gave it to Brandy's attorney a long time ago. When did he hand it over to you?"

"Recently."

"Why'd he hold onto it for so long? Could he be trying to manipulate the evidence?"

Washington shrugged. "Defense attorneys run on their own schedule. Unfortunately, it may not be the same as ours. It's part of the game."

Drat.

The detective returned the evidence bags to his file, then peered deep into my eyes. "Who do you think wrote these notes?"

"Could be anyone. Even Mr. Kingsbury. He was there when I found the white one. Strange, don't you think?" Didn't hurt to try one more time.

Washington didn't blink.

I had an idea. "Did you check them for fingerprints?"

"Yes."

"So you know who the writer is?"

"I can't discuss that."

"But if you know who wrote them, why—?"

"Ms. Newman, I'll ask the questions here, not you." He stood and paced to the entry.

My jaw clenched. I bit down harder.

Washington returned to the chair, but didn't sit. He scratched his head. "See, this is what I can't figure out. Why were they delivered to you? It makes me wonder if you are more involved than it seems."

I shot off the sofa. "No! We are not going there again. Just because I was staying next door to those people doesn't mean—"

He raised his hand. "You can relax, Ms. Newman. You and your friend are well-vetted. But you may know more than you are aware of. I need help here, and I feel like you're holding back."

He sat, tossed his pen onto the file and massaged his forehead. "After what happened to you the other night, I hoped you'd be more cooperative."

Carter's remark about my habit of waging war with the world came back to me. Why was I so defensive when I had nothing to hide? Brandy didn't need me. She had a lawyer to defend her, and I didn't owe Kingsbury anything but a boot to his backside.

I lowered myself onto the sofa again. "Sorry, Detective. I'd like to help you. Really." I offered a smile. "Can you please tell us who wrote the notes? After all, they could lead to the identity of the balcony intruder. My life may be in danger."

He shook his head and searched my face with tired eyes. "I cannot reveal the fingerprint results, other than to confirm what you know already. Yours and Mr. Kingsbury's were on both of them."

Of course they were, and I'd just confirmed how they got there. Drat. I'd botched a chance to mess with Kingsbury. "Go ahead. Ask your questions."

"I'd like to pick up where we left off, with the two notes. How were these delivered to you?"

"I figured they'd been slipped under the door. Then Kingsbury had a wild theory that someone came from the balcony and left them by the front door. Had me freaking out over it for a while. But when I mentioned it to you last time, you blew me off. The more I thought about it, I didn't think it was possible either. Until the day before yesterday."

"You had never seen anyone on the balcony before?"

"Window washers, and birds a couple of times." I hesitated. "Sometimes, at night, I've seen a shadow or heard a noise outside. But I'd look up and there'd be nothing. I'm not good with heights, so I don't spend a lot of time out there."

I felt Gertie stiffen again. She grabbed my arm.

Washington noticed. "What is it, Mrs. Gold?"

"It's probably nothing, but . . ." She covered her mouth with her hand, her wide eyes moving from me to Washington and back to me. "It could be something."

She tore her eyes from mine and addressed him. "I think I may have seen someone on the balcony, too, the night Irwin Bayne died."

She frowned, struggling with the memory. "I had finally managed to put Brandy to bed. She was cold, so I went in search of an extra blanket. I found one in the linen closet next to the master bedroom.

"As I turned off the closet light, I heard a noise behind me, very faint. I stepped into the room. Nothing was out of place, only a shadow moving across the curtains from outside. I opened them to see if anything had fallen onto the balcony, but Brandy started wailing again, so I took the blanket to her and forgot about it. Until now."

I took Gertie's hand. She was trembling. I was a little shaky, too.

The phantom on the balcony was not a figment of my imagination. Gertie had seen it. It had stalked me, watched me, and maybe even crept inside the apartment. But if it was the person who had killed Irwin Bayne, why had it bothered to save me?

CHAPTER TWENTY-EIGHT

Just in Case

Washington exhausted his list of questions and left. While we waited for Carter to return from wherever he'd gone, Gertie and I moved to the kitchen to make tea and mull over some questions of our own.

She poured Oolong into my cup with unsteady hands. "Do you think it was the murderer I saw out there on the balcony? Is it possible that Brandy didn't do it?" She must not have heard the news.

"The police are still working on it. It's possible that Irwin died from his own drunkenness."

"That's good for Brandy, I suppose." Relief played over her face before her eyebrows knit again.

"But, who did we see on the balcony?"

The question had been playing like background music in my head. I ran through the likely suspects again. The paperboy? He was there the morning Irwin died. But the young man seemed more like a hard-working, school-and-two-jobs kind of guy. Not a balcony lurker, or a murderer.

The valet? I hoped not. I liked him, and I'd promised not to tell anyone about his hallway encounter with Brandy. Another valet? They all had access to every part of the building. Or maybe it was someone else entirely, like . . . who?

The doorbell rang. I expected Carter to let himself in, so I didn't bother to get up until it rang again. I left Gertie in the kitchen and went to get the door.

It wasn't Carter. Instead, Pansy Gump rushed past

me and into the living room before I could stop her. She looked around the empty room. "Where is he?"

"He?"

"The police detective. I just spoke with the security manager downstairs about the monstrous murder in our building and he said the detective on the case was here in your apartment."

"He left."

Pansy stomped her foot. "I should not have to chase the man down when there is something important to tell him."

"You could call."

"I have, on numerous occasions, until I was told that he had received all the information from me he needed. Imagine!"

She plopped into the same chair that Washington had just vacated, then shot up again.

"The window washers! They are nothing but Peeping Toms. I'm certain they had something to do with it." She lowered herself again, draped the width of her caftan over the arms of the chair and waited for my reaction.

I hardly thought that a window washer would be hanging off the side of the building at night, but I didn't want to engage in a debate. "An interesting theory. However, the police are rethinking whether there really was a murder next door."

"Rethinking? There was a body, for Heaven's sake. And that woman, the wife, she's a troublemaker. I have an instinct for these things." She shook her head. "I must speak to the detective about the window washers. And remind him about the valet. I was once alone in the elevator with that one and he looked directly into my eyes. What if he is a serial killer? He must be stopped before he kills again!"

I fought a smile. "I think you owe it to yourself to go home immediately and call Detective Washington. Although, I'd go easy on the valet. He seems very mild-mannered."

"That's how they get you. Reel you in with their charm."

I imagined she was an Agatha Christie fan, fearing that she'd be the next victim if the killer wasn't apprehended in time.

I tried to offer comfort. "I'm having tea in the kitchen with an old friend. Would you like to join us?"

"An old friend? Someone I know?"

"I don't think so. She used to be my secretary."

"Secretary?" She shrugged. "I'd rather call the police."

Gertie was rinsing her cup when I returned to the kitchen. "I have to go, Samantha. Louis is picking me up for dinner before the symphony, and there's barely time to get home and change."

"But we've hardly caught up since dinner the other night. I want to know everything about you and Louis."

A grin spread across her face as she dried her hands. "And I want to tell you, but there's no time. And we're leaving for a two-week Mediterranean cruise at noon tomorrow." She lifted her bag from the counter. "Rain check when we return?"

As I followed her to the door, I considered my old friend. In her stylish dress, designer purse and smoothly tamed hair, she looked ten years younger and bushels happier than I'd ever seen her.

It was obvious that Louis Kleschevsky was working his magic on her. For her sake, I hoped it was real.

Gertie was long gone, and Carter still hadn't returned. When I calculated the time, it had been almost two hours. I shoved the possibility of another disappearing act out of mind.

I was putting up the tea things when the doorbell rang. I half-sprinted to the door and flung it open.

Lizzie looked up at me, her eyelashes damp. "Can I come in?"

I motioned her inside. "Are you okay?"

She sniffled and wiped a tear from her cheek with the back of her hand. "Do you still have ice cream?"

I attempted to inventory the contents of the freezer from memory, but like everything else that had happened during my inglorious binge, I couldn't call up anything for certain.

"Come to the kitchen and we'll look."

Lizzie sat on a barstool. "My Mom liked the kind you gave me before. Is there any more of that?"

I opened the freezer. Two pints glistened in frosty repose. "I've got Rocky Road or Cookies N' Cream. Why don't you take both? I won't be eating ice cream for a while."

"Okay." She made a half-hearted swivel on the stool and wiped her eyes on her sleeve.

It hurt to see her so sad. I wished I was a pro at dealing with children, but I'd never had any experience, except for my little brother, years ago. Still, I made a stab at it.

"I hope this isn't for a pity party. Ice cream's really best for having fun."

She lowered her eyes to the counter.

I didn't have the heart to press her. I grabbed the icy pints, found something to put them in and handed the sack to her. "Anything else?"

She shook her head and took the bag. "Thanks."

At the entry, I asked one more time if I could help,

but she opened the door herself and was about to walk out when Carter marched in and blocked her. He didn't look happy.

He lost his scowl and smiled down at her. "Hello there. Sorry I was in such a hurry. Are you all right?"

Lizzie backed a way and stared at the floor.

"Lizzie, this is my friend, Carter. He didn't mean to scare you."

She looked him in the eye. "I'm not scared. I've seen you before. I want to go home now."

He moved out of her way. We watched her progress down the hall before he shut the door. His frown had reappeared.

"Pack a travel bag, Samantha, enough for a week or so. We're not staying here tonight."

"But we just got here."

"Pack up and let's go. There's time to explain on the way back to the ranch." His tone alarmed me.

"Can you just tell me—"

"Where's your luggage?" He marched toward the bedroom. "I want to leave before dark."

I dressed and packed as fast as I could, but the cleaning crew had done such a good job, it took a while to find some things. I opened and shut a few drawers before I found my silver hoop earrings in the nightstand. Next to them was the mystery doo-dad I'd found under the bed. I pulled it out to give to Carter later, dropped them all into my cosmetics case and hurried out.

Once Carter had steered the Tesla onto the tollway, he seemed to relax a bit. I couldn't hold my curiosity any longer. "Can you please tell me why we had to leave so fast?"

He scanned the rearview mirror. "While you and

Gertie were busy with Washington, I took a closer look around the building. I originally chose that condo because it seemed secure. But I couldn't dismiss the fact that someone was on the balcony with you that night. I had to figure out how they got there."

"And?"

"I think it can be breached from outside the building. It would have to be someone with certain skills, but given the relationship of the parking garage to the building itself, and the balcony design, it can be done."

"Why would anyone want to?"

He gave me a quick glance. "I spoke with Washington before he left. He's positive Bayne was murdered. He had hoped you or Gertie could shed more light on it, but apparently—"

"What about the fingerprints? He said he had the notes tested for fingerprints, but he wouldn't tell me whose they found, besides mine and Kingsbury's."

Carter seemed to be considering how to answer me. "There was no match in the system for a third set of prints. And it's unlikely they'll get clearance to test for DNA anytime soon. There's one more clue they're pursuing, but so far, it's a dead end."

"What is it?"

Again, he struggled with an answer. "I'm not comfortable disclosing this, but they're grasping at straws now. Maybe it will jog something in your memory. They found a partial shoeprint in the blood near Irwin's bedroom door."

I worked the new clue over in my mind for a mile or so before I realized that Carter had managed to avoid answering my first question. I shifted in the seat and looked directly at him. "Why did we leave the condo in such a hurry?"

The answer came to me the instant I'd asked it. "You think I'm in danger."

He checked the rear-view mirror and steered toward the exit lane. "Let's take a break. I'll make a stop at Love's for coffee. Want some?"

I waited inside the Tesla, half of me frustrated, the other half, afraid. By the time Carter returned, I'd had enough.

I tore off my seatbelt. "If you don't tell me right now what's going on, I'm getting out of the car."

The threat sounded ridiculous, even to me. I shot him a serious glare and re-buckled my seatbelt. The sun was low in the sky. It pierced the windshield and stung my eyes. I searched my purse for sunglasses and put them on.

He checked the side mirror and returned to the road. "I don't mean to scare you. Once this thing about someone on the balcony is resolved, I'll stop worrying."

"Wouldn't a bad guy just let me fall when I was out there? Or kill me too?"

"It's probably nothing but my paranoia kicking in. I just want to be sure."

CHAPTER TWENTY-NINE

Sweetgum

It was dark when we arrived at Serenity. A full moon was rising. The big oaks along the entrance cast long, spidery shadows over the road. Carter's paranoia was catching. I shivered.

He stopped the Tesla in front of the house and turned to me. "Don't worry, Sam. You're safe here. My only concern is at the condo. There's a ring of security on this property under normal circumstances, and if we have to, we can take it up a notch or two."

"Like DEFCON One?"

He smiled. "Something like that."

I opened the car door and scanned the house and nearby trees for evidence of hidden cameras, which I figured would be feeding multiple images to the screens inside Carter's third-floor sanctum. I couldn't spot any.

Ralph greeted us at the door and carried our bags upstairs while Carter led me to the kitchen. He opened the refrigerator and plucked out some sandwich makings and a platter of cold sliced deli meat and cheese. There was a deep-dish pie on the island counter. Apple, it looked like, homemade, and probably delicious. I tried to ignore it.

Carter set the food on the counter. "Sandwiches okay?"

I nodded. "Now that you've scared the daylights out of me, I could also use a glass of wine."

Ralph appeared in the doorway and beckoned to him. Carter handed the bottle to me and joined him in the next room. They talked in low tones.

They were back in the kitchen before I had taken the first sip. They both seemed fairly relaxed. I took their cue and tried to relax, too.

Carter patted Ralph's shoulder. "Want a sandwich, buddy?"

Ralph shook his head. "Nah, I'm good, although I have been thinking about a slice of that pie since my Mom pulled it out of the oven. She made it for you, so I didn't want to be the first to cut into it."

Carter grabbed a clean knife and made a cut, then returned to his sandwich making. "Have at it. I'll catch up after this, assuming you leave me any."

"I can't eat the whole thing," Ralph said, "though I'd like to try."

"Actually, I was speaking to Samantha."

I sputtered into my wine. "I never said anything about pie."

Carter grinned. "I could feel your 'pie-dar' from across the room. The force is strong with you."

I stuck my tongue out at him. "Somebody has to keep Ralph company. Might as well be me."

Carter was gone when I woke in the morning. A note by the bed had two words on it: Third Floor. I plucked a fresh tee from my bag, pulled on my jeans, and went to wash my face and brush my teeth.

The bathroom was big enough to accommodate a small cocktail party. Natural light from the clerestory bounced over the walls. Cooler rays filtered through the oaks and floated in from the picture window that framed the claw-footed bathtub.

I wondered if anyone outside could spy in through the glass, but as I peered out, all I saw was dense greenery and an abandoned bird nest atop a high limb.

I retrieved the silver hoop earrings from my cosmetics case and stuck the little zipper pull—or whatever it was—into my pocket so I wouldn't forget to give it to Carter. After a swipe of lip-gloss, I bounded upstairs.

On my first visit to Serenity, I'd snuck up there out of curiosity while Carter was busy preparing dinner in the kitchen. I'd tripped a hidden alarm. He'd been good-natured about the whole thing, which had only slightly relieved my embarrassment.

I was there again after he'd abandoned me at the ranch. That's when Ralph let me peek inside and I'd seen Carter's shrine to his lost family: the children's violins, Katharine's cello, and that sad, abandoned guitar.

I knocked on the door. Nothing. I knocked again.

Carter's voice came through a speaker somewhere on the landing. "There's coffee in the kitchen. I'll be down in a minute."

So it wasn't an invitation after all. I waved above my head to whatever camera had identified me, turned around and made my way downstairs.

No food was laid out for breakfast, so I added milk and sugar to the coffee in my mug for sustenance. Then I caught sight of the pie—the remainder of the deep-dish apple from last night. Pie for breakfast: like buttered toast and jam, only better.

I debated whether Carter's "down in a minute" was the same as his "I won't be long" from yesterday. It could be hours before he appeared.

The sugar crystals on top of the piecrust sparkled in the morning sunlight that streamed through the window above the sink. I set my mug down, got a plate and sliced a two-inch wedge. A small larceny, hardly noticeable.

I was drying the plate when Carter joined me.

"Did you have enough for breakfast?"

Had he seen my thievery? "A tiny slice of pie with my coffee," I fessed. "Enough for now."

"Good. If you're up for it, let's go for a ride."

"Are you sure we'll be safe out there?"

A cloud crossed his eyes. "If you don't want to go—"

"I'm not talking about fire ants, Carter. What about last night?"

He cupped my face in his hand. "I told you, there's nothing to worry about here. As for the condo, I'm probably being over-cautious. I just want to give it a few days to make sure there's no more activity on the balcony. In the meantime, let's try to enjoy ourselves." He kissed me on the tip of my nose, took my hand and steered me out of the kitchen.

Our ride turned out to be on horseback. We waited in a patch of sunlight on the front veranda for Ralph to bring the horses. Gusts of varying temperatures, common in Central Texas when summer eases into autumn, wafted warm from one direction, cool from another, then warm and cool again.

Ralph rode toward us in a slow amble, the reins of our mounts in his hands, their glossy bodies flanking his roan mare. We left the porch to meet him at the bottom of the steps.

He unhooked a pair of boots from the saddle of a palomino and handed them down to Carter. "Are these the ones?"

Carter slowly inspected the tooled-leather cognac-colored cowboy boots, passing his hand tenderly over each curve of the raised scroll design. He held them out to me without looking up. "See if these fit."

They looked brand new. I wondered why a new pair

of boots would be lying around waiting for the right-sized person to wear them, until it dawned on me: they had been meant for Katharine.

It was eerie to have them in my hands. I tried to imagine what Carter was feeling. His face was masked by the shade of his cowboy hat.

No point making the moment more awkward by asking about them. I shucked my tennies and pulled the first one on. It was stiff, but it fit. I reached for its mate and tugged it on, too. Friction fired up the ant bites. I did my best to ignore them.

Carter was already astride his horse, a tall Appaloosa with solid chestnut blanketing its neck and shoulders and dappling its sturdy white hindquarters. As I stepped down join him, he glanced at the boots, then pointed to a path that led behind the house. "Meet me there."

Ralph boosted me onto my ride, the honey palomino. "This is Hollywood," he said. He gestured toward Carter's horse. "That's Remington. Have fun out there. It's a great day for a ride."

I did my best to turn the horse and catch up. My riding skills were rusty, to put it mildly. Truth was, I didn't have much experience. Fortunately, Hollywood was willing to follow my timid lead.

As soon as we pulled beside him, Carter took his horse into a leisurely trot and headed past century-old spreading oaks toward the meadowlands beyond. My horse followed with barely a hint from me. She was only slightly darker than the waist-high, tawny grasses that swayed around us. The breeze feathered through her creamy-white mane.

The trail wound around stands of pecan trees, their deep green canopies towering above us. The old well appeared under its tangled cover of desiccated dewberry brambles.

When we came to another meadow, Carter urged Remington into a canter and made for the tall trees on the bluff overlooking the creek. I recognized it as the place we'd walked to the last time, where the fire ants attacked.

By the time Hollywood and I caught up, Carter had dismounted and tied Remington to a low branch of the sweetgum. The tree's star-shaped leaves were broader than my hand, and hinted at an autumn display to come.

Carter caught me as I slid down from Hollywood's tall back. He gave me a quick kiss, took Hollywood's reins, and tethered her to a branch next to Remington.

As he spread a blanket over the fallen branch we'd sat on days before, I eyed it warily. "I'm pretty sure ants can crawl over that."

"It's just for comfort. I had this area treated while I was away. It should be fairly safe now."

With the old bites still flaring, I would have felt better if he'd said *totally* safe, but I braved it and sat on the blanket.

He reached up to pluck a sweetgum leaf. He crushed it in his hand, held it to his face, then pulled another one from the tree, scrunched it and handed it to me. I inhaled. Earthy sweetness filled my nostrils.

Carter pulled a burr off the tree. He seemed lost in thought as he walked to the edge of the bluff and tossed the burr into the water below. He stood there, hands on hips, head bowed.

After a while, he left the bluff and sat next to me. His arm swept the vista across the creek. "Any thoughts about my idea for that land?"

"It's spectacular. You could help so many people."

He made dirt circles on the ground between us with the toe of his boot. "It'll take a lot of people to make it happen."

"You'll have help. Gertie and Ralph and Dottie, to start with. Plenty of good people would love to work at a place like that."

I stood and walked to the edge of the bluff, taking in the open country that spread beyond the creek. It wouldn't be hard to be here more permanently, working on his dream with him. "I could help, too."

He lowered his eyes.

My words vibrated in the space between us. "Did I say something wrong?

His eyes searched mine. "It means a lot that you like the idea, Sam. A lot. I'm just not sure if now's the right time for you to commit to something like this. What about the job at KHTS?"

"But—"

"If that job's only on hold until the murder case is cleared, it's still yours. That's a pretty cool gig. I know how much you value your independence. Working with me would bind us together in a way you may not want."

I wasn't worried about the binding part anymore. I sat beside him again. "I want to stand for something good this time."

"The TV offer sounds like that kind of thing, too. Championing the little guy and all."

Between wanting, then not wanting, then landing the job at the station and losing it, I'd ended up understanding that it was a huge opportunity. If it were mine again, I'd be calling out slick operators like Kingsbury. That was doing good, too. I stared across the water and sifted through my feelings.

Carter's cell phone vibrated. He tossed the leaf away and dug into his pocket.

"What's up?" He listened for a while, then gave me

an apologetic look and walked a few feet toward the bluff to continue the conversation. When he returned, he looked more relieved than I'd seen him in the past twenty-four hours.

I squinted up at him. "Good news?"

"No action on the balconies."

"So it's safe?"

"I'd feel better if we gave it another day or so."

Ralph met us at the front steps of the house. He held Hollywood steady while I slid off. I gave her muzzle a pat and telepathically made a date with her to go riding again soon.

Something had been itching my thigh during the ride back. I needed to get my jeans off before fire ant panic set in. "See you guys in a minute."

I bolted up the grand staircase past the huge maps of Texas and flew down the hall into the master bedroom. Holding my breath, I unfastened my jeans and pushed them down. No bugs. At the top of my thigh, a half-peanut of a bump was the only mark that correlated to the stinging.

Thinking the bugger could be hiding in my jeans, I dropped them to my ankles, yanked off the boots, turned them upside down and gave the soles a couple of whacks, in case a crawly thing was hiding in there. Nothing. I pulled the jeans completely off, turned them inside out and tried again.

Something dropped to the floor: a sweetgum leaf, and the little object that I'd saved for Carter. That was the likely culprit.

The little piece hadn't bothered me on the ride out, but just before leaving the bluff to come back, I'd sat atop Hollywood and plucked the leaf off a low branch to bring back with me. I'd folded its five-point span into a small rectangle and stuffed it in my pocket. Most likely, I'd jammed the other doohickey down and accidentally shifted it to an awkward place on my thigh.

I lifted the leaf from the floor, unfolded it and held it to my face. It smelled like the breeze at the bluff. I put it back in the pocket and tugged my jeans and boots back on. I dropped the trinket on the nightstand.

My phone buzzed. Kingsbury.

My first instinct was to thumb his number into the blocked-call file on my phone. On second thought, I had unfinished business with the blabbermouth. I still wanted payback.

I said hello in my chilliest tone.

"Darlin'! How ya been?"

His voice sent my blood pressure spiking. "What do you want?"

"Thought you'd like to know that I'm callin' a press conference to announce the official close of the Bayne case."

"Official close?"

"If it ain't murder, there's no case, is there? I'm callin' the press, soon as Brandy comes back from her stay at the spa."

Spa. Sounded nice, and expensive. I wondered if that was part of his fee package.

He waited for me to say something, but I couldn't bring myself to congratulate him. Eventually, he filled the silence. "Anyway, just wanted to thank you for your help with, you know, the evidence and everything. If I can return the favor, just say the word."

The roof of my skull threatened to explode. I tamped the anger down and willed my voice to remain steady. "If I ever need a criminal defense lawyer, Mr. Kingsbury, it will likely be for murdering you. Despite your legendary reputation, I doubt you'd be much help beyond the grave."

"That's a little harsh, don'cha think? I was hopin' we could wind things up in a friendly fashion."

"Good luck with that." My thumb stretched to disconnect the call, but he kept talking.

"Really, if I caused you any consternation, I'd like to make amends."

"Meaning what?"

"Well, I'm a pretty good friend to have, if you ever need one."

"Goodbye, Mr. Kingsbury." I disconnected.

CHAPTER THIRTY

Garlic

Carter looked up from his desk as I entered the downstairs library. "You disappeared in a hurry." He must have read my scowl. "Something wrong?"

I didn't want to bring up Kingsbury's name. No sense ruining both our moods. I moved to reason number two. "I thought I had ants in my pants, so I rushed upstairs to check."

He frowned. "Ants, again?"

"Nope, no ants. Just something in my pocket that was poking me."

"That's a relief." He rose, came around the desk and kissed me. "I need to make some phone calls upstairs. Can you occupy yourself for a little while?"

"Whatever."

He peered into my eyes. "Are you sure everything's okay? You seem a little tense."

"Have you heard anything about the Bayne case being officially closed?"

"No. Why?"

No point repeating what was probably another Kingsbury gambit. If what the weasel had said was true, Carter would confirm the bad news soon enough. It was probably the reason for his pending disappearance.

I put on a happy face. "I think I heard Dottie puttering in the kitchen. I'll poke my head in to say hi."

Dottie was at the sink washing bowls and spatulas. Ralph's children, Courtney and Kerry, sat at the table eating their after-school snacks.

"Hi Samantha!" Kerry, the towhead, freckled nine-year-old, displayed a mouthful of half-chewed red apple as he greeted me.

"Gross!" Courtney whipped her dark French braid backward and made a face. "It's not polite to talk with your mouth full, dodo." She was older by a few years, too grown-up and girly to tolerate her brother's uncivilized behavior. She nibbled daintily on a slice of pear.

Kerry stuck out his tongue, which was coated in masticated apple. "A dodo is an extinct bird. Dead, and a bird, so I can't be a dodo, bat-face."

Dottie lifted a tray of cookies from the oven. "That's enough, you two."

"She doesn't even know what a dodo is, Gramma." His eyes lit up at the sight of the cookies. "Are those for us?"

His grandmother set the tray on the counter and scowled at him. "They are only for people who mind their manners."

Kerry shut his mouth, chewed quietly and swallowed. "Guess what, Samantha! I made a 'A' on my science test. It was on plants. My Dad says I could be a bot-tant-tist someday."

I poured a glass of Dottie's sun tea and joined the kids at the table. "A botanist? That sounds like fun. Let's see how good you are."

I took the sweetgum leaf from my shirt pocket and smoothed it open against the tabletop. "Know what kind of tree this came from?"

He set his apple down, lifted the leaf and smelled it. A triumphant smile spread over his face. "Sweetgum."

Courtney sniffed the leaf. "Gram taught us about it."

Dottie transferred cookies onto a plate. "We had

those trees back where I grew up. My grandmother used to chew the twigs. Said it was good for her constitution. When we moved here, I was glad to see something familiar. I have an old recipe to make medicine from the burrs. Good for the flu, they say, but I haven't tried it."

She brought the cookie plate to the table. Peanut butter and cinnamon-raisin aromas wafted over us. "Two only, then homework."

Kerry grabbed one of each. Courtney scooted her chair away from the table. "May I be excused, please? Cookies are for babies."

Dottie nodded and watched her granddaughter exit the kitchen. "Growin' up too fast, that one."

"Can I have her cookies, Gramma?" Kerry reached for the platter.

Dottie lifted the plate out of his reach. "One more now, or two after supper. You choose." She sat beside him and put the cookies in front of him again.

Kerry was weighing his options when Carter walked in. Dottie rose from the table. "Want some lunch?"

"Thanks, but I think we'll just have an early dinner today." He popped a pear slice into his mouth.

I was hungry, but first I wanted to know what he'd been doing upstairs.

Dottie frowned. "My quilting group is tonight. I wasn't planning to cook."

"No problem. It's Samantha's turn to cook, anyway." He shot me a wicked glance.

My face heated. "I . . . I . . ." The longer I stammered, the bigger his grin grew. "I don't really cook much."

"I can cook," Kerry boasted. "Gramma taught me how. I can make macaroni out of the box."

I'd mastered that art in college, but real cooking had always eluded me. "There's so much good food in

Houston, it's easy to pick up whatever you want."

Carter's grin had a mischievous kink in it. "Let's see what we can come up with." He rummaged through the refrigerator, then moved to the pantry. "Yup. We've got all the fixings for spaghetti and meat sauce. How 'bout a cooking lesson?"

"Pasgetti!" Kerry clapped his hands together. "Can I have some, too?"

"There'll be enough for everybody." Carter turned to me, a challenge in his eyes. "That okay with you?"

There were plenty of reasons why it wasn't a good idea. After college, I'd tried to teach myself to cook and failed miserably. When I confessed my kitchen disasters to Gertie, she'd suggested that the set of Julia Child cookbooks I'd bought were too advanced for a beginner. Spaghetti sounded easier. "Sure. Why not?"

Kerry finished his apple and sped out of the kitchen clutching his third cookie. Carter and I helped Dottie clean up before she excused herself. Once we were alone, I stole the last slice of pie from the pan and refilled my tea.

Carter plucked two large onions from the wire basket on the counter and held them in front of me. "Ready for your lesson?"

"Kinda early for dinner, don't you think?"

He ignored me and set the onions on a chopping board, then drew a knife from the butcher's block. "First secret of successful meat sauce is to take your time. Slow and steady. Treat every ingredient with respect."

He reached into a bowl of homegrown tomatoes on the counter. As he plucked them one by one from the bowl, he gave each a gentle squeeze, playing his fingers over the plump circumference and measuring its heft in his palm. "You have to wait until everything's ripe."

He diced the tomatoes, guiding their liquid into the

shallow well of the cutting board. "See, the juice flows better if they're primed and ready. Then you add the other ingredients together and let them simmer gently, as slow and as long as you can stand it until their essence blossoms and you feel like you'll explode if you don't dig in and drown your angel hair in it."

I felt my cheeks flush. "You make cooking sound sexy."

"Takes time and technique, that's all I'm saying."

He grinned as he nudged the tomatoes off the cutting board and into a glass bowl. He poured their juice on top and set them aside. "Why don't you cut some fresh basil and oregano from the herb garden while I chop the rest of this?"

He grabbed a garlic bulb from a clay pot near the sink and began to separate the cloves, fingering each one with a gentle rub until the naked kernel popped out from its papery skin.

Back when I was struggling with the Julia Child cookbooks, I'd browsed the fresh herb section of the supermarket a few times. I knew what rosemary looked like, with its woody stem and spiky leaves, but identifying fresh basil and oregano would be a challenge. Still, I didn't want to show my ignorance of all things culinary. I finished the last bite of pie, found the shears, headed out the door and hoped for the best.

The herb garden was just to the side of the back steps. Mercifully, all the plantings were labeled. There were two kinds of basil, one with green leaves and one with purple. I clipped a few stems from each, found the oregano and clipped it, too. The fresh-cut mix smelled clean and delicious.

When I returned to the kitchen, Carter had just finished chopping the garlic.

"That's a lot of garlic."

He scraped the minced garlic into a small bowl. "It's not the amount of garlic that matters. It's when you add it in. Too soon and you overcook it, and it turns bitter. You have to respect all the subtleties of flavor, aroma, moisture, texture." He looked up from the cutting board. "Come to think of it, it *is* a lot like sex."

"Stop, please. Stop now, or we'll never make it to the cooking part."

He laughed. "By the way, I spoke to Washington when I was upstairs. He said he's being pressured to suspend the case."

"I know."

He paused the knife in mid-air. "Who told you?"

I laid the herbs in the sink and turned on the tap to rinse them. "Rufus Kingsbury called when I was upstairs. Told me he was setting up a press conference. He said the case was closed."

He frowned. "Not closed, according to Washington. That so-called attorney is full of it." He started on the onions, assaulting them with a savagery that rattled the cutting board.

I shook excess water off the herbs and pictured Kingsbury in front of the cameras, gloating and claiming victory. "There must be something they've missed, some clue that would keep the investigation going."

"They have plenty of clues already, but they've led nowhere." Carter ceased his onion butchery and raised a finger. "The balcony prowler." Another finger went up. "The unidentified fingerprint on one of the envelopes." A third finger rose. "That partial shoeprint in Irwin's blood at the door to the bedroom. All still unresolved. And we could throw in your balcony prowler, if we could find a connection to the case."

"And the autopsy?"

"Washington said they might be able to refute the report offered by the defense. It's probably their last hope for ruling it a homicide. If that happens, the investigation will continue."

"So, Kingsbury's press conference is a big show of bravado. It's not a done deal."

Carter scraped the diced onions into a big sauté pan. "The good news is, if he convinces everyone that the case is closed, your TV job could open up again. And soon. Decided what you want to do about it?"

I shook my head. A few weeks ago I'd had no future. To have the choice of a television career, if the chance came around again, versus working with Carter on his life-affirming project was a lot to wrap my head around.

Thinking about the TV job jogged something lose from my subconscious. In a burst of inspiration, I suddenly knew how to get back at Kingsbury.

I dropped the herbs on the counter where Carter was sautéing the onions. "Gotta go upstairs." I kissed his cheek and rushed out.

CHAPTER THIRTY-ONE

Wrazzmatazz

Carter poked his head into the bedroom just as I had disconnected my phone call. He leaned on the doorframe and crossed his arms.

"Good job of ducking out on your first cooking lesson, Ms. Newman."

I hadn't realized how long I'd been gone. "Sorry."

He eyed the phone. "Long conversation?"

Hmm. If I let him in on my scheme to rattle Kingsbury's cage, he'd only try to talk me out of it. I couldn't let that happen.

"I wanted to update Gertie about Brandy's case."

"Isn't she on a cruise in Europe?"

"Mmm, yeah."

"So you called her at . . ." he looked at his watch, " . . . midnight, her time?"

My face heated. "I . . . I thought she'd want to know."

He crossed the threshold towards me and put his hands on my waist. The crinkles at the corners of his eyes told me he knew I was hiding something.

"So, how is she?"

"Gertie?" I stared at the blank face of my phone. "I didn't connect. Voicemail."

His smile deepened. "You must have left a really long message."

I cobbled shards of truth into a reasonable excuse. "I also called Jay Patel at KHTS."

"You did? How'd it go?"

"I told him about Kingsbury's press conference.

Thought he'd appreciate the heads-up."

"And?"

"He was happy to hear from me."

Carter waited for more.

I produced another nugget. "We talked about the case."

"Did you ask about your job?"

"Patel mentioned it."

"And?"

Carter was getting dangerously close to my motive for the call. I needed to change the subject fast.

"I think everything would be easier if we knew who was prowling the balcony, and why."

"We'll figure it out soon. I promise. Then you can do whatever makes you happy."

He lifted my chin and kissed me. "By the way, your timing is perfect. The sauce is made. I left it on low simmer downstairs. Long and slow, until the essences melt together."

"Sorry I ran out on the chef."

"The chef forgives you. He is very impressed with your appreciation of his sexy technique." He kissed me again, his lips lingering on my neck. His breath tickled my ear. "You know, we have a little time to do some simmering ourselves."

"Pssst, Sam, it's suppertime."

I opened my eyes. Carter bent down and kissed my forehead. The bed was still warm from the heat of our bodies. Early evening sun streamed in through the bedroom windows, bathing his torso in radiant gold.

He pulled on a shirt and leaned in to kiss me again. "Time to boil the pasta. Meet me in the kitchen."

"Okay." As I raised up, a ray of sun glinted off the

little object that I'd been meaning to give him. "Carter?"

He stopped in the doorway and pivoted.

I picked the piece up and held it out to him. "This was under the bed at the condo. I saved it for you." I dropped it in his hand.

He looked at it, then at me. "What is it?"

"A charm, or a zipper pull, I think. Is it yours?"

He shrugged. "Nope."

"I found it in the condo a few days ago and saved it, in case you'd lost it."

He studied it again. "Don't think so."

"Okay. Just checking before I tossed it."

I plucked it from his hand and aimed for the wastebasket by the nightstand, then stopped in mid-toss.

The same thought seemed to hit both of us at the same time.

"Wait!" He held out his hand. "Let me see it again."

I dropped it onto his palm again. He played his thumb across it, flipping it over and back. "Looks kind of like an astrological sign. Virgo, I think."

My heartbeat zoomed. "Could it be from the prowler?"

"Don't know." His brow knit. "Ralph's probably still up in the office. I'll get him to start an object search before dinner." He kissed me on the forehead again. "See you downstairs."

Carter was tossing a salad when I entered the kitchen. Pasta boiled in a big pot next to the huge pan of sauce. Kerry and Courtney were already in their chairs at the table.

I waved to the kids and caught Carter's eye. "Smells good. Can I help?"

Carter laughed. "You managed to stay away just long

enough." He pushed past me with the big wooden salad bowl and set it on the table. "Sit and partake."

Kerry tucked a corner of his napkin into his T-shirt. "Sit by me, Samantha!"

Courtney rolled her eyes. "He's in love with you, in case you couldn't tell."

Kerry covered his face with his napkin.

I sat next to him. "What a nice compliment, Kerry. I like you, too. I'm glad we're friends."

He lowered the napkin. His face was red as a ripe tomato.

Carter brought a basket of ciabatta to the table and joined us. "Dig in, everybody."

Kerry grabbed the salad bowl and shoveled a pile of greens onto his plate. Courtney crossed her arms. "I'm waiting for Dad."

Carter dropped salad onto my plate and then served himself. "He'll be here soon. He's doing a little search right now."

"On that unidentified object?" I ground pepper over my salad.

Carter's brows knit. His eyes traveled from me to the children. "Let's save that for later."

Kerry looked up from his salad. "You don't have to talk like we're little kids. We can tell when you and my Dad are trying to solve a mystery."

Carter and I exchanged a look.

Kerry's eyes lit up. "Ple-e-ease let me help. My teacher says I'm a good problem solver." He bounced up and down in his chair. "*Ple-e-ease?*"

Carter stifled a smile and set his fork down. "Okay, Kerry. Let's say a person had sneaked into somewhere he didn't belong, and he left something behind. It could be a clue to his identity, but you don't exactly know what it is."

The boy's eyes widened. "Cool! What's it look like?"

Carter studied him for a second. "I'll draw you a picture." He got a paper and pencil from a nearby drawer, sat on the other side of Kerry and started sketching.

The boy watched intently, then scrunched up his face and pivoted the paper until the image was upside down. "If it goes like this, it's from a Wrazzer."

Carter and I reacted in unison. "Wrazzer?"

"Wrazzers are from the planet Khyton. They live in Ziggurat Citadel, and they're awesome. They're defending their city from the Dokuks. Those guys are like, total bullies." He looked at us as if that explained everything.

Carter seemed to get it. "Is that a video game?"

"Yeah, Khyton Tetrallax. My Dad won't buy it for me. He says I'm too young, but sometimes I play it over at my friend Kyle's."

Carter smiled. "Interesting. This is a logo from the game?"

"It's like, on all the Khyton shields, and their flag and stuff."

"So this might have come from a gamer?"

Kerry nodded. "Yeah, like, from gamer gear. There's T-shirts and other stuff for Wrazzers and Dokuks. I even saw a guy with a tattoo like this when we were at the mall."

Carter and I locked eyes. He took his cell phone from his jeans and spoke into it.

"Ralph, dinner's ready. Stop what you're working on, and bring the object with you."

A grin spread over Kerry's face. He sprang from the table. "Did I guess it? Did I?"

Carter put a hand on his shoulder. "We'll see when

your Dad gets here."

The boy jumped up and down behind his chair. "I did it! I solved it. Do I get a reward?"

"Let's wait and see if you're right."

"I'm rich!" Kerry exclaimed. "I'm gonna win a million dollars!" He took off from the table and tore around the kitchen, shouting, "I'm rich! I'm rich!"

When he saw Ralph in the doorway, he flew to him. "Let's see it, Dad. Lemme see the Wrazzer."

Ralph was almost knocked over by his son's exuberance. "Whoa, boy. The what?"

Carter held his hand out. "The piece you were trying to match online. I think your kid may know what it is."

Ralph handed the thing to Carter, who set it on top of the paper with the drawing. We all peered in.

Kerry shot his fist in the air. "Yes! A Wrazzer, like I said. Can I get my reward now?"

Carter scratched his ear. "I'll be darned."

"What's a Wrazzer?" Ralph asked.

The boy blew out a frustrated sigh. "Do I have to explain it all over again?"

Carter took up the question. "It's a video game logo. Probably came off a gamer's gear."

Gamers. A tickle of recognition began to creep from my brain to the hairs on the nape of my neck. I grabbed Carter's arm.

He turned to me. "Sam? You look a little pale."

My thoughts jumbled in a clash of possibilities. In each scenario, the phantom on the balcony had a different face, and each led to a different and unpleasant conclusion. I heard myself thinking out loud. "Maybe it's nothing."

Everyone gaped at me like they expected me to say more, but I couldn't. Which face zooming through my head was the one?

Or, I could be off the mark entirely. I shook my head, stood and made for the back door. "I need some air."

Adrenaline propelled me around to the western veranda. I stared through the branches toward the pink and orange glow of dying sunlight, searching for an answer.

Carter found me. He put his hand on my shoulder. "Are you all right?"

"No, I'm not."

He wrapped me in his arms. Normally, that would be enough to calm me down, but my brain kept scrolling through probabilities like an endless wheel of sevens and cherries and diamonds on a slot machine. Which face would be there when it stopped?

I pulled away and leaned on the railing. My thoughts became words.

"I think I know who the balcony prowler is."

CHAPTER THIRTY-TWO

Parkay, Anyone?

"Why won't you tell me, Sam?"

Carter had followed me up to the bedroom where I was packing to return to Houston. "Yesterday you were afraid of a murderous balcony stalker, and now you have to get back to the condo tonight?"

I dropped clothes into my travel bag. "I'm not afraid anymore. Not for myself, anyway."

"Then why not tell me who you think it is?"

"If I give you a name, you'll grab your superhero cape and spring into action. I need time to think it over."

Steam could have spouted from the top of his head. "Before I take you back, I have to know what we're walking into."

I pressed my hand to his chest. His heart thumped hard against my palm. "I know you want to protect me, but I'm pretty sure I'm not in danger anymore. Probably never was."

He put his hands on his hips. "You've got to give me more to make it okay to leave."

Unless I wanted to thumb a ride to the city, I had to offer something. "All right, here's what I'm thinking. I'm not exactly certain who the prowler is, but I think we can narrow it down."

His frown softened. "To . . .?"

I sat on the bed. "The Irwin Bayne case is not over, right?"

"Not yet."

"What if the phantom is not the killer, but he did

witness Irwin's death?"

Carter's eyebrows inched toward his forehead. "And?"

"I'm thinking that the same person who was out there when I nearly went over the railing, and who pulled me back from certain death, is someone who cares, not someone who kills."

"Where are you going with this?"

"I'm saying that the prowler may be, at worst, a Peeping Tom, like you said. If we can figure out why he was on the balcony, we could get closer to knowing who it was, and eliminate a murder suspect. Or convict one."

I let the idea sink in before I offered a compromise. "Can we talk it over on our way to the city."

"You'll tell me everything?"

"If you promise not to go off like a rocket. Deal?"

"I'll be ready in ten minutes. Unless you want to finish dinner first."

Returning to the pasta was tempting, but I couldn't imagine calmly sitting and sharing dinner with Ralph and the kids while my mind raced off in another direction. "Doggie bag?"

Half an hour later, we were on the road to Houston. Twilight tempered the glare of the cars around us. The highway grew more and more congested as we approached the city.

Carter listened as I ran through all the possibilities. "So, you're ruling out the paperboy? What made you think of him in the first place?"

I put my sunglasses away. "His age, I guess, and his clothes. I don't know if he's a gamer, but he looked like he could be. He was in the hallway when I arrived that morning. That, and the fact that the note in the yellow envelope was written on a scrap of newsprint."

Carter took his eyes from the road to glance at me. "Are you sure he's not the one?"

I shook my head. "He seemed too calm that morning to have just killed someone, or witnessed someone die. Besides, I can't think of anything to connect him to me, or to Irwin or Brandy, other than delivering the paper. It doesn't feel like he's it."

Carter glanced at me again. "Intuition can be a strong indicator of reality, or it can be total horseshit."

I poked him in the shoulder. "Are you saying my judgment is poop?"

"I was making a general statement." He smiled. "Who's next?"

A rush of heat coursed through me as I searched for what to say about Harland, the valet. I'd promised not to tattle about his hallway encounter with naked Brandy. He'd broken a major security rule by sneaking off with a key, but he'd done it out of compassion for her. His modesty and the way he'd talked about his family seemed genuine when he confessed the incident to me. I couldn't bring myself to say his name.

"Is it warm in here?" I punched the temperature down a notch.

"Who's next on the list?"

I fanned myself with my hand. "I'm still hot."

He glared at me sideways. "You promised. Give it up or I'm turning around."

I lowered the control another couple of degrees and exhaled. "One of the valets."

"Valets." His eyes narrowed slightly as he pondered the idea. "That's a strong possibility. Those balconies can be breached only by someone with crazy physical strength and special training. It would be unusual for a civilian to manage it, but a few of the young ones look fit enough."

I remembered Harland's behavior the morning of Irwin's death: his rush from the elevator, his muscular arm holding the doors apart for me. Had he suckered me into believing him? I couldn't eliminate him from the conversation, but I wanted to keep my promise, at least for now.

"Sam?" Carter waved a hand in front of my face. "The valets? Do you have one in mind?"

"Remember Pansy Gump, the woman who thought you and Brandy were lovers?"

Carter winced.

"Well, she told me the same story about Brandy and one of the valets."

He laughed. "I hesitate to ask, but for the sake of being thorough, which valet was it?"

"By her description, it must have been Harland. Pansy said she saw him helping Brandy with one of the exercise machines, and according to her, the two of them seemed a little too intimate."

"Sounds like the woman has a recurring fantasy."

"You wanted me to tell you everything, so there it is. Harland was also the valet on the shift when Irwin died. When I arrived at the condo that morning, he was in a hurry to get out of the elevator. And he looks really strong."

Carter seemed to be weighing the possibility. His silence came as a welcome relief. I stared out at the darkening landscape. A mile or so later, he emerged from his ruminations. "Could be something there, the idea of a valet. Any valet, really."

I raised a point I'd been struggling with. "But why would a valet be prowling on the balcony, when any one of them could enter an apartment with a key?"

He glanced at me. "Good question. Still, I think I'll

have a chat with the security manager about the staff. There's a chance that something significant wasn't caught in a normal background check."

"Discreetly, please. No names yet. You promised."

After another couple of miles, Carter turned to me. "So, is that it? All your suspects?"

I shivered and hiked the thermostat up. A sign on the highway signaled that we were approaching the exit for Love's. "I'm freezing. Let's stop for coffee."

Back inside the car again, I turned the thermostat up another couple of degrees and cupped the styrene mug between my hands. Hardly any warmth penetrated through. I took a sip from the steaming vent in the lid.

Carter eased the Tesla onto the highway. "So, anyone else on your list?"

I raised the coffee to my lips again. The cup shook. I clung tight, lowered it to my lap and stared at the lid.

He repeated his question. "Anyone else?"

I struggled to quiet my thoughts. Something like a sob escaped.

Carter touched my wrist. "Sam?"

His face blurred through my tears. "Promise to keep this between us, until we know for sure?"

"Know what?"

"You have to promise."

He shrugged. "I don't know what I'm promising, but, okay, I promise."

"That you'll keep this between us."

"Yes. Okay. Now, where are you going with this?"

I wiped my eyes. "There's someone else Pansy mentioned who could be—"

"That woman again?" Carter's fingers gripped the steering wheel tight enough to make his knuckles blanch. "You're getting worked up over another loony theory?"

"Believe me, she's the last person I'd take seriously, but she mentioned something that made me wonder."

"About what? Who?"

I took a deep breath. "You know my little friend, Lizzie?"

Carter shook his head. "She's way too young."

"I know, but—" My mouth went dry. "Her older brother . . ."

"What about him?"

"He's extremely shy, and a little strange."

"And that's why he's on your list?"

"Pansy said she'd seen him with Brandy, more than once. She thinks he's sweet on her."

"He's the one into Krav Maga?"

"Yes, and one other thing Lizzie mentioned. It sounded like Parkay or Parker, some kind of game. When the piece I'd found turned out to be a gamer thing, her brother came to mind."

Carter's eyes widened. "What did you say the last one was, the one you thought was a game?"

"Parker."

He took his foot off the gas and steered toward the shoulder. When the Tesla rolled to a stop, he turned to me. "Could she have meant *parkour*?"

CHAPTER THIRTY-THREE

Daisies

In the remaining miles to the city, Carter tried to explain parkour to me, but I could only picture people running and jumping around like maniacs. Once we were back at the condo, while he warmed the pasta sauce and boiled fresh linguini on the stove, I sat at the counter and watched a few web clips on his tablet.

In one video, young men vaulted over barriers, jumped from rooftop to rooftop, and scaled high walls in one fluid motion. They bounced, flipped and rolled as they navigated city landscapes. Without tools or ropes, one ran up the vertical side of a building, flipped backward and landed on the ground, then sprang up off a trash dumpster and pulled himself through an open window on the second floor. An instant later, he reappeared in the window, leaned out, twisted, dropped and hung from the sill, pushed off with his feet, somersaulted to the ground, ran to a nearby tree and swung up through its high branches before landing again and running out of the camera frame.

"Wow."

Carter smiled. "That's what I meant by special skills."

"Can you do this stuff?"

"Could, back when I did more physical work. Parkour began as a military training regimen before it became a free-styling urban sport. Even though it looks like fun, you have to practice every day, or it can be dangerous."

I set the tablet aside and wondered about the

prowler on the balcony. Most of the videos showed daredevils working from one or two stories up. I couldn't imagine someone trying those stunts from ten floors higher. My vertigo kicked in.

Carter must have read my face. "A regular Peeping Tom prefers a target with easy access. They're cowards, not risk-takers. I don't think anyone, even your little friend's brother, would be doing it to peep." He waggled a bottle of Paolo cabernet at me. "Want some?"

I began a search for the corkscrew. "So, either we're not looking for a Peeping Tom, or there's someone with a different motive, and possibly a strong death wish, who's climbing around out there."

"Basically, yes. Or, back to your idea about the valets, it still could be someone with access through the front door who sneaks onto the balcony without being seen. And who might be Irwin Bayne's killer."

I opened the bottle, the parkour videos replaying in my head. Carter drained the pasta, divided it into two bowls and spooned sauce over the top. "Why don't we suspend this discussion for now? There's not much to be done anyway, until the security manager gets here in the morning. Let's enjoy dinner and relax."

"That may be impossible."

"You're the one who wanted to be here, remember?" He grated a knob of Parmesan over our bowls, sat across from me and lifted his glass. "Buon appetito."

I took a deep gulp of wine and held the half empty goblet out to him. "More please."

He made a face. "Seriously?"

"I'm trying to relax."

"Dig into the pasta first. My sauce is guaranteed to transform your senses."

I started to protest, but Carter was firm. "Pasta first. Then more wine."

I plunged my fork into the bowl, swirled the narrow strands around the tines and tasted Heaven. "Who taught you to cook like this?"

He grinned. "I never reveal the source of my sauce."

Once we'd put away the leftovers and cleaned up the kitchen, Carter wanted to go down to the terrace. On the way out, he grabbed a couple of brandy glasses and picked a bottle from the serving cart in the music room.

From below, The Wellbourne loomed against the dark sky, framed by a smattering of stars that twinkled beyond its roof lights. The evening was mild, sweetened by a sea breeze from the Gulf of Mexico, forty miles away. A faint hint of chlorine wafted across the swimming pool and mixed with the salty air.

Although he had chosen a table with a view of the downtown skyline, Carter sat facing the building. I swiveled and followed his gaze as his eyes traced up the façade and across the balconies.

I didn't have to ask what he was thinking. "I saw him—the prowler—didn't I? The afternoon of the pool party, he was the one sitting on the railing."

"In all likelihood, yes."

We were quiet together for a long time, serenaded by the whirr of the city. I must have dozed a little. My eyes were shut when Carter's voice came to me.

"Ready to go upstairs?" He extended his hand to help me up.

Just before we left the terrace, I raised my eyes to the balconies once more. Some of them had gone dark. Others glowed in varying intensities, hinting of activity within: a vertical neighborhood, where residents went about their lives in private. And where a prowler lurked.

We waited for the elevator for what seemed like an

hour. When the doors finally opened, the Gumps were aboard. Carter shot a glance at me before we entered.

Pansy sniffed. "Hubert and I have just returned from the opera." She shook her head, which sent strands of pearls rolling side to side across her ample breasts. "I simply abhor these modern interpretations. Carmen, the poor woman, was practically naked onstage. I have a mind to cancel our season subscription."

Carter squeezed my hand, hard. I knew if I met his eyes, I'd start giggling. I gave him a subtle kick to the ankle, looked straight ahead and held my breath. I'd almost made it to our floor without cracking up, but just as the doors opened, I ran out of air and a huge giggle escaped. As the doors closed on the Gumps, I heard Pansy mutter, "Gesundheit."

The aroma of breakfast beckoned. I pulled on a tee and gym shorts and followed the scent to the kitchen.

Carter was already dressed for the day. He poured coffee into my mug. "I was about to leave you a note. The security manager gets in about now. I want to catch him, first thing."

I swiped a piece of toast from his plate. "Remember your promise."

He held up three fingers in a Boy Scout pledge. "I will not name names until we are absolutely certain." He gave me a peck on the cheek and headed out.

I stayed in the kitchen and finished his toast with my coffee. As anxious as I was about what his meeting with the security manager might reveal, I had my own agenda. I refilled my mug, retrieved my phone from its charger and called the TV station.

After I'd phoned him from the ranch, Jay Patel wanted to see me as soon as I returned to the city. I'd asked a favor of him, and he'd requested a commitment from me in return, details I hadn't yet shared with Carter.

Patel wasn't in. I left a message, grabbed my mug and headed toward the bedroom to get dressed. Halfway there, the doorbell rang.

I expected to see Carter's face when I opened the door. Instead, Lizzie stood there, hands deep inside the pockets of freshly ironed pink shorts. Her matching pink flowered shirt was neatly tucked in, and her normally tangled hair was combed and held back from her face with a barrette of plastic daisies.

She pulled something from her pocket and offered it to me.

I backed away and stared.

In her hand was a neon yellow envelope.

CHAPTER THIRTY-FOUR

The Yellow

You can't uncrack an egg.

My mind was blank, except for that old epigram blinking on and off behind my eyes like a lotto sign. I couldn't tear my eyes off the envelope.

She lifted it nearer. "It's for you. See, I wrote your name on it."

Printed in red ballpoint on the front was a very wobbly *Samantha*. I cleared my throat. "Lizzie, I . . . uh, why don't you come in?"

She shrugged. "Okay, but I'm kinda in a hurry." She walked straight to the kitchen, set the envelope on the breakfast island and hiked herself onto a stool. "My Dad's taking us to the zoo."

"Your father?"

"Yeah. He's home."

I reconsidered the envelope. The red scrawl looked similar to the writing in the first note, but I couldn't be sure it was the same. Half of me wanted to tear it open. The other half wanted to tear it up.

Lizzie swiveled on the stool. "You look funny. Are you sick?"

"Sick? No, I . . ." I turned my back and put my mug in the microwave. "I just woke up."

While the coffee reheated, I drummed my fingers on the counter and mentally counted down the seconds until the timer beeped. I grabbed the mug and faced her again with a happy face.

"So, Lizzie. Your father! You must be really happy to

see him. Was he gone long?"

She lowered her eyes to the envelope. "You gonna open it? It's from him."

"From your father?"

"Yeah. When he came home, he wanted to know what's been going on, and I told him about how you gave me ice cream for Mom. I told him you were a real nice person." She offered a shy smile.

With her sudden good grooming, she barely resembled the disheveled child who had sat there days before. Perhaps her father's presence had something to do with it.

I took a slug of coffee and reached for the envelope. Before I could touch it, my phone came to life from the pocket of my shorts. I dug it out. Without bothering to look at the screen, I toggled it to vibrate, slipped it back into my pocket and picked up the envelope.

A second thought popped in. If it was Jay Patel, calling to set up a meeting, I didn't want to miss him. My pocket was still vibrating. One more time, and I'd lose the connection.

Lizzie seemed happily occupied with swiveling, so I retrieved the phone. But it wasn't Patel who lit the screen. It was Gertie.

With everything else happening, I'd lost track of where in the world she was and when she'd be home. I couldn't blow her off, despite the bad timing. I shot a glance at Lizzie and set the envelope down.

Gertie's voice leapt through the phone. "Samantha! You won't believe what just happened!"

"Hey, where are you?"

"In New York."

"I'll call you right ba—"

"I have some news!"

Lizzie jumped off the stool and waved goodbye. I pulled the phone from my cheek. "No, Lizzie, don't go!"

At the kitchen door, she stopped. "My Dad said not to be too long if I want to go to the zoo. Bye." She waved again and walked out.

I scurried out the door behind her. "Lizzie, wait!"

Gertie's faint voice squawked up at me. "Samantha?"

I raised the phone to my mouth. "Just a sec, Gertie."

It took less than an instant to say that, but it was long enough for Lizzie to gain distance. As I rounded the hallway corner, she disappeared into the elevator. The doors shut her inside.

More squawks emanated from the phone. "Samantha, are you there?"

I raised it to my cheek. "I'm here."

"Everything okay?"

I exhaled and retraced my steps to the apartment. "Long story. What's going on with you?"

"Well, as I was saying, you won't believe—"

"Aaack!"

I jiggled the front doorknob, twisting it right, left and back again before it became clear that, in my haste to catch up to Lizzie, I'd locked myself out. Again.

Gertie's tone deflated. "Should I call back later?"

I leaned on the door and shut my eyes. The yellow envelope was on the kitchen counter, unopened.

If I hung up and called security, they'd send a valet to unlock the door for me. On the other hand, Carter had a key, and he would likely return soon from downstairs.

Gertie was dying to tell me something. I couldn't bring myself to disappoint her. I took a deep breath and sagged to the floor. "Plenty of time now. What's up?"

"Louis proposed!"

My eyes flew open. "What?"

"He proposed! Can you believe it? I'm going to be

Mrs. Louis Kleschevsky!"

No, I couldn't, actually. They had met only weeks ago, officially anyway. Gertie's story about their first encounter at the hospital a few months back didn't amount to much, in my opinion. Still, I wanted to be supportive. "You sound very happy."

"I am."

"So, tell me about it."

"On the flight back to the States, we were set to change planes in New York, and I confessed to Louis that I'd never been to the Big Apple. He immediately summoned the flight attendant and asked her to change our tickets so we could stay here for a few days. He's originally from Brooklyn, did you know that?"

"No."

"Anyway, he's treating me to a whole New York City experience. We've seen three Broadway shows, two off-Broadway, and oh, the food, Samantha, the restaurants are amazing! We did four museums, too."

"Sounds like you're having a good time."

"I haven't even gotten to the good part. Louis is a Veteran, you know, and he loves this country. Yesterday, we visited The Statue of Liberty. We went all the way up to the crown! Imagine me and all those stairs!

"This morning we took a ferry to Ellis Island, where his grandparents arrived in America. We were standing in the middle of the Great Hall where the immigrants used to register, and he dropped to one knee. At first, I thought he'd collapsed. Then I saw the ring!"

I had to hand it to the guy. A whirlwind romance like that and even I might say yes. "He sounds like he knows how to woo a girl. That's some proposal."

The sight of Carter coming around the corner took

my attention away. He was studying at a sheet of paper as he walked.

I stood and mimed my locked-out predicament. "I'm talking to Gertie."

He rolled his eyes. "Really?"

"Yes, really. She's calling from New York."

I returned my attention to the phone as he unlocked the front door. "Listen, Gertie, you know that I wish you every happiness. I want to hear more about everything, but Carter just came in and I have to tell him something right away. Can I call you later?"

"Louis and I will be busy while we're here. Let's get together when we're back in Houston."

"See you soon." I disconnected and followed Carter inside.

He proceeded to the music room and sat on the leather sofa. "Everything okay with Gertie?"

"Louis proposed to her this morning. She's ecstatic."

He glanced up briefly, and then returned to the paper. "Good for them."

"I wish I knew more about him."

"He's a solid citizen."

I raised my hands to my hips. "You know this, how?"

Carter looked up at me and smiled. "Gertie's a good woman. And she works for me. He checks out fine."

He'd investigated Louis. Of course. I eyed the paper he was studying. "Who are you checking out now?"

"Employees of The Wellbourne. The manager didn't want to turn over their personnel files, but when I threatened to have the police investigate every one of them, he had a change of heart and gave me this list of names. As for your little friend's family, all he would tell me is that the Dad is in the military."

"Well, I have something better—or worse, maybe. Lizzie came by while you were gone and delivered a note to me from her father. In a yellow envelope."

Carter set the list aside and looked up. "What does it say?"

"I don't know. I was about to open it when Gertie called. Lizzie got up to leave and I tried to stop her. That's when I locked myself out. It's still in the kitchen."

"Let's see it."

I marched into the kitchen, but I only made it halfway to the breakfast island before my cell rang. The TV station ID lit the screen. "I have to take this."

I headed out of the kitchen and down the hall.

When I reentered the kitchen, Carter was on his phone, reading off the list of Wellbourne employee names. He disconnected. "Ralph will let me know if anything interesting comes up."

His eyes swept over my fresh clothes. "Going somewhere?"

"That was Jay Patel on the phone. He wants to see me at the station today."

"The job's on again?"

"It may be. I need to scoot over there."

Carter tapped the yellow envelope. "Let's open this before you go." He nudged it toward me. We stared at it as if it were a ticking time bomb.

CHAPTER THIRTY-FIVE

Two, Extra-Large

Carter nudged the envelope nearer. "I never saw the first one. Is it the same?"

My heart pounded like crazy. "Identical, except this has my name on it."

His hand touched mine. "I know you're worried. No matter what we may discover, we'll deal with it."

I pushed away from the breakfast island. As I paced the kitchen, Carter drew a paring knife from the rack and brandished it over the envelope. "Want me to do the honors?"

"I'll open it."

He handed the knife to me. I held my breath and carefully slit the flap. Inside was a matching yellow note card. Even though it was sturdy, it might as well have been a fragment of a Dead Sea Scroll. My hands shook as I gingerly extracted it and set it on the counter between us. The ink was black, in a precise and bold cursive.

Dear Samantha,

My daughter told me of your kindness to her and her mother while I was away. She speaks of you as someone she turns to when she gets sad. I'm afraid that happens all too often lately, and I'm happy she has found someone to help her through a difficult time. I look forward to meeting you to thank you in person. In the meantime, please know how grateful I am for your friendship with my lonely little girl.

Best personal regards,

LTC Thomas J. Mason

I tapped the LTC. "Lieutenant Colonel?"

Carter nodded.

"So, he is in the military." My mind wandered to Carter's description of parkour. My heart sank. "He couldn't be the balcony intruder, could he?"

"Another to add to the list."

I shook my head. "He sounds too nice."

Carter looked at his watch. "Don't you have to be somewhere?"

"Blast! I almost forgot." I paced the kitchen again. "I feel like I'm being ripped in two." I eyed the note. "What should I do about that?"

Carter took the note and slipped it into its envelope. "Go to your meeting. I'll hold onto it while you're gone."

I drove to KHTS wishing I could be in two places at once. Leaving Carter alone with the note from Lizzie's father was a dicey proposition. I could only imagine what he would do with it.

It was hard to accept this new addition to the suspect list. I didn't know much about Lizzie, but I knew enough to want to shield her from any more sadness.

The receptionist handed over my visitor's badge. "Mr. Patel is waiting for you in his office."

I slipped the badge over my navy blazer. Patel had seen me decked out a couple of times already, so I'd decided to dress casually, just a white long-sleeved tee and jacket over dark jeans.

As I entered the corridor to his office, the station's star news anchor Alicia Sultana emerged from hers. She wore jeans and a jacket too, though her blazer was blood red. She looked like she'd just stepped out of a fashion shoot for Ebony.

"Hello." She sounded almost friendly.

"Hi."

She stopped in front of me, leaned down and flashed her sizable teeth. "Jay tells me you're going to be working with us again. Congratulations."

"Well, it's a little premature . . ." Overwhelmed by her Shalimar awesomeness, I stepped sideways toward the wall.

Her smile disappeared as she pressed nearer. "A word of advice. Save your money. You're great looking now, but one day you'll be too old, even for Botox. And plastic surgery will kill your soul."

At first I thought she was trying to intimidate me, but with her face inches from mine, faint scar lines revealed a different picture. She was talking about herself.

From down the hall I heard a familiar voice. "Hey, Miss Thang. I got your hot rollers hot and your Chardonnay on ice." Jojo, the makeup guy, strolled up behind Alicia and peered at me over her shoulder. "Hello, you."

Alicia backed off and beamed her on-camera smile at me. "Good luck."

I watched as she and Jojo sashayed away. Her perfume clung to my jacket. I attempted to brush it off and continued toward Jay Patel's office.

Patel greeted me from behind his desk. "You're here! Come in. We have a lot of work to do." I took a chair across from him.

He pressed a button on his desk phone and spoke into it. "Sedgwick, come to my office, please." He hung up and turned his attention to me. "Since the press conference is tomorrow, I thought we'd start you there."

That caught me off-guard. After the last cycle of being hired-and-fired, I'd assumed there would be a little more wooing this time. Besides, I hadn't told

Carter yet.

Patel's face fell. "You did say you still wanted the job when we spoke on the phone."

I marshaled my wits. "Of course I do. I just didn't think I'd be starting so soon, although, I . . . I'm happy, and eager to begin. But don't we have a few things to settle first?"

"Your salary, benefits, the whole package is the same as before, so if—"

"No, I meant, how we'll be positioning me on air. The name of my segments, and all that."

Patel looked relieved. "We'll work that out. No problem."

I was about to respond when a slightly pudgy and balding man poked his head in. "You wanted to see me, boss?"

Patel waved him in. "Samantha, this is Lloyd Sedgwick, one of our reporters. He covers the police department and the courthouse."

I recognized Sedgwick as the one who had interviewed Kingsbury in the clip that doomed my last first day at work here. He smiled and shook my hand. "Great to meet you."

Sedgwick took the chair next to mine. Patel leaned on his elbows and spread his hands wide. "The press conference is set for tomorrow. There's not much time to prepare." He looked at me. "Tell Lloyd what you told me on the phone yesterday about Kingsbury."

As I recounted my idea to embarrass Kingsbury with his envelope flimflam, it sounded less solid than when I'd thought it up. On the other hand, Patel seemed to be a guy who liked pushing boundaries. After all, he had pursued me—a rank beginner in the news business—to shake things up.

Once I'd filled Sedgwick in, he was eager to play along. "I've heard rumors for years about how Kingsbury crosses the line, manipulating witnesses and evidence. I'd love to get his reaction to this new one on camera."

For better or worse, the plan was a go. My job looked like a go, too. After almost an hour of hashing out details, Patel and I shook hands.

I filled out new employee forms—again—and got a new parking space: number eighteen this time. Despite the balcony prowler and the unresolved Bayne case, for the first time in a long time, I was ready to celebrate.

It was almost dark by the time I left the station. My stomach growled. I called Carter as soon as I got to the car. He didn't pick up. My mind whipped through a million scenarios of what that meant.

The phone buzzed. "Sorry I couldn't catch your call," Carter said. "I'm with someone."

"Who?"

"It can wait until you get here."

I ran through the possibilities of who might be with Carter. I hoped it was Gertie, freshly returned from her adventures with Louis. Sharing my good news with her would be a bonus.

"It's almost eight. Should I pick up dinner on the way? I was thinking pizza. There's that new place—"

"Perfect. Make it two, extra-large."

Half an hour later, I pulled up to the entrance of The Wellbourne. Harland, the valet, met me at the car. He lifted the pizza boxes from the passenger seat. "I'll carry these for you, Ms. Newman."

I could have managed them myself, but he insisted, so we headed for the elevators together. Halfway there, Harland froze in his tracks. Two others were waiting to ride up: Brandy Bayne and Rufus Kingsbury.

I tapped Harland on the arm. "Let's wait for the next one." He looked relieved, but before we could escape, a familiar voice called out.

"Hello, darlin'!"

Harland and I were still half a lobby away when the elevator arrived. Brandy disappeared inside, but Kingsbury held the doors apart for us and waved for us to join them. "C'mon!"

Harland closed his eyes in what looked like silent prayer. I tugged at the pizza boxes. "I'll carry them. You don't have to come."

He held on. "It's my job, Ms. Newman. I'm okay, really."

Kingsbury grinned as we made our way toward him. "Y'all are a coupl'a slowpokes."

I steeled myself and stepped in. Harland followed. As we rode up, Brandy gave Harland a shy smile. He turned the color of rust and concentrated on the marble floor.

I ran my mind through several greetings before I settled on one. "Welcome back, Brandy."

"Thanks." Her eyes traveled to the floor, too.

I held my breath and studied the numbers above the door as we rode up. Kingsbury eyeballed me. "Long time no see. Whatcha been up to?"

His self-satisfied attitude pierced my resolve not to engage. "Actually, I'm working at a TV station now, and looking forward to your press conference tomorrow."

A slightly bewildered look crossed his face, but he quickly recovered. His eyes twinkled. "Yes, now that Brandy's all set, I'll be ready to take on new challenges."

My pulse surged. "That's good, because I have one for you."

"You do?"

"Yes. I know how you like to push the envelope."

The twinkling stopped. "What do you mean?" He eyed me suspiciously. "What kind of challenge?"

The doors opened on our floor. I thanked Harland, took the pizzas from him and escaped, scurrying down the hall ahead of Brandy and Kingsbury as fast as I could. At the door to the apartment, I struggled with the boxes while I maneuvered the key into the lock. Brandy and Kingsbury rounded the corner behind me.

"Need help?" Kingsbury reached for the pizzas. I tried to yank them away, but his tug pulled them from my grip. They landed on the carpet between us.

"Oops." Kingsbury toed one of the boxes that had sprung slightly open. "It's probably okay."

"Thanks a lot." I rang the doorbell and knelt to retrieve the pizzas, wondering if I'd have to scrape pepperoni from inside their cardboard tops. At least nothing had spilled out.

The front door opened. Carter barely acknowledged Brandy and Kingsbury. He caught my eyes as I popped up in front of him, pizzas in hand. I escaped inside.

He took the boxes from me. "We're in the living room."

I was happy to remove myself from Kingsbury's presence, but when I followed Carter inside, the person I saw made me wish that I could be anywhere else but there.

CHAPTER THIRTY-SIX

The Other Man

Detective Washington swiveled his head in our direction as Carter and I entered the living room. He stood from his chair and turned to face me. "Hello, Ms. Newman."

For a moment I doubted it was really him, because he was dressed casually in a green polo shirt and khakis. A nanosecond later, my eye caught sight of a familiar yellow envelope glowing neon on the coffee table. It was the one Lizzie had addressed to me, with the thank-you note from her father inside.

I wobbled to a stop. Speechless, I looked to Carter.

If he sensed my discomfort, he didn't show it. "I think we've solved the mystery of the balcony prowler. We were just discussing how to proceed from here."

He set the pizza boxes on the coffee table and pivoted toward the kitchen. "I'll be right back."

Alone with Washington, I panicked. "I'll go see if he needs help." I spun around and chased after Carter.

He was calmly gathering plates and forks and napkins. "I forgot to ask what the detective wants to drink. Could you grab a few sodas and beers?"

My pulse ticked up. "What the . . . what's going on?" I wasn't sure if I was actually yelling, or if the screaming was all in my head. I lowered my voice to a shaky rumble. "You could have clued me in when I called."

"I didn't know how to tell you without a long, involved conversation. We were at a critical point in our discussion. I figured you'd be home soon anyway."

I controlled the urge to throw a punch. "What happened to your promise?"

"I made one phone call, that's all. Not to Washington. I never intended to get him involved. But one thing led to another, and . . . I didn't mean to spring this on you. It's not as bad as you think. You'll see."

Before I could let another word fly, it occurred to me that I had arrived with news of my own to spring on him. I crossed my arms and took a deep breath.

Carter tried again. "Can we at least call a truce until you know the whole story?"

With Washington in the living room, things looked serious, but there was nothing to be done except to trust Carter. I unfolded my arms. "Truce. For now."

It took a moment to reset my anger meter before I reached into the fridge and pulled out the beers and sodas. I caught Carter's eye. "You're lucky you didn't have to peel me off the floor."

He turned in the doorway and grinned. "I'm getting to be pretty good at it."

I stifled a smile and followed him out of the kitchen. "Speaking of peeling things off the floor, there may be a problem with the pizzas."

When we returned to the living room, Washington was at the balcony door, looking out. He shook his head. "What a crazy fool. How on earth—why on earth— would anyone try such a stupid stunt?"

"I think we know the answer to that." Carter twisted the cap off a beer and handed it to him.

That Washington was drinking on the job seemed odd, until I recalled Carter's assurance that the detective's presence wasn't as bad as it looked. The beer, and his casual attire, seemed to indicate that this wasn't an official visit. Still, his presence was unsettling.

I sat in a side chair across the coffee table from him.

Carter took the one next to me and opened the first pizza box. Mercifully, only a few olives had popped off. The men each took a piece.

Hungry as I was, I couldn't focus on food, not with a million questions spooling in my head. I shut the pizza box. "Could someone please explain what's going on?"

Carter set down his slice and turned to me. "We know who's been on the balcony, and why. After you left, I called Tom Mason."

"Lizzie's father?"

"Yes. I didn't think a call to him would violate my promise to you, since he had reached out first. I told him a little about who I was and said that I was curious about his background. He turned out to be very appreciative of my interest, and he opened up about the family issues he's been dealing with. Actually, he seemed grateful to have someone to talk to.

"After that, with Mason's permission, I called Detective Washington and invited him over unofficially, as a courtesy."

I shot a glance toward Washington. "Why?"

Carter answered. "The balcony issue may have a bearing on the Bayne case. He needs to know."

Washington glanced at my hand. I'd been spinning my Mom's ring around my finger at a furious pace. I tucked my thumb under to hold it still.

My eyes shot daggers at Carter. "But you promised."

"Just hear us out, Sam."

Washington set his beer on the table. "We believe the person on the balcony didn't kill Irwin Bayne, but may have seen him die. And was probably the one who wrote the note saying that Mrs. Bayne didn't kill him. To get that kind of eye witness testimony could be critical to solving the case."

My theory, exactly. I unruffled my feathers. "So, who was it out there?"

The doorbell rang. Carter popped out of his chair. "Hold that thought. We have company."

Three people followed Carter into the living room. Lizzie entered first and waved when she saw me. Her brother slumped in, eyes downward. There was a fresh-looking cast on his arm. Directly behind him was a tall, broad-shouldered man. He was tan and fit, with a deeply creased face like outdoorsmen get from sun and weather. By his light brown buzz cut and straight arrow military posture, I assumed he was their father.

Carter introduced him. "Samantha, meet Lieutenant Colonel Thomas J. Mason."

"Call me Tom, please." He crossed the room and held out his hand. I shook it automatically, but words escaped me. He smiled. "I'm so glad to meet you in person, Ms. Newman."

Carter gestured for the family to sit on the sofa. Lizzie picked the end nearest me, her father sat next to her in the middle. The boy reluctantly twisted himself onto the other end.

Carter opened the pizza box again and returned to the chair beside mine. "Now that everyone's here, perhaps we can resolve some things."

Lizzie's brother grabbed a slice of pizza with his good arm and stuffed it in his mouth. He struggled to get his lips around the half he'd bitten off.

His father touched his arm gently. "T.J., we're guests in someone's home. Let's mind our manners."

T.J. So that was his name.

Barely able to talk through the wad of food in his mouth, T.J. managed a "Yes, sir." He covered his mouth and planted his eyes on his knees while he chewed and swallowed the rest.

Lizzie eyed the pizza expectantly. I took a plate and handed it to her. She lowered her gaze to the unopened box underneath. "Are they the same kind?"

"The bottom one's Margherita. No meat, just tomatoes, cheese and basil. Kinda plain, but I like it."

She settled into the sofa. "Okay, I'll have it too."

The Margherita was miraculously intact. I served her a slice, opened a soda and handed it over, then lifted another plate and gestured to Tom Mason.

He waved me off. "No thanks. I understand that the Detective needs to get back to the police station soon."

T.J.'s eyes shot toward Washington. As he downed another wad of pizza, his face turned bright red. He sat back and attempted to cross his arms, but his cast stymied him. He winced and dropped his eyes again.

I took a quick glance around the assembly and tried to grasp what was happening. My eyes landed on Carter. I twisted to face him directly. "You were saying?"

I hoped my eyebrows were arched high enough to signal what I really wanted to convey: Tell me right now what's going on, or I'll explode, and it will not be pretty.

He got the message. "Tom, Samantha's just arrived and needs catching up. Why don't you explain why we're gathered here?"

"Yes, sir." Mason leaned forward, rubbed his palms together, and turned his eyes to me. "I'm responsible for the training of Army Rangers. The job requires me to be away from my family for large chunks of time. That was all manageable, until my wife's stroke last year.

"I moved her and the kids to Houston because her mother lived here. Her Mom set up a team of caregivers and helped me manage them. I'd hoped that would be enough to keep things steady until I completed my twenty and retired in the next couple of years, but unfortunately, my mother-in-law died last month.

"Yesterday, I came home on leave to find everything in disarray. My wife was okay, but her caregiver hadn't showed up, which had been happening on and off, unbeknownst to me. The kids thought they were big enough to handle everything, so they never told me.

"The house was a mess, and my children . . . well, to start with, Lizzie had changed from a bright, energetic sprite to a sad little urchin. And T.J.—" Sadness clouded Mason's face. His jaw tightened.

He took a deep breath and continued. "I am blessed with two great kids. T.J. is super-motivated. He wants to be an Army Ranger, like me. I've encouraged him to do his best toward that goal." He shook his head. "I don't know, maybe I pushed him too hard."

Carter leaned forward and took up the story. "When I called Tom, he had just returned from the emergency room. T.J. had attempted a parkour maneuver in the dark, early this morning, and failed. Fortunately, he fell backward onto their balcony and not over the edge."

I couldn't move a muscle.

Carter sat back. "T.J.'s mishap compelled me to give Tom a brief history of the Bayne case next door, the balcony visits here, and the first yellow envelope. He immediately understood what was at stake and invited me to join him when he asked T.J. about it. To the boy's credit, he cooperated, and Tom agreed to invite Detective Washington over so we all could hear T.J.'s story."

The boy had not raised his eyes from his knees. His dad wrapped an arm around his shoulder. "You okay, buddy?" T.J. nodded. A tear glistened from the corner of his eye and fell onto his lap.

I stopped twirling my ring. "So, what now?"

Tom wrapped his other arm around Lizzie's

shoulder. "I brought Lizzie here because I want her to understand how serious this is. She knew her brother was sneaking out the balcony and climbing around, but she kept his secret. She said she was trying to follow Ranger code to always have her brother's back. Now I hope she understands the difference between having his back and acting responsibly."

He patted her hand. "I want you to go home now and be with your Mom while the detective talks to your brother. I hope he finds it in his heart not to arrest him."

The boy slumped deeper into the sofa.

Lizzie pulled her hand away. "No! I want to stay. Can't I stay, please?"

Mason shook his head. Lizzie turned to me, her eyes brimming. "Please, can you tell him to let me stay?"

A knot twisted inside my chest. "Your father wants you to go home. That's best for now. I'll see you again soon, I promise."

She stood and slouched out the door.

Washington started to speak, but he didn't get two words out before I jumped out of the chair.

"Okay, you guys have taken this far enough. I need to speak to Detective Washington, privately, right now. Sir, please meet me in the kitchen." I stormed out before he could protest.

The detective tiptoed into the kitchen like it was a tiger cage and I was the angry cat. I half expected Carter to come too, but he didn't.

I chose my words carefully. "You, sir, have a way of talking to a person that is rude and intimidating. That boy in the living room has misbehaved, no doubt. He's scared me half to death from the balcony more than once, but he also saved my life."

That comment seemed to puzzle the detective. I wasn't about to sidetrack my tirade with details, so I pushed on. "If you believe he had nothing to do with Irwin Bayne's death, you need to be gentle with him. He's clearly terrified, and in physical pain, too. That family has enough troubles already."

Washington's eyes clouded. "I'm aware of my job here, Ms. Newman. This is my business, and none of yours."

My ears burned. "I am warning you. No bullying. Do not treat him like a hardened criminal."

Carter popped his head in. "Samantha? Detective? Everything okay?"

I was about to yell at him, too, but stopped myself. I had started badly with Washington. I nodded to Carter and he backed out.

I took a deep breath and recalibrated. "Sir, I—"

He held up his hand to stop me. "This might go better if you call me by my first name. It's Buron. I'm here unofficially, remember?"

"Yes, but—"

"I am not a heartless man. I have no intention of talking to that boy any differently than I would my own son. His father and I have already spoken, and I pretty much know the kid's involvement. His Dad thinks my presence will scare him straight regarding his dangerous activity. As long as you don't push for a trespassing charge, he's out of the woods. Besides, I'm a homicide cop. I only want his account of what he saw from the balcony the night Irwin Bayne died."

"You won't arrest him?"

"Not part of the plan." He set his hands on his hips and locked eyes with me. "So, are we good?"

I put my hands on my hips too. "If you promise not to bully him."

"Cop's honor." He saluted, and then broke into a grin that changed his whole face. The man I had wanted to strangle two minutes ago—and on numerous other occasions—morphed into a human being.

"Okay then." Something compelled me to show him some gratitude. "You have nice teeth, by the way. You should smile more often."

He beamed even wider. "My wife tells me that all the time." His face turned serious again. "Can we move on?"

By the time Washington and I returned to the living room, Mason was sitting where Lizzie had been and Carter had taken my chair. Their heads were bowed together in deep conversation. T.J. remained on his end of the sofa, eyes closed. They popped again when the detective sat next to him.

I took a seat next to Carter. Mason moved back to the sofa, beside his son.

Washington cleared his throat and addressed the boy. "T.J., I'd like you to tell me what you saw the night Irwin Bayne died. Let's start from the time you climbed onto their balcony."

The boy's eyes were full of fear. Mason patted his hand. "Tell him what you told me, son."

T.J. lowered his eyes. "When I pulled myself over, I accidentally knocked into a big planter with a bush in it. It didn't break or anything, but it made a noise, so I looked through the glass door to make sure nobody had heard it. That's when I saw him."

Washington took a small notebook from the pocket of his slacks and pulled out a pen. "You saw Irwin Bayne?"

T.J. nodded. "I didn't know his name, but I'd seen him before."

Mason's eyes squeezed shut. "You'd been on that balcony before?"

T.J.'s lips tightened.

Washington stepped in. "Can you describe what Mr. Bayne looked like?"

"He was in his underwear, on his hands and knees, like he'd tripped or something. His face was all bloody. The blood was, like, in his hair and running down his neck and stuff, and there was some on the floor. He tried to stand up, but he couldn't. He . . . he looked right at me. I don't think he saw me, because the balcony was dark. I was afraid to move, so I just froze."

Washington made a brief note, nothing like the volumes he'd taken when he interrogated me. "And then?"

"His eyes kept closing, like he was falling asleep. He tried to stand up again, but he slipped on some blood, so he gave up and laid down and closed his eyes."

The detective made another note. "On his back?"

T.J. shook his head. "Not then, but after a minute or so, he opened his eyes and kinda tried to raise himself, but he gave up again and rolled over on his back. Then he got real still. I thought he was asleep, but he raised his head and let it fall again, and kinda jerked a little bit."

Washington looked up from his notes. "That it?"

The boy returned his eyes to his knees and didn't answer.

Mason spoke. "The detective asked you a question, T.J."

Still no answer. Mason nudged his son. "Is there anything you haven't told us?"

I stepped in. "I'm sure it's traumatic for T.J. to talk about this, especially since he knows that the man died while he was watching."

T.J mumbled something. Washington leaned closer.

"What did you say?"

T.J. eye-checked his father, then the detective. Tears welled up in his eyes. "He was laying there, kinda shaking all over. And then I saw the other man standing in the doorway . . ."

Washington lowered his notebook and gaped at the boy. "What other man?"

All eyes were on T.J., which rendered him mute.

Mason turned to his son. "Someone else was in the room? Why didn't you tell me this before?"

The boy's eyes fell to his quaking knees. "I didn't want to get her in trouble."

"Her?" Washington stood and towered over him. "T.J., if you're trying to protect someone, you could become an accessory to murder. Do you understand what I'm saying?"

T.J. nodded. Another tear dropped into his lap.

Mason wrapped his arm around the boy's shoulder. "Son, this is really important. Who did you see?"

CHAPTER THIRTY-SEVEN

Tongues

Washington shut down the interview as soon as he realized T.J. could add vital information to the case. He instructed the boy not to say any more until he made a formal statement at the police station. As soon as the detective left, Carter drove T.J. and Tom Mason downtown.

Waiting for him to return had me on edge. I made myself a cup of ginger tea and booted up my tablet to surf the KHTS website. Carter's comment—about the TV job and how I'd be championing the little guy—had been circling my brain. Once it merged with my need to expose Kingsbury for the fraud he was, it wasn't so hard to reconsider the whistleblower's role. Still, I had a lot of catching up to do.

By the time Carter finally walked in, I'd moved on to shopping websites. I pounced. "Everything. I want to know it all. Is T.J. okay? Who did he see next door?"

He set his keys on the counter. "The kid did fine. He's home, safe and sound. That's all I can say, for now. Washington asked that I not disclose anything until he can act on it."

"But I'm the one who led him to—"

"You're still a material witness, Sam. Can't talk to you about it yet."

I gave him the stinkeye.

He shrugged it off. "How was your meeting at the TV station?"

"I have the job."

"That's great! Tell me about it."

Much as I wanted to share my big triumph, I wasn't about to let him off the hook. "I will if you will."

It was his turn to give me the stinkeye. I returned to the laptop and pretended to concentrate on the screen. No way I'd crack first.

He got a glass of water and drank it down. "We're both tired. Maybe we should call it a night." He kissed me on the cheek and disappeared down the hall.

I felt like a dog without a bone. How could I go to bed without knowing what T.J. had revealed? Still, it was well past midnight. Tomorrow would be too important a day to sleepwalk through. I wanted to inform Sedgwick and Patel about the new evidence in the Bayne case first thing in the morning, enough time to work it into the questions they'd prepared.

Excitement over the press conference and Kingsbury's comeuppance buzzed in my head. It jockeyed for the space where my snit with Carter sizzled, until they merged into a giant mind-freak. No way I could sleep until I knew what T.J. had seen. I powered down the laptop and headed to the bedroom.

Carter was already under the covers. I considered turning on all the lights and harassing him until he told me what I wanted, but that was unlikely to work.

I undressed and got into bed, making as much noise as possible. When that didn't get him to roll over, I punched the pillow hard against the headboard. I coughed. Nothing.

I gave up, leaned back and blinked into the darkness. Half my brain worked through various possibilities of who T.J. might have seen the night Irwin Bayne died; the other half sped through hopeful scenarios of tomorrow's press conference. I tossed around all night.

At the first crack of daylight, I got up and dressed, trying not to wake Carter. He was probably fake-sleeping again, but I didn't care. There was no time to rekindle last night's squabble anyway.

Today was the day I'd finally get back at Kingsbury, if Lloyd Sedgwick played along like he'd promised. To seal the deal, I was about to give him a legitimate scoop. Carter may have kept the details of T.J.'s statement from me, but still I knew more about the investigation than Kingsbury did. More ammo to catch him off-guard, in public and on camera, like he'd embarrassed me.

I pulled into the number-eighteen employee parking space at KHTS, picked up my employee badge at the front desk, and bee-lined toward Jay Patel's office.

I plopped into a chair across from him. "You won't believe what's happened!"

He dropped the document he'd been studying onto his desk. "Come in, Samantha. Take a seat."

"Sorry to interrupt, but I think this will make your day."

He set his reading glasses down and leaned back. "Let's hear it."

"There's a new development in the Bayne case."

"Shall I call in Lloyd Sedgwick?"

I nodded. "Could he bring coffee?"

Patel looked at me strangely. "You're certainly making yourself at home here."

"Sorry. I've been up all night."

"I like it. I was worried that you weren't a hundred percent sure about joining us."

He pressed a button on his desk phone and spoke into it. "Lloyd, come to my office, please. Bring your notes on the Kingsbury press conference, and an extra coffee."

Waiting for Sedgwick gave me a chance to address Patel's doubts. "I know I seemed reluctant to take this job. It's been a wild ride for me the last year or so, and I guess I needed the fog to clear before I could move on. But I'm ready now—eager—and grateful for the opportunity."

"Glad to hear it."

I craned my neck toward the door. "Will he be here soon with the coffee?"

Sedgwick finally appeared. I took the mug from him and sipped while he settled himself into the chair next to me.

Patel opened the conversation. "Samantha has something to add to your file."

I ignored Sedgwick's eye roll. "There's new evidence in the Irwin Bayne case."

He ruffled the papers on his lap. "So, this stuff gets dumped? A coupl'a hours, wasted." He cursed and slumped in his chair.

Patel's eyebrows rose. "I'm sure there's background you can salvage, Lloyd. Samantha may have brought us something bigger. Let's hear her out."

I turned to Sedgwick. "You have contacts at the D.A.'s office, right?"

"Yeah. There, and the police department, too. What's up?"

"I've heard that they're not going to close the Bayne case. And Kingsbury doesn't know it yet."

That got his attention. "What's the evidence?"

"An eyewitness."

Sedgwick's eyes popped. "Who is it?"

"Mmmm . . . sorry . . . I can't say."

Patel frowned. "We don't play twenty questions here, Samantha."

I couldn't expose T.J. "Can't you check with your source at the police department?"

Sedgwick bolted out the door. Patel called the news director and asked her to join us. I'd had one brief interview with her and liked her. A good thing, since we'd probably be working together.

Sedgwick was back in a flash, his face radiant. "It's confirmed! They wouldn't say who, but they have an eyewitness! The case isn't closed. They seemed pretty confident."

I listened as the three journalists worked out the timing and placement of the breaking news. They debated whether to preempt a popular late afternoon game show for a live transmission of the press conference, or run an edited version in a regular segment of the five o'clock newscast. Then they considered the need for a junior reporter to assemble footage for a background segment.

Sedgwick started reviewing the copy he'd prepared, slashing through lines and adding more notes. By the time he sailed out, everything was a go. The news director left to order a revised schedule.

Patel stood and shut the door. Back in his chair, he tented his fingers and pressed them to his lips. Something in his face changed the rhythm of my pulse.

I locked my thumb firmly against my palm. "Is something wrong?"

Patel scratched his chin. "If the Bayne case is reopened, it will put us in the same position as last time, with a news department employee—you—involved in an open criminal case. And a sensational one, at that."

"But this is different. I'm not . . . it's not . . . you can't . . ." I lost breath.

"You're right, Samantha. This isn't exactly the same. Before, the implication was that you might be directly involved. With an eyewitness, you'll probably be clear of that. Still, you seem to know more about the case than you can tell us, which leads me to believe—" His phone buzzed, but he didn't move to pick it up.

While my heart and stomach switched places, I tried to keep my voice even. "You once said that I was in a unique position to do good by calling out the cheaters and liars who make life hell for the good guys. I thought it was a crazy idea. But now I want to do it. I have to."

"So, how do you propose we get around this?"

"I have a lot to learn here. Watching all of you work through the options for covering the press conference was an eye-opener. I realized that I don't know enough about how a television station operates, and I don't want to be on-air until I do. I don't mind starting as an intern until the Bayne case is resolved. A paid intern, hopefully."

Patel looked doubtful. "You'd still be an employee."

"With no visibility."

He shook his head. "I don't see how we can have you in the news department."

I panicked. "I'll do anything—receptionist, file clerk, kitchen supervisor." Kitchen supervisor? Thank goodness another option came to me. "What about marketing, the promotions job I originally applied for? That's not in the news department, right?"

He brightened a little. A slow smile traveled over his face. "My instincts about you were accurate. You'll do well here." He stood and offered his hand. I shook it, hoping it meant we had a deal.

He strode to the door and opened it. "I'll have HR draw up papers for a new start date."

"Not today?"

"Let's see what develops at the press conference this

afternoon. Call me tomorrow."

I left, uncertain if I had a job. Since no one asked for my employee badge and parking pass, I kept them. My HR file was probably upwards of an inch thick already, and I hadn't yet logged a single hour of work.

Counting down the time until Kingsbury's press conference, I was completely rattled when I pulled into The Wellbourne. I raced into the lobby and pressed the up button, heart pumping.

The wait for the doors to open was agony. But when they finally spread, they revealed a sight I wished I could unsee: Brandy Bayne and Rufus Kingsbury locked in a kiss. A sloppy one. With tongues.

I gasped. They sprung apart.

Kingsbury wiped his mouth with the back of his hand and grinned at me. "Hey, darlin'. What's up?" He took Brandy by the elbow and ushered her out of the elevator.

As they passed, he brushed against me. His pumpkin aura curled my nostrils. Over his shoulder, he offered one last comment. "Cheer up, honey. It's gonna be a great day."

The doors shut before I could board. I pressed the up button again, hoping for an empty elevator this time.

My phone beeped and lit with the TV station's ID.

Jay Patel sounded jubilant. "You're all clear, Samantha. It's a provisional position in the marketing department, for now. You can start tomorrow."

I hadn't fully recovered from the Kingsbury encounter. I mustered a weak, "That's great."

"Sure you're okay with it?"

"Yes, yes, it's fine. Is the plan still on for the press conference?"

"It's a go."

"Okay if I come, just to observe?"

"Well, you were the one with the scoop. I suppose it's only fair. Besides, it's in a public space. I can't stop you."

The elevator arrived. A faint hint of Eau de Kingsbury greeted me when I stepped inside, but I didn't care. The weasel had been right about one thing. It was turning into a great day.

CHAPTER THIRTY-EIGHT

Not a Bird

By the time I opened the door to the apartment, my head was buzzing. Kingsbury would soon be getting a taste of his own medicine. And to top it off, I had job. No way I'd let it dissolve into nothingness again. I danced around the living room like a maniac.

I stopped to catch my breath and saw Carter standing in the doorway of the music room, laughing. I flew into his arms and buried my face in his neck.

His voice vibrated in my ear. "Good news?"

I tilted my head and planted a kiss. He answered with a long, deep kiss of his own. I didn't want it to end, but the start of the press conference loomed like a hot air balloon coming in for a landing. I peeled myself away, took his hand and pulled him toward the bedroom. "I'll tell you all about it while I change."

"Change? What for?"

I swallowed hard. "I'm not talking until you tell me more about last night with T.J. at the police station."

"I can't. Not yet, anyway."

"Promise me he's not in trouble."

Carter stopped our progress at the bedroom door. "Relax, Sam. Washington was very pleased with the boy's statement. There won't be any criminal charges against him. And I don't think he'll be prowling the balconies, ever again."

"Thank goodness for that. Did he say why he was out there in the first place?"

Carter squinted like he was considering how much

more to tell. "Apparently, T.J. had developed a crush on Brandy. They'd talked in the gym a couple of times. He said she was really nice to him. When he found out that she lived only one balcony up and across, he got it in his head to try a parkour gambit to get there."

I winced. "I hope that's not as creepy as it sounds."

"After hearing him talk, I think it's more of a Mom-crush thing, like his little sister has on you."

"Me?" I leaned on the doorframe. I'd never stopped to analyze Lizzie's attachment to me, and I'd certainly never thought of myself as a mother figure. I still missed my own Mom too much. Yet, Lizzie and T.J. were pitifully bereft of maternal comfort. It was possible that the boy simply needed an older woman's attention.

My brain shifted to a different, more unpleasant thought. "Although, teenage hormones being what they are, and Brandy being . . . " The idea was too grimy to contemplate. "Nope, I'm gonna go with your Mom-crush theory."

Carter nodded. "Anyway, T.J.'s first try to get there was the night he saw Irwin die. That was enough to keep him from going back again."

"So, he came here instead?"

"Not on purpose. He thought the person he'd seen inside the Bayne apartment had seen him, too."

I turned to face Carter. "Who?"

He crossed his arms. "Nice try, Sam. Anyway, T.J. figured that his quickest escape that night was toward our place. Once he'd made it over, he was too rattled to move. That's when he saw Brandy and 'an old lady', as he put it."

"That must have been when Gertie caught a glimpse of him."

"Yes. The next morning, he wrote the note. He said

he'd planned to slip it under our front door, but it wouldn't go through. He went home and climbed out later to deliver it from the balcony.

"When he didn't see anyone in the living room, he came in through that door and dropped the envelope on the floor in the entry, so it would look like it came from the hallway."

I'd probably been asleep down the hall, or in the shower when T.J. was in the apartment. I shuddered. "Why did he come back after that?"

"He worried that nobody had paid attention to the first note, so he wrote another one. But when he climbed over to deliver it, he saw you through the glass and took off."

"So, I didn't imagine it. And it wasn't a bird. Or a phantom."

"No. But we're lucky he persevered, because the last time he tried was when you burst onto the balcony and did a header toward the railing. He says his instincts took over and he grabbed you. He made sure you were breathing and climbed off without leaving the note."

Goosebumps spread over me. I stepped toward the balcony window and scanned the railing and the city skyline beyond. "T.J. saved me. I knew it."

"In a way, you saved him, too. After witnessing the Bayne horror on his first venture, then later, yanking you back from certain death, and breaking his arm on the next try—his enthusiasm for parkour from thirteen stories up is history."

Carter's phone beeped. He pulled it from his khakis, checked the screen and gave me quick glance before he turned away to concentrate on the call.

I moved closer and attempted to read his face for clues to the caller's identity.

At last, he spoke. "Interesting." Unperturbed, he

listened without comment long enough for me to start spinning my mom's ring. His eyes slid to my hand. "One moment, Detective."

Washington. I stopped twisting.

Carter covered the phone and whispered. "Nothing to worry about, Sam. I'll just be a minute."

I was too frazzled to bother with changing clothes. I stared out past the balcony. Thin white clouds skidded over the tops of the downtown skyscrapers. A siren from somewhere below grew louder, louder, then fainter as it passed.

Carter seemed to be winding down. "Okay, Detective. Thanks for the update. Good luck."

I wheeled around. "And?"

"And nothing, Sam. I've told you T.J. is safe. It's your turn to tell me about your job."

Him and his darned secrets.

I doled out bits of my convoluted journey from the on-camera offer back to the desk in marketing, but I left out the Kingsbury payback I'd wrangled for today. I didn't see the harm in keeping Carter in the dark until it was over.

It was almost time to leave. "Anyway, I'm going to the press conference. Wanna come?"

"That's not a good idea."

"Okay." I slung my bag onto my shoulder.

His brows knit. "Not a good idea for you to be there either."

I waggled my KHTS employee badge at him. "I work there. I'm going. Are you coming, or not?"

CHAPTER THIRTY-NINE

Plutonium

On the way to the press conference, I had second, third and fourth thoughts about bringing Carter along. For most of the ride, he grilled me on why a promotions person was needed at this kind of event. I dodged his questions, hoping he'd understand later.

Kingsbury knew how to draw a crowd. In front of the office building, production vans from every local news outlet lined the street. I spotted my station's van.

There was an open space behind the KHTS truck. I pointed. "Park there."

As soon as he'd maneuvered the Tesla into the spot, I jumped out, raced to the truck and beat on the door. A sound tech opened it. She pulled an earphone away from her head and glared at me. "Yeah?"

"I'm looking for Lloyd Sedgwick."

She gestured across the small plaza that fronted the building. A raised podium had been set at the entrance. With a parting frown, she readjusted her headset and banged the door shut. Above it, an amber On Air sign flashed.

Carter came up behind me. He was not looking happy. "We shouldn't be here, Sam."

"It's just a press conference."

"I know what it is." He put his hands on his hips.

"I have to find Lloyd." I worked my way through a crowd of onlookers. Reporters milled around the podium. I moved closer.

Lloyd Sedgwick was reading copy into his

microphone. When he caught sight of me, he held his finger up, covered the mike and whispered, "Sound check."

I whispered back. "All set?"

"Yeah."

I gave him a thumbs up and backed off, retracing my steps to look for Carter. He was where I'd left him, standing next to the production van, scowling.

The crowd noise kicked up a few decibels. I searched across the plaza for a clear view of Sedgwick and saw that Kingsbury was about to take the podium. Brandy trailed behind.

I grabbed Carter's arm. "C'mon. I want to get closer."

He wouldn't budge, so I left him and returned to a spot near Sedgwick. With one hand holding the mike and the other pressing on his earpiece, he seemed to be waiting for a cue.

At last, he nodded and looked into the camera. "Yes, Alicia. As our viewers may remember, Brandy Bayne was accused of allegedly murdering her husband, Irwin. Her attorney Rufus Kingsbury is here, ostensibly to comment on the rumor that the investigation is about to be closed, due to lack of definitive evidence. However, our sources tell us that may not be accurate."

Someone nudged me from behind. Carter had followed me after all. His face knotted in a scowl. "Did you tell . . .?"

I shrugged and held a finger to my lips.

Kingsbury stood at the podium behind an array of microphones, his eyes twinkling wildly as he took in the moment. "Can y'all hear me?"

He looked into the crowd and grinned, then rearranged his features into a stern courtroom face. "I'm here today with my wrongfully-accused client, Mrs.

Brandy Bayne, to announce that the case against her for allegedly murdering her beloved husband is at an end. Come here, darlin'. Let the people see you."

Brandy stepped up to the podium. Kingsbury wrapped his arm around her shoulders and squeezed, a move that highlighted more bosom than early evening newscasts usually featured. She smiled shyly. Murmurs rose from the crowd.

Kingsbury yammered on. "I had expected this announcement to be preceded by an official statement from the D.A.'s office. Unfortunately, they've delayed their briefing. No doubt they're embarrassed at having blundered so badly on this case. We, however, are confident that it is not too early to proclaim that Brandy Bayne is as innocent as the day is long. She is merely a bereft widow who has lost the love of her life in a tragic, tragic accident."

He squeezed Brandy's shoulders again, giving everyone another peek at her assets. There was more hubbub from onlookers. Eyes a-twinkle, he let it settle before he leaned into the microphone again. "That's all for now. Justice is served. Thanks for coming out."

Before Kingsbury could turn away, Lloyd Sedgwick's voice carried over the crowd. "What do you say to the fact that police have uncovered new evidence?"

Kingsbury chuckled, returned to the microphone and peered down at Sedgwick. "New evidence?"

My pulse ticked up. For an instant, everybody stopped moving, speaking and breathing. When life resumed, reporters from the other stations moved closer to Sedgwick, and their camera operators followed.

Sedgwick continued. "Yes, counselor. We've learned that an eyewitness has come forward. We're also told that an old piece of evidence has become pertinent to the case." Sedgwick checked his notes. "A white envelope, I believe."

I gave myself a mental high-five as Kingsbury reacted. His jaw moved, but no words came from his mouth. A struggle played across his face as he whispered, "That's impossible."

His eyes darted about until he seemed to catch sight of something. I followed his gaze and spotted Detective Washington on the other side of the podium amid a phalanx of uniformed officers.

At first, I figured that the detective had arrived to make a statement to the press after all. But Kingsbury's reaction was puzzling. He spun around, grabbed Brandy and pushed her ahead of him toward the entrance to the building, calling back over his shoulder as he ran. "Excuse us, folks, there's somewhere else we gotta be."

Sedgwick scurried behind the pair. A scuffle broke out in front of him between Kingsbury and Washington. They tussled for a few seconds before two policemen grabbed Kingsbury and pulled him off the detective. One of them cuffed him; the other one took Brandy.

Sedgwick backed away. From a safe distance, he addressed the camera. "As you can see, Rufus Kingsbury was wrong about the disposition of his client's case. A reliable source has told us that the attorney is, in fact, a new person of interest in the alleged murder. We'll be reporting further, as details develop. Back to you in the studio, Alicia."

My mind reeled. I'd only meant to poke Kingsbury in the gut with the bogus white envelope—publicly embarrass him, like he'd tried on me. Catching him off-guard with news of an eyewitness was the cherry on top.

The cops hauling him away on camera? What was

that about?

My heart pumped like I'd just run the hundred-meter sprint. Every conversation I'd ever had with Kingsbury compressed into one tiny bead of plutonium that threatened to explode my skull.

That disgusting kiss I'd witnessed between him and Brandy in the elevator popped into focus. I'd taken it for the same kind of spur-of-the-moment flirtation he'd tried with me. Now it seemed like something much, much worse.

CHAPTER FORTY

Smog

The crowd melted away. Some people continued on to nearby shops and restaurants, others returned to their cars. The television technicians and reporters packed their vans and departed.

I spotted Carter, leaning on the passenger door of the Tesla, his arms crossed tight over his chest. "Either that reporter's clairvoyant, or somebody tipped him off."

My head was still spinning with salacious images of Kingsbury and Brandy as I slid into the passenger seat.

The sun had disappeared, and street lights illuminated the road. Cars inched forward in a rush-hour crawl. Carter got behind the wheel and stared out the front window, a scowl deepening the shadows on his face. "Any idea who told him about the eye witness?"

I buckled my seatbelt and stared ahead. We sat like that until the pressure almost burst the windows. Carter jolted the car onto the road.

Awkward silence poisoned the air inside the car for the entire traffic-jammed drive back to The Wellbourne. Carter eased the Tesla into its parking slot in the garage, wrapped his arms over the top of the steering wheel and leaned his forehead on them. "Why did you put yourself in the middle of that spectacle?"

"I didn't put myself in the middle of anything. I was off-camera the whole time."

"You know what I mean."

My thumb moved to Mom's ring. "Remember when Kingsbury's big mouth cost me the TV job in the first place? And that bogus white envelope he made me believe was real? Not to mention almost splitting you and me apart? He's a bullying, smug liar, and I wanted payback."

Carter raised his head. "Payback?"

"Payback, revenge, whatever. I'm tired of people like him, flouting the truth to get what they want. I wanted to see him squirm in public."

"You leaked privileged information for your own personal satisfaction? You could have ruined the entire investigation!"

"I . . . what?" If the sunroof were open, I'd have shot up through it. No way I'd let him pin that on me. "What privileged information?"

"Why do you think the police took those two into custody?"

I'd figured that the weasel's shenanigans had finally caught up with him somehow. If not that, then what?

Goosebumps covered my arms as a different possibility dawned. "Kingsbury! He was the person T.J. saw from the balcony that night?"

Carter didn't answer. He didn't need to.

I exploded. "How was I supposed to know? I would have backed off, if you had told me what was happening. But everything with you has to be a deep dark secret!"

Another Tesla pulled into the charging slot beside Carter's. Based on the driver's look of alarm as he got out, our discussion had escalated to a shouting match.

I waited for him to connect the power cable and walk away before I pounced again. "You didn't trust me, and that's on you."

It occurred to me that if I'd shared my stupid plan for revenge, it might have forced Carter to tell me that Kingsbury was the man T.J. identified. But I hadn't trusted him to let me play things out my way.

Perhaps we both were at fault. I covered my face with my hands.

He touched my arm. "Let's go upstairs."

The wait for an elevator was excruciating. I spent the time studying the marble floor and anticipating the seventh perversity of elevators: Anger between two people is certain to intensify by a factor of a zillion for every floor they're stuck inside together.

Relief, of a sort, came when the doors opened to reveal Hubert and Pansy Gump. She pushed Hubert out and charged toward me. "Have you seen the news?"

Carter moved past the pair and boarded. I followed, hoping my silence would discourage her, but she circled back. Astonishment lit her tiny black eyes. "They have apprehended another perpetrator!"

I looked away as if I hadn't heard her and pressed the up button. The doors began to close. As the gap between them narrowed, she wedged her handbag through and they shuddered open again.

"We must speak!" She grabbed Hubert and yanked him in with her. Carter and I retreated to opposite corners. The doors closed and we lifted off.

"I knew it all along, of course," Pansy sniffed. "The moment I laid eyes on that redheaded monster in the elevator the other day, I said to Hubert, 'Hubert, that man is up to something.' I did not like the way he looked at me."

A noise came from Hubert: his voice, which I'd never heard before. It was remarkably soft and measured. "We'll be late to the symphony, dear." He pressed the button for the next floor, and when the doors opened, he ushered his flummoxed wife out into the hallway. She spun around and was about to say something, but the doors shut before she could speak another word.

Carter turned the key in the lock. As I followed him inside, I touched his back. "We need to talk."

"Not now."

"You still don't understand what happened."

"I saw what happened. The entire television viewing audience saw what happened." He shut the door behind us little too hard and headed for the kitchen.

I followed. "Yes, but I didn't . . . I wasn't . . ."

He stopped at the refrigerator and stuck his head in. "You weren't what?"

"Can you turn around and look at me?"

"I'm hungry." He pulled out the remaining pizza box from yesterday, set it on the counter and finally, met my eyes. "Wanna share?"

The disappointment on his face made me ache. "I'm trying to explain."

"I meant the pizza."

"Oh." A peek inside the box went straight to my tummy. "Sure. But only if you'll listen."

We scarfed down the pizza without bothering to heat it. Tension thick as smog hung between us as I laid out my role in framing Sedgwick's questions.

Carter got himself a beer. "So, the bogus white envelope. Your plan was to make Kingsbury think the police were interested in it?"

"It seems lame now, I know. I couldn't prove it was fake, but I thought if I could scare Kingsbury with it . . . I told the guys at KHTS about it, and they agreed to use it at the press conference. The worst thing I did was imply that it could be an important piece of evidence. I wanted to embarrass the weasel, mess with his mind. That's all."

"How did they know about the eyewitness, and all

the rest?"

I felt my face flush. "I never gave them details. The reporter checked with his contacts downtown before the press conference started."

Carter eyebrows knit. "You gave him the tip."

His frown deepened. He flattened the empty pizza box and stuffed it into the recycling bin. "I'm going to the ranch."

I watched the late news broadcast in the bedroom. The segment was almost an exact replay of what I'd witnessed, with Alicia providing bookends to Sedgwick's report. They had also cobbled together some file footage for a backstory about Kingsbury's career. I'd seen too much of his smug face already, so I shut it off.

I pulled my feet under me and settled against the headboard. A full moon cast shadows as crisp as sunlight onto the balcony. I pictured T.J., crouching outside, and me, rushing headlong out the door toward oblivion. I'd never be able to look out there again and not think of that brave boy and his broken-hearted family.

Hard to say if that's what sent tears streaming from my eyes, or if it was because I'd disappointed Carter, or my anger at his holier-than-thou attitude. If he had trusted me with what he knew, I'd never have gone through with the scheme. The secrets we'd each clung to were tearing us apart.

CHAPTER FORTY-ONE

Peace Offer

Good thing I arrived at KHTS early. The receptionist detoured me to Jay Patel's office before I headed to the marketing department.

A party atmosphere greeted me as soon as I stepped into the corridor. We had been the only news department prepared for Kingsbury's downfall, and it seemed as though everybody knew that I was the reason why. Lloyd Sedgwick gave me a hug like a long-lost friend and introduced me around.

Patel offered a hearty handshake. "We scored a little coup last night, thanks to you. Pretty good for someone who insists she's not a whistleblower."

Sedgwick gave me a KHTS mug filled with coffee. When he and Patel made a toast to my first day at the station, I tried to appear grateful, but I didn't feel heroic.

The press conference had turned everything upside down. Now, my little game of payback seemed juvenile. Revenge and justice were like two sides of a coin, and I'd skated on the thin edge in between.

I excused myself as soon as I could and headed to the promotions office on the opposite side of the building. The hallway there was festooned with glossy photos of Alicia Sultana and her co-anchors smiling alongside various civic leaders and sports figures. There were posters from past clothing drives, fun runs and golf tournaments sponsored by KHTS.

Missy Eton, the public affairs manager, did not look happy to see me. Her handshake could have iced a watermelon in August.

She led me to an area shared by two other people. By their UH and Go Coogs! pullovers, they looked to be college interns of the unpaid variety. My new boss brushed by them without speaking. I nodded to them and said a quiet hello.

"That's where you sit." Eton pointed to a bare desk with a huge arrangement of pink roses on it. From Carter? My heart did a hopeful flip. "Wow."

I detected an eye roll from Eton as I plucked the card from a plastic stalk among the flowers. Welcome Aboard! it read, from your colleagues at KHTS.

The bouquet did seem over the top for a lowly newbie. Perhaps that was what had annoyed Eton. She probably knew my job under her tutelage was temporary, and she didn't want to waste time getting to know me, or train me, or—by her sudden exit from the room—speak to me again. It would be a task in itself to avoid ruffling her feathers, but compared to my previous homicidal co-workers, she didn't scare me.

That afternoon she held a staff meeting to update us on the projects in the pipeline, and for the first time I got a handle on the current activities of the department. Thanksgiving Day Parade coverage was the big one.

To my surprise, Eton picked me to assist the promotions coordinator and work with the news staff assigned to the event. I'd be spending time back on the other side of the building with Alicia and another news anchor. Things were looking up after all, job-wise anyway.

Carter called in the evening. "How was the first day of the rest of your life?"

"Fine." Certain that he wouldn't want to hear about

the celebration that had started my day, I searched for something neutral. "I'm working on the Thanksgiving Day Parade."

"Sounds like fun." He didn't mention our quarrel. Still, it hung heavy in the silences. "I had a closing this morning in Brenham for the land adjacent to Serenity."

I figured that was his way of excusing his exit last night. "Congratulations."

"Why don't you come out for the weekend?"

While I wavered between accepting the invitation and hanging up on him, he asked again. "I'd like to show you the property, if you want to see it."

It sounded like a peace offering.

On Saturday, I left for Serenity around mid-morning. Driving up to the great house, I could see Dottie on the veranda. I waved, grabbed my bag and headed up the front steps. Two tables had been set for lunch.

Carter hadn't mentioned that he'd invited other people. Typical.

"Hey, Dottie. Who else is coming?"

She didn't stop to look up. "All I know is, I hope the six chickens I'm about to fry are enough. It's gonna be a crowd. Ask the boss."

He was at his desk in the library. My pulse skipped at the sight of him. He crossed the room and took me in his arms. I wasn't sure if we were in one of those long goodbye embraces or if he was really happy I'd come. Either way, I wouldn't be the first to let go.

The front door creaked open. "S'cuse me, folks," Dottie called from the entry. "Thought you'd want to know that the guests are arriving."

Carter took my hand. By the time we reached the front porch, a large blue van had parked beside the steps. Doors opened on all sides.

Lizzie emerged from the front passenger seat, ran up the steps and hugged me around the waist. She seemed as surprised as I was by her spontaneous show of affection. She backed away, lowered her eyes and mumbled, "Hi, Samantha."

Tom Mason opened the van's side panel and lifted his wife out. She wore the same floppy hat and sunglasses she'd had on at The Wellbourne pool party. Despite his arm cast, T.J. managed to unhitch her wheelchair and set it on the ground.

Tom studied the steps leading up to the porch, then hoisted Elizabeth a little higher and carried her all the way. T.J. followed with the wheelchair in an effortless one-armed carry.

Carter frowned. "Sorry. The ramp is around back. I'll have Ralph move it up here before you leave."

"No worries. " He spoke to his wife. "You're not heavy, are you dear?"

She gave no discernable response. Mason settled her into the wheelchair, carefully placing her feet on their rests and securing them.

He took in the view. The live oaks held their deep green foliage year-round, but the maples and sweetgum fizzed with color, from bright yellow to deep maroon. He shook hands with Carter. "Your description of the place didn't do it justice. It's spectacular."

The front door opened, and Kerry and Courtney spilled onto the porch. Kerry saw me and exploded into a grin. "Hi Samantha!" Courtney rolled her eyes.

Carter gently pivoted them to face the Masons. "I want you to meet some new friends. This is Tom and Elizabeth Mason and their children, T.J. and Lizzie."

Kerry straightened himself into a big boy stance and offered his hand to Lizzie, who was nearest to him.

"Pleased to meet you." Then he shook hands with T.J. and Tom. When his eyes landed on Elizabeth, he offered his hand, but quickly withdrew it. Courtney and T.J. exchanged shy glances.

Carter smiled. "Courtney, why don't you and your brother take T.J. and Lizzie to the stables. You can pick horses for a ride after lunch, if you want."

Kerry and Lizzie whooped and sped down the steps, heading for the path to the stables. Courtney shrugged and glanced at T.J., who shrugged in response, each too cool to give in.

"Go on, T.J.," Mason said. "Let her show you the horses."

Reluctantly, the teens ambled down the steps.

I was curious about why Carter had invited the Masons. One thing was for sure: with other people around, the two of us weren't going to be rehashing the ups and downs of our relationship anytime soon.

Carter ushered us into the library. Mason wheeled Elizabeth to a window so she could look out, then took a side chair beside the leather sofa where Carter and I had settled. Dottie came in with iced tea.

Carter took a glass from the tray. "Thanks, Dottie. We'll probably be ready to eat in half an hour or so, after the last guests arrive."

I flinched. The last time Carter invited an unknown guest to lunch at the ranch, Roland Birney had showed up and snatched him away without warning.

"Who else is coming?"

"Gertie and Louis. I have business to discuss with Tom after lunch, and I thought you'd enjoy spending time with Gertie while we're gone."

"Gone?"

"I'm taking Tom for a tour of the new acreage."

I was eager for time with Gertie, but hadn't Carter

invited me to see the land? "I'm not going too?"

"We'll go later. I want Tom to see it while he's here."
Carter took my hand. "I haven't had a chance to tell you.
I offered him a job, once he retires from the Rangers, to
help me build and eventually, run the new project."

Mason smiled. "It is an unbelievable offer. I can keep
my family together while I work on such a meaningful
project. I'm humbled and excited."

Carter turned to me. "What do you think?"

For families in distress, Carter had said, when he'd
laid out his vision for the sanctuary. To engage someone
like Mason, who knew what that meant, and was capable
as a Ranger Lieutenant Colonel . . .

"It would be wonderful for Lizzie and T.J."

Mason finished my thought. "Elizabeth, too."

I glanced at the pitiful figure by the window and
went to kneel beside her. I patted her wrist. "You'll be
happy here, don't you think?"

I wasn't sure she could feel my touch, until a slight
movement tickled my palm. It made my heart squeeze
with hope.

A car drove up to the house. From the window, I
watched Louis exit the driver's side and circle around to
open the passenger door for Gertie. "That's my friend," I
told Elizabeth. "You'll like her. She just got engaged."

The four of us moved out to the porch to greet them.
I rushed down the steps and nearly smothered Gertie
with a hug. As she let me hold on, I realized I was
reenacting Lizzie's greeting from a few minutes earlier. I
backed away. "I'm glad you're here."

She caught her breath and took my hand. "I'm glad
too. I was beginning to think you were angry with me."

My eyes fell to a rock-hard chunk on her finger: a
square-cut ruby, nestled in a diamond bezel, sparkling in

the sun.

She blushed. "It's not too too, is it?"

Dottie stepped out and banged her triangle to announce lunch. I took Gertie's hand and led her and Louis up to the veranda, where the rest of the grown-ups were gathering around the big table.

The kids soon appeared on the path from the stables, laughing and talking. They found their seats at the smaller table, where they hungrily sucked and nibbled at their fried chicken. Dottie had cooked the birds to a perfect crispy finish.

Mason cut Elizabeth's food and fed her while the rest of us took our share of chicken, broccoli slaw, ranch beans and corn on the cob. We were on seconds before he touched his own plate.

Once Mason dug in, Carter clinked his beer with a fork and addressed the table. "I'd like to welcome you all to Serenity. And offer congratulations to our friends Gertrude and Louis on their engagement to be married."

After we raised our glasses to the happy couple, Carter turned to me. "Shall we toast to your new job at the TV station?"

Until the two of us could bridge our quarrel, it didn't feel right. "Let's toast to something better. Like justice."

Gertie's eyes widened. "Are you talking about the Bayne case?

"Justice in general, though I wouldn't mind if it started with that."

She winced. "I read about it in the paper, and I can't believe it. Brandy really played us for fools."

I set my glass down. "She wasn't the only one."

"What do you mean?"

I'd told her about my first kitchen drama with Kingsbury and Carter, but as for the bogus envelope and the predicament the weasel had put me in with my job, she had no clue. "It doesn't matter now. Let's toast to justice. May it be as swift as a kick in the pants."

Carter shook his head. "There's a long road ahead before justice is done in this case."

Mason glanced toward the children's table. They appeared to be happily occupied in their own conversation. He lowered his voice and leaned in. "If my boy didn't actually see the murder being committed, will they still be able to get a conviction?"

Carter shrugged. "They've definitely classified it as homicide. They'll charge Brandy for sure. She already admitted to inflicting the blow. Now that they can place Kingsbury in the apartment at time of death, he'll face criminal charges, too. Could be murder, conspiracy, or something less."

Gertie leaned in. "Does anybody know what really happened?"

Carter's brows knit. "They're still piecing it together. One theory is that Brandy and Kingsbury were lovers, and they used her husband's habitual drunkenness to stage his murder."

A vision of the disgusting kiss between the two of them popped into my head. "That gets my vote."

"Or it could be that Brandy whacked Irwin and Kingsbury devised a cover-up," Carter added. "Truth is, without a confession, we may never know for sure."

Gertie frowned. "With DNA and all the modern-day science, someone must be able to figure it out. If not, there's no justice."

Carter's phone buzzed. He glanced at the screen and excused himself. A pall settled over the table.

I had little sympathy for Irwin Bayne—wife beater and sexual predator that he was. With Brandy's looks and the history of abuse at Irwin's hand, she'd probably land a lighter sentence.

As for Kingsbury, murderer or accessory to murder, either way he'd serve prison time. And he'd never be allowed to practice law again. That might not be the perfect justice Gertie was looking for, but it was close enough for me.

We busied ourselves with small talk and food while Carter finished his conversation at the far end of the veranda. When he rejoined us at the table, a slight smile played across his face.

He patted Gertie on the shoulder. "Well, Ms. Gold, you may get your wish."

CHAPTER FORTY-TWO

Self-Defense

Everyone at the table looked up at Carter, trying to figure out what he meant.

Gertie was the only one who understood. She brightened. "They found some DNA?"

"Close." He turned to me. "Remember the partial shoeprint they couldn't find a match for? When they searched Kingsbury's place, they discovered blood under the toe of one of his Topsiders. Turned out to match Irwin Bayne."

My mind returned to the night Kingsbury had barged in with that repulsive pizza, saying he was on the way to his boat. He'd probably been wearing those shoes, right there in the kitchen, already stained with blood.

Nausea threatened, then glee took over. Killer or not, mastermind or conspirator, Kingsbury was done. Eyewitness + Physical Evidence = Throw Away the Key.

"That's not even the best part." Carter sat back and folded his arms. "Brandy confessed."

It didn't seem like big news to me. "Confessed to what? She admitted hitting Irwin over the head from the very beginning."

"True, and she'd already claimed it was in self-defense. But Kingsbury had threatened to turn against her if she talked about what happened after.

"Washington convinced her that her former attorney had accused her of masterminding a plot to kill Irwin, which meant she'd be facing premeditated homicide. She decided it was in her best interest to tell her side."

I spoke for all of us. "Which was?"

"According to Brandy, everything happened as she said, in the beginning. But when Irwin collapsed in the bedroom, she thought he was already dead, so she called Kingsbury. Apparently the two of them had carried on an affair for years, before she married Irwin. When the lawyer got to the condo, he concocted the cover up."

I worked to put the pieces together. "So, she didn't know Irwin was still alive?"

"Not until Washington told her. Knowing that Kingsbury watched Irwin die was probably what made her open up."

The table grew silent as we each mentally conjured the scenario.

Gertie gasped. "It's all my fault!" She gripped Louis's hand. "If I'd never opened the door, their plan wouldn't have worked."

I remembered Harland and his hallway encounter with Brandy. "That's not exactly true. Any valet making night rounds would have found her, eventually. That's probably what they were counting on. You just stepped in a little early."

"I definitely stepped in something! I'm so sorry, for landing all of us in the mess."

Carter shook his head. "No need to apologize. You tried to do the right thing."

It hurt to see Gertie slip into misguided guilt. "Why don't we move back to the happy place we were before the conversation turned." I picked up my glass. "A toast to the good guys. May they always win."

Carter raised his beer and we all clinked. "Speaking of good guys . . . Gertie, have you and Louis set a date?"

She threw her hands in the air. "There's hardly been time to think about it!"

Louis grinned. "I told her not to keep me waiting too

long. I'm not getting any younger. Plus, I already booked a honeymoon cruise for next month." He winked. "I'm a bit of a fast worker."

Carter offered the last square of jalapeño cornbread around the table. With no takers, he put it on his plate and grabbed the butter. "Serenity's a good place for a wedding."

I set my fork down and stared at him. His eyes met mine for an instant, then moved to Gertie. "If you and Louis like the idea, I would be happy to host a little country affair."

"Oh my!" Gertie lit up at the suggestion, until she looked my way and sobered. "It is beautiful here, but I'd like to talk it over with Samantha first."

I don't know why Carter's idea made me feel so odd, but when Dottie came to serve dessert and the subject changed to her delicious cooking, I was relieved. She pooh-poohed everyone's compliments, all the while basking in the attention as she served hot-fudge sundaes to the children and pecan pie a la mode to the rest of us.

It wasn't long before Ralph appeared on the path from the stables, leading four horses toward the house. Kerry popped out of his chair and sprinted down the steps.

"He's so rude," Courtney said to her table guests.

Lizzie sprang from her chair, ready to bolt after Kerry. She cast a glance toward her father. "May I please be excused, sir?"

With her father's nod, she raced to catch up.

Carter rose. "Now that lunch is over, I'm going to take Tom down the road to look at a piece of land. Louis, you're welcome to come along, or you can stay here with the ladies. Ralph will take care of the kids. That okay with everyone?"

The horses had made it up to the house. Ralph helped T.J. onto a quarter horse named Flash, and gave the boy a couple of pointers on how to manage him. Courtney rode Winnie, a bay mare. Kerry hopped on his gray pony, Sancho.

They waited as Ralph lifted Lizzie onto the back of the horse she had chosen. Hollywood.

Ralph hoisted himself onto his horse, took the reins and clucked a giddy-up. Just before the group disappeared down the path, Lizzie turned in the saddle, beamed a smile at me and waved.

Gertie and I stayed at the table and watched the men drive away in Carter's Jeep. Dottie brought coffee and disappeared inside again, wheeling Elizabeth with her.

Gertie set her mug down and took in the view. "This is a lovely setting for a wedding."

"Will you take Carter up on his offer?"

Her eyes scanned mine. "Let me ask you something first, Samantha. What's going on between you two?"

I studied my coffee. "Nothing."

"That's one way to describe it."

"What do you mean?"

"Not one friendly glance or one touch passed between you today."

"We hugged. You just didn't see it."

She screwed up her face. "What happened while I was gone?"

Tears sprouted inside my lids. "I'm not sure."

She didn't press again, but the silence between us teased out my thoughts. "I think we've realized how different we are."

"Different? In what way?"

"I used to believe we were exactly alike. We'd each lost people we loved, and we're pretty much alone in the world. We've been through so much together, when

I was searching for Lista, and after. It seemed like we had so much in common."

"And now?"

"We seem to be pulling in different directions."

"How?"

"My new job's in the city and he's got the new project here."

Gertie shook her head. "My goodness, dear, that's just geography. And why does it matter if the two of you aren't exactly alike? That's got nothing to do with love."

"We had a fight."

"About what?"

"It's too long a story."

"We have time."

I shook my head. "Can't we talk about something else? Something happy, like your wedding."

"Okay, but promise me you'll settle this soon."

Dottie showed up with a plate of sand cookies dusted with powdered sugar. She turned to go inside, then stopped and pivoted in place. "I know it's none of my business, Samantha, but I hope you're staying the weekend. There's been too much moping around here lately, if you ask me."

Gertie pounced. "I've just been telling her the same thing."

I pushed away from the table and crossed my arms. I knew they both cared, and I was truly grateful. But I wasn't ready for an open forum on my love life.

I looked up at Dottie. "Thanks. We're working on it, I think. Lunch was delicious."

"I'd be pleased to cook for a wedding."

I winced. Dottie and Gertie exchanged eye rolls.

Dottie turned to me. "For Gertie, I mean, if she decides to have it here."

"It would be an honor," Gertie said.

They both eyed me again before Dottie left for the kitchen.

Gertie did not break her gaze. "Did you hear what she said, Samantha? It may not be clear to you, but you belong together, and everyone knows it."

"How?"

"I see how he looks at you."

"You're marrying someone you hardly know. How do you know that's even real?"

Gertie smiled. "I may have just met him, but I have known him all my life."

What could I say to that? I watched a wispy cloud float aimlessly in the bright autumn sky.

Gertie reached for my hand. "Forgive me dear, but I must say this. When I was your secretary, I thought you were the smartest, gutsiest young woman I'd ever known, a trailblazing executive and fearless seeker.

"I don't blame you for feeling wrung out after all you've been through, but it's time to be that person again. You have a wonderful man who loves you, and a new career . . ."

"That's what caused our fight. My job." She waited for me to say more. I looked away.

"Don't miss this chance for joy, Samantha."

I searched the sky for the little wispy cloud. Only a trace of it was left, floating on the breeze.

CHAPTER FORTY-THREE

Conclude Away

I managed to move the conversation away from my problems with Carter. By the time the men returned to the house, Gertie had unspooled a blow-by-blow of her whirlwind courtship.

Louis bounded up the front steps like a teenager and kissed her. "That's a great piece of property over there. Chapman's plan for it is a worthy one. I think we should donate a little something for a bunkhouse or a clinic. How about it, Gert?"

"That would be lovely, Louis."

Carter mounted the steps with Mason. They were winding down their conversation.

"I'm in, sir, if you want me," I heard Mason say. "I'll do everything to get here as soon as I separate from the Rangers."

On the path from the stables, the children were in a footrace race toward the house. Courtney and T.J. gave up early, but Kerry and Lizzie fought it out to the end.

"I won!" Kerry claimed as he tagged the bottom step.

Lizzie didn't seem to care. She kept going, all the way up to the porch, stopping only when she knocked into her father. Her eyes were huge.

"Kerry's dad says I can ride Hollywood anytime. Can we come back tomorrow? Please!"

Mason looked down at her. "Not tomorrow, but we'll come back soon. We need to pack up for home now."

Lizzie hung her head and trudged down the steps toward the van. T.J. was already there, leaning against the side panel, deep into a conversation with Courtney. Mason disappeared inside to get his wife.

Gertie and Louis said their goodbyes, too. I hugged her almost as tight as I had when she'd arrived. She whispered in my ear. "Talk to him."

Carter and I stood on the porch and watched the cars pull away. He jingled the key to the Jeep. "Ready?"

We headed down the front drive and onto the highway. "How was your visit with Gertie?"

"I hadn't realized how much I missed her."

"They seem happy, don't they?"

"Very." Drat. My eyes were filling up behind my sunglasses.

We had traveled less than a mile when Carter turned the Jeep onto a gravel road. A few yards in, we came to a metal gate that had been left open, its lock dangling from a post.

The Jeep rumbled over a cattle guard and down a small slope before the land spread out in all directions. It was more rugged than Carter's ranch, at least from our vantage point. The same high grasses swayed between rocky outcroppings and over open pasture. Oaks and cottonwoods lay in the distance.

Carter steered down an almost imperceptible path through the tall grass and headed toward the trees. We bounced along another few hundred yards until the ridge where we had sat on the opposite bank came into view. Under an old spreading oak, he cut the engine.

"There's a lot to show you. I thought I'd start here, because you've seen this piece from the other side. It'll give you a sense of how this property lines up with Serenity. If it gets too late to see the rest, we can always come back tomorrow."

Tomorrow. "Sure," I said, though I wasn't.

This side of the creek looked much like its twin. I opened the door to get out and walk to the ridge for a closer look. Carter held me back. "Careful, Sam. I haven't had a chance to sweep for fire ants."

At his touch, a flush of warmth spread through me. I sat back and shut the door. "You saved me. Again."

"Any time." His hand clasped mine. "I don't ever want to rain on your parade, Samantha. You deserve happiness."

It might as well have been fire ants, the way he'd come out of nowhere with that stinger. I willed myself to speak. "So do you."

He squeezed my hand. "I'm always happy with you around."

I pulled away. "Was that happiness on your face when you left me after the press conference?"

He started to speak but stopped, then started again. "I've been thinking a lot about that, and how we ended up in a fight."

"Any conclusions?"

"Yes. Want to hear them?"

"Conclude away."

He leaned his back against the driver's door and looked me straight in the eye. "First, I'm an ass."

I chuckled. "Interesting theory."

"It's true." He smiled. "I love it when you laugh, by the way."

I tried to ignore that. "Why do you think you're an ass?"

"I don't trust easily. Partly because of my work, but truth is, I was born that way."

"Pathologically secretive?"

"Ouch. When you put it that way."

"Go on."

He played his fingers over the steering wheel. "How I acted at the press conference, and after. That was my fault too."

"And?"

"That's about it. Otherwise, I'm perfect." His grin was as wide as the afternoon sky.

I struggled not to grin back. "You forgot control freak."

He shook his head. "Nope. That one's on you. And childish, I might add."

I crossed my arms. "You were doing so well for a minute there."

He took off his sunglasses and set them on the dash. "Here's the thing, and I'm serious now. We both know what it's like to live with grief."

"What does that have to do with anything?"

"Sometimes, if a person lives in darkness too long, the light can be blinding when it starts to shine again. But that's no reason to run from it. It doesn't matter if we disagree on some things. We're not clones, after all."

"You sound like Gertie."

"A wise woman." He leaned in and pulled off my sunglasses. I reached out to take them back, but he handed them over without a struggle. I set them on the dashboard next to his.

His fingers played the top of the steering wheel again. "All I'm saying is, our timing may be a little off right now. You're feeling your way into a whole new career, and I've got this project to develop. We have time to sort things out. I'm not going anywhere."

"That's what you usually say just before you disappear."

"I'm cutting back on my client list. Way back. Like I said, whenever you're ready, I'll be right here."

His sad toffee eyes: If it weren't for them, I could

have made another snarky comeback. The little girl in me wanted more than anything to fall into his arms and hear him promise we'd live happily ever after. But the grown-up me didn't believe in fairy tales.

Maybe he was right about the timing. Maybe things would work themselves out.

He dropped something into my hand: a small box, robin's egg blue. Tiffany. I searched his face for an explanation.

"Open it. I promise it won't bite."

I untied the white silk ribbon. Inside, wrapped in white tissue paper, lay a blue flannel pouch holding something long and narrow as my pinkie finger. A thin sterling necklace slipped out. Hanging from it was a silver police whistle.

"I figured you could use it to call out evildoers."

I raised it to my lips and blew. From up in the trees, a mockingbird replied with a trill of its own.

Carter smiled. "I considered giving you a cape, but this seemed more your style."

I kissed him on the cheek. "Thanks, Superman. You keep the cape. You never know when I might need saving again."

He lifted the chain and draped it over my head. "I'm guessing that won't be necessary anymore. Besides, anytime you want me, all you have to do is—"

"Whistle?"

"Something like that."

I leaned into him and felt his warmth encircle me. He took my hand, and this time, I held on tight.

THE END

ABOUT THE AUTHOR

Gay Yellen has been sneezed on by an elephant, held at gunpoint and survived a killer California earthquake, which may explain her penchant for writing cliffhangers. She began her working life as a stage and TV actress, then happily moved behind the camera at The American Film Institute (AFI) as Assistant to the Director of Production.

A former magazine editor and national journalism award winner, she was the contributing book editor for *Five Minutes to Midnight* (Delacorte Press), an international thriller. Her Samantha Newman Series of mystery novels includes *The Body Business* and *The Body Next Door*.

Gay lives in Texas. She loves connecting with book clubs and community groups in person and online. You can contact her through her website, GayYellen.com.

FROM THE AUTHOR

Acknowledgments

The Body Next Door made it through to publication only because readers of *The Body Business* enjoyed that book and encouraged me to continue the story of Samantha, Carter and Gertie. I am grateful to each and every one of you. Special thanks go to those who posted reviews and recommended it to their friends.

To writing group regulars Carla Conrad, David Welling, Melissa Algood and Bill Mays, thank you for your honesty and attention. Your abiding enthusiasm kept me going throughout the first draft. To part-timers Kyle Russell, Nandita Banerjee and Louis Epstein, your comments were very much appreciated.

Big thanks go to author Donna Hill for the spot-on critique that helped to clarify the storytelling. To beta readers Rebecca Nolen, Claire Hart-Palumbo, Jackie Mazow, Heidi Hancock, and Cyvia Reiser, thank you for your time, and for catching last-minute glitches.

Very special thanks to Patricia Flaherty Pagan and Pamela Fagan Hutchins, two exceptional authors who generously shared their wisdom with me. And also to the remarkable Heidi Dorey, who turned my vague suggestions into wonderfully evocative cover art.

My deepest gratitude to Donald, for his unwavering support and quiet patience during the long months it took to navigate this book to The End. I love you, now and always.

Now that you have read *The Body Next Door*, would you please consider taking a moment to leave a brief honest review on the book's Amazon.com or Goodreads.com page? It's a great way to share your thoughts and to help other readers decide if they might enjoy the book as well.

The author would greatly appreciate it. Thank you!

The Samantha Newman Series

*

The Body Business
The Body Next Door

CPSIA information can be obtained
at www.ICGtesting.com
Printed in the USA
LVOW07s2323180817
545593LV00001B/45/P